A DOCTOR FOR LADY DENBY

Book 2—The Hope Clinic

TRISHA MESSMER

DEDICATION

To embracing our differences.

CONTENTS

ACKNOWLEDGMENTS

As always, first and foremost a big thank you to my family. My oldest son admitted it's a little disconcerting to know his mother writes romance. He'll live. And to the rest of them who cheer me on, thank you for your support. I love you all.

To my loyal group of critique partners at Critique Circle. What would I do without you? Seriously. You keep me honest, cheer me on, slap me upside the head when I do something stupid, and continue to make me strive to be a better writer.

To my growing list of readers. I wouldn't be able to continue if it weren't for your support and encouraging words. Please stay safe and keep reading!

CHAPTER 1—THE TROUBLE WITH WOMEN

LONDON, ENGLAND, NOVEMBER 1823

Oliver Somersby glanced at his pocket watch as he raced down the street. *Late again!* If only he hadn't stayed so long at home. But how could he refuse Tori's request to stay a few moments longer? The chaos of the morning had him at sixes and sevens. His fingers clutched around—air? *Blast!* He had forgotten his medical bag.

As he spun around to head back, a soft, fragrant lilac barrier slammed into him. Or was it the other way around?

Instinctively, he reached out, attempting to regain his balance when he stumbled forward, his hands landing on two distinctly soft —pillows?

A hard slap to his face brought him to his senses, and his hands dropped to his sides.

Dark brown eyes, the rich color of coffee, glared at him. "How dare you!" The woman staggered back, catching the hem of her pelisse in the heel of her half boot. A ripping sound followed.

The sweat beading his brow appeared in direct contrast to the chilly late autumn temperature, and his greatcoat abruptly seemed unnecessary. "I beg your pardon," he blurted, anxious to remove himself from the situation yet unable to tear his eyes from her heaving bosom with which he'd collided. "It was an accident. If you'll excuse me." He edged around her and sprinted back to the hackney stand from whence he came.

"Someone needs to teach you some manners, sir," the woman called after him.

"And someone needs to teach you to be more tolerant of people's mistakes," he mumbled to himself.

After retrieving his bag, he hurried to the clinic. As expected, a crowd three deep waited outside its doors.

"Late again, Doctor," a skinny man with a red nose said. "If you'd get a wife, that'd cure that 'abit fast. I can't wait to get out of my 'ouse and away from 'er naggin'."

Oliver unlocked the door, and the crowd streamed in. He made a mental note to write to Harry and ask permission to obtain additional assistance. The problem was where to address his letter as Harry, the Duke of Ashton, was currently on his wedding trip to Italy. He would have to wait to hear from Harry first. Neither of them had expected the clinic to be such a tremendous success.

He performed a quick assessment of each person and made a list of their ailments in an effort to prioritize their care. If nothing else, time passed quickly, and he often discovered he had worked the entire day without eating anything. He anticipated another similar day.

He finished with the third patient and stepped out of the treatment area to call the next. The same woman—the soft, fragrant barrier, with the alluring warm, brown eyes—stood out like a rose among a field of brambles. *What is she doing here?*

Her eyes flared. "You!"

His eyes narrowed. "Yes, me. What are *you* doing here? This is a medical facility for the less fortunate." The arrangement of her rich brown hair with a few tendrils draping seductively down her neck made his fingers yearn to touch them. His eyes roamed over her figure, taking in every luscious curve. She wore a green pelisse and a matching bonnet. He waved a hand at her. "Didn't you have on something pink earlier?"

"Mauve, yes, but your clumsiness tore it."

"No, as I recall, *your* clumsiness tore it when *you* stepped on it."

"Because *you* pushed me and," she leaned close to whisper, "touched me inappropriately."

"Because *you* ran into me."

She huffed, her eyes seething. "You . . . ran . . . into . . . me. I had to go home and change, otherwise I would have been here sooner."

"Which brings me back to my first question. What are you doing here? And who the deuce are you?"

She lifted her chin in the way high-born ladies did. He hated that gesture. "I'm Lady Denby, and I've come to see how things are progressing. It seems I arrived not a moment too soon. The clinic appears to be a disaster. Why are all these people waiting to be treated?"

He tamped down the frustration building in his chest. It wasn't that Oliver didn't like women. In fact, it was the exact opposite. He loved them, perhaps a little too much. However, the particular female before him was currently setting him on the verge of apoplexy.

"I assure you, madam," he said through gritted teeth. "I'm doing my utmost to attend to all the patients in an expeditious and thorough manner. I would remind you that you have not been trained in the field of medicine, and I have."

"Since you've failed to introduce yourself as a gentleman would, I will presume you're Dr. Somersby." She sighed, the sound both alluring and unsettling. "I'm merely trying to help. Ashton instructed me to see if you needed anything in his absence and to make sure things are going well while he and Margaret are on their wedding trip."

"Did he now?" Oliver raised a questioning eyebrow at the infuriating woman. "Are you certain you didn't assign that task yourself?"

From the fire in her eyes, he expected another hard slap to his face. She jutted her lovely chin again, which only drew his eyes to her full mouth and kissable lips. *Damnation! Stop it, man.*

Her dark brown eyes sparkled with intelligence as she perused the room, assessing, probably calculating the many ways in which he fell short of her high standards. The hair on the back of his neck tingled, and he resisted the urge to scratch it. She'd most likely think he had lice.

"You need help," she said, causing his head to snap back.

He did, but admitting that to her clawed at his gut. "I'm managing."

Those brown eyes narrowed. "You, sir, are a liar as well as a clumsy oaf. I'm offering you help, and unless you are also slow-witted, you'll accept."

His jaw clenched so tight, he feared he would break a molar. "What I need, you can't provide. Word is spreading, and the clinic is prospering. We need another physician."

"I shall place an advertisement today."

He blinked. *What?*

She gave a curt nod as if her statement solved everything. "I'll write to Ashton and advise him. Now, I suggest you return to your duties posthaste. These people need assistance." She turned on her heel and headed toward the door without so much as a good day.

Damn if he'd let her have the last word. "Lady Denby," he called, and she turned back. "Please warn me next time you decide to pay a visit. I'll keep my hands to myself."

Although brief, her composure wavered as she stumbled, and color rose to her cheeks, giving him the satisfaction he desperately craved. She recovered quickly with one final thrust of her chin as she left.

He stared at the closed door. The sweet fragrance of lilac still clung to the air around him, and his mind swam, struggling to break free of the morass threatening to drown him. That was the trouble with women, they addled your brain.

Someone cleared their throat, drawing his attention to the faces of his patients watching him with interest. A few of them grinned. One woman giggled.

"Who's next?" He veritably snarled the question.

One of the men laughed. "I'd say *you* were, doctor."

CHAPTER 2—THE TROUBLE WITH MEN

W ith astonishing clarity, Camilla Denby finally understood the attraction of Gentleman Jackson's Boxing Academy. She wanted to hit something—hard.

What an infuriating, rude . . .

The image of the man she'd left mere moments ago coalesced in her mind. Eyes bluer than the sunniest summer day contrasted sharply with his swarthy complexion. Thick black hair so unruly she wanted to run her fingers through it, the generous mouth with full lips that would be so attractive if he only smiled. Thoughts of doing something other than hitting that face bombarded her—a colossal mistake.

No, no, no!

Her heart stuttered and lightheadedness overcame her. Thank goodness she reached her waiting carriage before she embarrassed herself twice in the same morning. She instructed her coachman to return home, then sat back on the plush seat, closing her eyes.

"Oh, Hugh," she whispered, calling the name of the man she had loved and lost. Eight years had not lessened the pain and emptiness. Yet something sparked to life during her repartee with

Dr. Somersby. How she'd missed such lively exchanges with a handsome man, no matter how atrocious his manners.

Upon arriving home, she informed Stratton, her butler, that she wished to remain undisturbed, then proceeded to her room. The box she pulled from the bottom of her drawer had been left unopened for a year, and her fingers trembled as they ran across the rich cherry wood. With only a moment's hesitation, she flipped the small gold latch and revealed the contents.

Hugh's letters rested within. Light perfume from the sachet lying alongside them drifted up, teasing her nostrils. She stroked tentative fingertips over the pale-blue ribbon securing the bundled missives. The bittersweet pain they evoked stirred in her chest as she lifted them from their resting place, and she smiled through the tears welling.

Stop being a ninny.

With a gentle tug of the ribbon, the letters cascaded loose in her hands, falling into her lap. She had read through them all, in order, so many times she had lost count. Today, one in particular called to her.

Easily identified, it remained the one with splotched handwriting on the outside where it had been addressed as well as the missive itself. The writing had been executed in a neat hand; it had been her own tears that had forever marked it. And Camilla was not prone to tears.

With great care, she opened it—the creases so fragile from unfolding and folding it, the slightest movement would rip it into pieces—and skimmed the beginning.

Written in Captain Harrison Radcliffe's hand, he informed her of her husband's death.

My dear Lady Denby,

It grieves my heart to tell you that your husband, Major Hugh Denby, has made the utmost sacrifice for King and country—his very life. His valor on the battlefield will not be forgotten. Words fail me, dear lady, at the loss I regrettably must convey.

Hugh requested I take down his words precisely as he dictated them to me. And so, I write:

My darling Camilla,

Well, like a fool, I've gone and managed to get myself shot. Not the great hero you thought, eh?

I'm not much for pretty words, but I hope you know how much I love you. You made my world better, made me better. Thank you for giving me that happiness.

Don't stop living, Cam. Soldier on. Did you like my little joke? Ha! Remember me, but don't let my memory stop you from living. You know what I mean, Cam. Be happy, make someone else happy.

Yours always,

Hugh

More followed in Harry's words regarding Hugh's bravery in battle, but she didn't need to read further. Once again, she folded the letter and placed it back among its brothers. She brushed away the moisture from her cheeks, the salty tang reaching her lips.

Closing her eyes, she called forth Hugh's face, the task becoming more difficult with each passing year. *Ah, there!* In her mind, he smiled, exposing that heart-stopping dimple.

By all accounts, he wasn't the handsomest man, but that dimple always undid her, and in her opinion, no other man measured up. If Helen of Troy had the face that launched a thousand ships, Hugh Denby had the smile that initiated a thousand swoons.

Don't stop living. Be happy, make someone else happy. The words ricocheted in her brain until her head hurt.

The desire to yell *I'm trying* swelled, and she huffed an exasperated breath. There simply wasn't anyone worthy. Instead, day in and day out, men like that infuriating Dr. Somersby crossed her path.

Like an unwelcome intruder, the uncouth doctor's face surfaced in her mind. His eyes full of fire and passion. *No, no, no! Go away!* She tried in vain to push him out.

And that was the trouble with men. They always did what they wanted.

CHAPTER 3—PRESUMPTIONS

A month had passed and Oliver still hadn't been able to find a suitable physician to assist at the clinic. Many who initially had shown interest, ultimately balked at the idea of treating the less fortunate, especially for the minimal wages offered. Oliver regretted not examining the posting made by the high-and-mighty Lady Denby. Unfortunately, he'd been too busy struggling to keep up with the grueling pace to place his own advertisement.

Consumed with a troublesome case involving an infant who was failing to thrive, Oliver decided to consult with Harry. Luckily, he'd returned from Italy and was spending Christmas at his estate in Kent, allowing Oliver to reach him via correspondence. The infant's condition itself wasn't surprising, given the living conditions of the East End, but he trusted the mother when she insisted she'd been following his instructions to the letter. Something else was wrong.

As he composed his letter to Harry, Lady Denby once again invaded his thoughts. He'd been unable to put her from his mind, try as he might. He'd spoken about her with his grandmother, who had only laughed and accused him of being smitten.

"You've lost your mind," he'd said, brushing off her assessment.

"Is that your professional diagnosis?" his grandmother had asked.

He forced his attention back to his letter. With luck, he would avoid any additional contact with Lady Denby. So why did he endlessly search the street where he had first encountered her? Why did he scan the waiting area of the clinic each time he stepped out from the treatment room?

Blast!

Several days before Christmas, he received a reply from Harry, who made a few suggestions regarding his troubling case. Harry also stated he and Margaret would be arriving in London at the beginning of the new year, and he looked forward to becoming useful again at the clinic. Oliver breathed a sigh of relief that Harry would provide a much needed extra set of hands.

After preparing a sign stating the clinic would be closed on Christmas day, he threw on his greatcoat, preparing to head home after another long day. As he hung the sign in the window, much to his surprise—or was it dismay—Lady Denby appeared, her expression dour as she glared at him through the glass then moved toward the door.

The knob of the locked door rattled, a sharp knock following. "Dr. Somersby, open the door. I know you're there."

He huffed a breath—bidding goodbye to his pleasant day—and unlocked and opened the door. As she breezed in, the air in the room chilled more from her demeanor than the frigid temperature outside.

"Lady Denby," he said, his jaw tensing. "To what do I owe the *pleasure?*"

Her icy stare cut him as precisely as a sharp scalpel. "It's no *pleasure* to see you, sir. I've come to see if you've hired another physician."

"I have not."

Her brown eyes narrowed—accusing, condemning. "Why not?"

"None of the applicants have proven suitable."

She rolled her entrancing eyes. "Might you be a little more specific? In what way were they not suitable?"

Damn her. Is she questioning my ability to select an appropriate candidate?

"If you must know," he said, taking a deep breath to calm his throbbing pulse, "they weren't agreeable to the salary or conditions. It seems they were expecting something offering a little more"—he struggled to find the right word—"posh."

Her delicate eyebrows arched. "I'm sorry?"

"Of course. Being a high-born lady you wouldn't know. It's slang for money."

She snorted, a sound he found strangely alluring. "In the East End? Don't be ridiculous."

He wanted to go home to a warm fire and a nice cup of tea. "Perhaps if you told me what the posting said, I might identify the problem."

She squared her lovely shoulders and adjusted her pelisse. "Simply that the Duke of Ashton requested a physician for his medical facility."

His head dropped as he shook it in disgust. "Well, there's the problem. Mentioning a duke is bound to bring in people expecting something grand and well-paying."

"Oh, I hadn't thought . . ." She spoke the words so softly, had the clinic been filled with the usual commotion he wouldn't have heard her.

For a brief moment, she appeared helpless and vulnerable, and he had a strange urge to comfort her.

She eradicated his momentary weakness as soon as she opened her mouth again. "Well, an educated person should have deduced the salary was minimal based on the location."

"Would they now?" His patience was worn as thin as his grandmother's coat . . . which reminded him. Before heading home, he had somewhere to go, a promise to keep.

"Yes, well." She cleared her throat with a delicate, almost musical cough. "I'll admit the posting could have been phrased more clearly. I'll write another straight away."

"Don't bother. I'll take care of it. I'll mimic Harry's posting. It proved effective."

She tilted her head at a forty-five-degree angle, drawing his attention to her slim throat. "How so?"

He fought back a smile. "It brought *me* here, didn't it?" He fastened his greatcoat about him. "Now, if you'll excuse me, I was about to leave. I have somewhere to be." He held his hand out, motioning her toward the door and escorting her out.

She walked a few feet down the street where her high-and-mighty carriage waited. The coachman leapt from his perch and assisted her inside.

Satisfied she was safe, Oliver locked the clinic door and strode down to the hackney carriage stand a street away. After giving his destination to the coachman who protested until promised an extra two pence, Oliver climbed in and settled onto the bench.

He huffed a breath, realizing he left one stubborn woman to immediately head toward another. And here it *had* been a relatively pleasant day.

The coach lurched forward, heading to the outskirts of London where few chose to go.

CHAPTER 4—THE WOMAN WHO PROTESTS TOO MUCH

S omething about Dr. Somersby's behavior niggled at Camilla's brain. The nervous tic in his left eye alerted her that something was afoot, and she intended to discover what he was up to.

She instructed her coachman to follow the hackney carriage Dr. Somersby boarded. As her carriage moved through the crowded streets of the East End, she fully expected to turn and head back into the better part of the city. Instead, as she gazed out the carriage window, passing buildings disappeared, replaced by an open stretch of road and then dense woods. Her coach jolted to a stop.

Langley, her coachman, appeared at the carriage door, and, even in the darkness, his face expressed concern. "My lady, we're heading into a dangerous area. Are you certain you wish me to proceed?"

"Dangerous in what way?"

The man shifted nervously on his feet. "There's a gypsy camp ahead, my lady."

Hugh had accused her of being too curious for her own safety, but the prospect of gypsies did nothing to deter her—in fact, it enticed her more.

"Continue on, keep the coach in your sight, but stay far enough back to remain unnoticed."

"Yes, my lady."

The carriage dipped under Langley's weight as he climbed back on, the snap of reins and forward motion following. They traveled a short distance further, then came to another stop.

When Langley didn't immediately appear, Camilla opened the carriage door. "What is it?" she asked.

"The coach stopped, my lady, and the passenger alighted. Seems he's exchanging some words with the driver."

Camilla descended from the carriage. Light from campfires and lanterns rimmed the camp in an eerie glow. Wagons and tents peppered the area, and people moved about, their strides purposeful. Soft, melancholy strands of music from a violin sweetened the night air.

The lone figure by the hackney carriage moved toward the encampment, his greatcoat swinging against his legs—Dr. Somersby. He disappeared from her view, engulfed in the activity around him.

"My lady?" Langley called from his perch above, shakiness coloring his voice. "You're not going in there, are you?"

"No," she said, although she very much wanted to. *What is he up to?*

The hackney carriage remained, presumably waiting for Dr. Somersby's return. Who knows how long he would be?

She climbed back into the carriage. "You may take me home, Langley." She envisioned her coachman uttering a sigh of relief. *And they say women are the weaker sex. Rubbish!*

On her journey home, her mind swirled with questions. *Is he providing medical care? If so, does Ashton know, approve? Does he put stock in gypsy fortune tellers? Is he there for a woman?* The last question gnawed at her craw a little more than she wished to admit. She'd heard tales of gypsy women enticing English men, their exotic beauty irresistible. He said he had somewhere to be, so they apparently expected him.

Dr. Somersby, what is your secret? She intended to find out.

THE FESTIVITIES OF THE CHRISTMAS HOLIDAY OCCUPIED CAMILLA, and she had little time to think about Dr. Somersby and his suspicious activity. She prepared for the expected melancholy to steal its way into her mind.

Hugh had loved the Christmas season, and she often accused him of acting like a small child. He had answered her with a grin. The memories softened, becoming bittersweet, but nonetheless, the ache of his absence remained.

"When is Ashton expected back in London?"

Her father's question jolted her from her daydreaming, and tea from the cup she held sloshed over the rim onto the saucer. "Soon, I believe. In her letter, Margaret said Harry is anxious to return to the clinic."

Her father raised a quizzical brow. His knowing gaze conveyed he recognized the pain lurking behind her practiced composure. "Is she happy? I worry it doesn't bode well if her husband wishes to return from a wedding trip."

"No, nothing like that. She's deliriously happy. She mentioned Harry spent some time with an eminent Italian physician and is anxious to implement the techniques he learned."

Her father shook his head but smiled. "A duke who's a doctor. I fear my world is crumbling around me."

"Pshaw, Father. The aristocracy remains solid. Besides, I thought you liked Harry."

"Ashton, Camilla, Ashton. The least you can do is address the man by his title. And I do like him. It pleases me that Margaret has found happiness after what she endured at the hands of his brother. It gives me hope for you."

The bone china of her cup clinked against the saucer, and her spine straightened to the verge of snapping. "What about me?"

He held up a hand in defense. "Now, Camilla. Don't be angry. It's been eight years. You're still young and vibrant. You should start living again."

The words of Hugh's letter echoed. "You mean find another husband."

"Well, yes."

She used her typical tactic and deflected. "Have I suddenly become a burden? I maintain my own household, so I'm hardly underfoot. Is it the money?"

Her father cringed, and she regretted her unjust words. Although Hugh left her a treasure trove of memories, he left her very little financially. Her father generously provided for her living expenses.

"Camilla." His eyes implored. "I only wish for your happiness."

"I *had* happiness, one short but glorious year of it. It's impossible to find a love like that again."

"You don't know that unless you try."

Be happy. Make someone else happy.

Mercifully, Holmes, his butler appeared, announcing Christmas dinner was ready.

❦

A WEEK AFTER CHRISTMAS, CAMILLA RECEIVED A LETTER FROM Margaret, announcing her arrival in London and her intention of calling upon Camilla soon. Guilt tugged at Camilla as a fleeting wave of envy passed through her. Maggie deserved happiness, just as her father had said.

There had been a time in their friendship when Camilla had spoken of her blissful marriage with Hugh and witnessed a longing in her friend's eyes. Margaret had been much younger, still clinging to the hope that she too would find such a match.

Later, a different guilt had assaulted Camilla when Margaret's marriage to George Radcliffe had proven quite the opposite of the dreams of her youth. It didn't seem fair that she had experienced such a great love when Margaret only knew sorrow.

Camilla blew out a breath. Maudlin thoughts were not part of her makeup, and she vowed to be an enthusiastic supporter of Margaret's happiness. However, as she listened to Margaret recounting the details of her wedding trip, a small, uncomfortable part of Camilla grew envious of her friend's joy, and she struggled to tamp it down.

Margaret bubbled with happiness, glowing with the radiance of a new bride. Camilla smiled and nodded, as a friend should, but her mind wandered, as a friend's should not.

Margaret settled her teacup on its saucer. "Cam, what's wrong?"

Camilla lifted her eyes from her cooling tea to meet her friend's knowing gaze. "Nothing. I'm sorry. What were you saying?"

"Oh, no you don't. Something's bothering you." Margaret's brows drew down, her eyes narrowing.

Camilla was well acquainted with that look. Margaret scrutinized her. She had always been adept at reading people's behaviors. The queasy uneasiness of shame left a sour taste in Camilla's mouth.

"Cam, you should have stopped me. I'm being terribly insensitive."

Leave it to Margaret to blame herself. Years of conditioning were a hard pattern to break. Camilla shook her head. "You? I'm the one who's a terrible friend."

"Nonsense. Here I am going on and on about my Christmas gift to Harry, when Christmastide had been so important to Hugh. Even after all these years, this must be such a difficult time for you."

Camilla nodded. "He did love the season, much like a small child." Her eyes widened as Margaret laid a hand on her abdomen. Something in her mind clicked. "Maggie, what did you say about the gift?"

"It was a small fawn. The son of one of our tenants carved it to go with Harry's stag and my doe. Of course we have a young buck with sprouts of antlers for Manny, but . . ."

Camilla's mind froze on her friend's words, Margaret's radiant glow making perfect sense. "You're carrying?"

Margaret sprang from her seat and joined Camilla on the sofa, enveloping her in an embrace. "Isn't it wonderful, Cam? I never thought I'd be able to have a child. Harry said we shouldn't announce it so soon, but I just had to tell someone or burst."

Tears welled in her friend's eyes, and Camilla joined her as they both wept with happiness.

"Will it be difficult for you, Cam, being around me?"

"Don't be a ninny. Of course not. I will expect all the privileges of a big sister, though. Foremost, holding that precious bundle as much as possible when he arrives."

"You think it will be a boy? Harry says he doesn't care, but I know deep down he wants an heir." Margaret ran her hand over her abdomen again.

"Boy or girl, you will love it beyond measure." Another pang of jealousy crept up Camilla's spine, along with the accompanying realization she would never experience the joy of having life quicken within her.

Although Camilla fought to contain the emotion, Margaret's astute observation read her friend's expression. "Cam, I never thought I would have this, yet here I am. Why don't you consider marrying again? You're young and have so much to give."

Her friend's simple words dealt the final blow to the wall holding back the tide of Camilla's feelings. The crack that had formed re-reading Hugh's final letter, now split wide, and Camilla heaved a sob.

Margaret embraced her instantly. "Cam, I'm sorry. What did I say?"

Camilla shook her head, unable to form the words to express the muddled mix of emotions swirling through her.

Margaret rubbed Cam's back, silently waiting for her friend to speak.

Camilla lifted her head, her eyes wet from her tears, and met Margaret's compassionate gaze. "I've been wondering the same thing."

Margaret blinked. "Why does that upset you?"

"Because it's a betrayal of Hugh, of what we had."

"You can't truly believe that? Hugh adored you and would want you to be happy. How is that a betrayal?"

Camilla shook her head, unable to answer.

"Cam," Margaret said, her voice firm. "If I didn't know better, I'd say you were afraid."

"And just what am I afraid of?" Camilla withdrew her lace handkerchief from her reticule and blew her nose.

"Of being happy."

A laugh broke free, a strange accompaniment to her sobs, and Camilla stared at her friend. "That's the most ridiculous thing you've ever said."

No amusement shone in Margaret's incredible violet eyes; they remained dead serious as they penetrated Camilla's defenses. "Ah, I see I've hit the mark. You're afraid if you find happiness with someone else, it somehow lessens what you had with Hugh."

Unable to form a response, Camilla's mouth hung open.

Margaret pressed on. "After my disastrous marriage to George, I wanted to avoid another at all costs. Years of his lies made me believe I was incapable of being a proper wife—that I wasn't worthy or deserving of love." Her eyes met Camilla's. "I was afraid. Although my fear was different from yours, it sealed off my heart as surely as fear has sealed off yours. If anything, your past with Hugh proves you're capable of a loving union—if you give yourself a chance."

Camilla wanted to deny Margaret's accusation, but she could not. Often truth proves a difficult thing to accept, even when presented by a dear friend.

After a few minutes of silence, Margaret circumvented the uncomfortable topic. "Harry wishes to thank you for your efforts to secure another physician for the clinic."

And yet, the change of subject only served to bring to the forefront what she struggled to avoid. The image of Oliver Somersby sprang forth, criticizing those very efforts. "He should only thank me if I had been successful."

Margaret sipped her tea, eyeing Camilla over the rim of her cup. Something about Margaret's knowing gaze unsettled Camilla to her core. "You tried your best. We couldn't expect to be as fortunate as we were with Dr. Somersby. It was pure destiny that he arrived, allowing Harry and me to leave for our wedding trip. Harry says he's been a godsend."

Camilla muttered, "More like a demon. The man's a menace."

Blast Margaret's superior hearing. Her eyebrows rose, almost reaching the line of her raven hair. A smile crept across her lips, quirking slightly at one corner. "Why, Cam, what has Dr. Somersby done to earn such a judgment?"

The need for an escape from the conversation pressed in on Camilla, and she squirmed in her seat. "Nothing," she forced out the lie. "I simply find him extremely disagreeable."

"In what way? Certainly not his appearance? He's very handsome, although in a somewhat dangerous way. Those crystal blue eyes appear almost out of place with his swarthy complexion and black hair. He's much like the pirates I imagined as a young girl."

"How quickly you forget your husband," Camilla teased.

"I only mean to imply most women would find him very appealing, and his smile could melt the snow."

He smiles? "Since I've yet to experience it, he must reserve that snow-melting smile for special occasions. However, I can attest the man scowls with great skill."

How Margaret's eyebrows reached even higher, Camilla wasn't sure. "Cam, what on earth happened between the two of you?"

"Not a thing, Maggie, and I intend to keep it that way."

Margaret raised her teacup, smiling over the rim. "Didn't Shakespeare have a line about protesting too much?"

CHAPTER 5—THE MAN WHO PROTESTS TOO MUCH

Oliver shoved the jar of white willow bark onto the shelf with a bit too much vigor. The glass jars next to it rattled in protest.

"We would have had another physician a month ago had it not been for that useless advert the high-and-mighty Lady Denby placed. I swear, when God created women, He must have shaken his head and then decided to make them attractive to counteract their utter lack of reasoning." He turned toward Harry who stared, his mouth agape.

"Oliver, I'll have you remember that Lady Denby is a dear friend of my wife's . . . and mine. I'm certain she only tried to help," Harry said.

"I apologize, Harry. But the woman is a menace. She needs to confine her helpful assistance to hosting sewing circles and garden parties, or whatever the beau monde does."

He stopped short, realizing he had just criticized the man who employed him, had proven to be a loyal and valuable friend, not to mention saved his life—and who was a duke. "I apologize again, Your Grace. That statement was uncalled for and unfair to you.

However, you must admit, you and your dear wife are not cut from the same cloth as much of the aristocracy."

"You're forgiven, but I'd point out, you're quick with your judgments based on little fact. Are there members of the nobility who exemplify everything you detest? Most certainly. But the majority of us are like you, and we put our trousers on one leg at a time."

Oliver snorted his disagreement. *With the help of a valet. If only you knew the depth of my knowledge of the aristocracy.* "I'll take you at your word." He slid the next jar containing leeches into place, this time more gently.

"Perhaps an opportunity to come to your own conclusion is in order. Although our funds are holding up well, I thought I might throw a charity ball. People love to show off their finery, and what better time to ask them to loosen their purse strings for a worthy cause than when they're in a good mood."

Oliver paused midway as he lifted a stack of bandages to the shelf. "You're not suggesting I attend?"

"Well, of course I am. I need the man who's in the thick of it day in and day out while I waste away each evening in the House of Lords. What better way to garner healthy contributions from our benefactors than to regale them with stories of the work their donations allow."

Oliver's lips pursed, and he gave his head a slight shake. "I don't know."

"Come now, you deserve some relaxation and fun in your life."

"I have Tori, she's enough to keep me entertained."

"Although I find her endearingly amusing, your ten-year-old sister is hardly entertainment for a grown man."

Oliver's gut twisted in a sailor's knot at the lie he'd told about Tori. A lie borne from the desire to protect and ease the pain now clawing to escape. How long could he keep up the pretense?

Harry continued, undaunted by Oliver's silence. "I won't take no for an answer. Who knows, perhaps some lovely young woman might catch your eye and break through that coat of armor you wear."

If he was anything, Harry was persistent. Oliver barked a laugh. "And again, I'll remind you that no woman who belongs to the *ton* would have interest in me. Lady Denby is proof enough of that." *Blast! Why on earth did I say that?*

Harry's eyebrow quirked. "Do you want her to have interest in you?"

"No," Oliver insisted emphatically, the falsehood souring on his tongue. "I'd rather be drawn and quartered than be leg-shackled to that harpy."

"Hmm." Harry rubbed his chin. "I see. Yet, she's the first woman to pop into your mind."

"Only because we had just been discussing her." Oliver turned his back to Harry, hoping to hide his discomfort in the conversation.

"Fear not, my friend." Harry patted him on the shoulder. "Your secret is safe with me. Now, let's open the doors and get to work."

The question remained, which secret had Harry discerned?

۞

OLIVER'S FOUL MOOD PERSISTED THE REST OF THE MORNING. Several times, Harry had to remind him not to take his frustrations out on his patients. When he snapped at a woman for burning her hand on a flat iron, Harry sent him home.

"Whatever demon is crawling under your skin, exorcise it before you come back. I will not allow you to disabuse our patients."

For the first time, Oliver witnessed his friend acting in the full power of his title. Harry had slipped into his role as duke seamlessly. If they hadn't been so shorthanded, Oliver was certain Harry would have sacked him on the spot.

Oliver tromped down the street to the hackney carriage stand. His temper didn't often get the better of him, but when it did, it was like breaking a festering boil. What came out was vile.

Boarding a coach, he bellowed the destination to the driver and settled back in the seat, his blood still boiling. *Deep breath in, exhale out. Deep breath in, exhale out.* He repeated the exercise all the way home.

Marginally calmer, he descended from the coach and entered

the modest house. After discarding his greatcoat and hat, he headed to the parlor.

The women in his life were a study in contrast. His mother sat in her usual spot, staring out the window with glazed eyes, oblivious to the world around her. He made a mental note to check the laudanum bottle. Tori looked up from her lessons with wide eyes and ran to him, wrapping her arms about his waist. Her tutor gave him a harsh look.

"Ollie, you're home! It's only midday." Tori pulled back from her embrace and gazed up at him with her all-seeing blue eyes. "What did you do?"

He snorted a laugh. "And why must it be that I've done something to bring me home? Perhaps I simply missed my scrap of a sister." He nodded to the frowning woman. "Miss Evers."

She nodded back, her face scrunched up like a prune. "Doctor. You've interrupted an important lesson."

Of course I did. The whole day has been a fiasco. "I apologize, Miss Evers. Victoria will study twice as hard tomorrow, won't you poppet?"

"Oh, I will, Miss Evers. I promise."

Oliver doubted the sincerity of Tori's words, and Miss Evers made it clear she did as well. Or it could have been her perpetual scowl. He swore her hair, so tightly fashioned in the bun at the top of her head, was the only thing preventing her face from dissolving entirely into her neck. He shuddered at the thought of her letting her hair loose.

"How is she today?" he asked, glancing toward his mother.

"She asked for tea this morning, Ollie," Tori said, her voice ringing with a ray of hope.

He girded himself and strode over to his mother then squatted before her, noticing the half-empty bottle on the table. "Mother?"

The injury she sustained while working as a silk weaver in a London factory had incapacitated her and deprived her of her livelihood. He had ended his career as ship's surgeon aboard *The Destiny* to secure employment in London to care for her.

It had been fate that led him to Harry's clinic—effectively going from one destiny to another. It provided the perfect solution—and today he'd come dangerously close to botching it.

Although recovered from her physical injuries, the use of laudanum provided by his mother's first physician had become a crutch to numb a pain deeper than those in her body. He tried to monitor and limit her usage, but her cries wore him down, and he inevitably relented.

She stared at him with lifeless eyes. His heart sped up when they quickened with recognition. "Charles?"

The name she spoke dashed the brief moment of hope as swiftly as it had arisen, and he cursed his father under his breath. "No, Mother. It's me, Oliver."

"Oh," she said, her voice so feeble it broke his heart. Like her people, she had been a fiery woman, full of life and spirit. Now, no longer able to busy herself with work, he watched helplessly as her mind strayed to another time, and the opioids provided escape from the memory of his bastard of a father.

He choked back a derisive laugh. Bastard indeed, poor choice of words when it was he, not his father, who bore the epithet like an open wound.

She lifted a hand and caressed his face. "Oliver? Are you home from school?"

Odd, how she always went back in time before his father had crushed her heart. He brought her hand to his lips and kissed her palm. "No, Mother. I've come from the clinic, remember? Tori said you had a good day." *Best to keep things positive.*

"Tori?" Her hand slipped from his and went instinctively to her abdomen. "Oh, yes, Victoria." She smiled weakly. "Will you play for me, Oliver? You know which one."

Of course he knew. He played it from memory now. He'd learned at his grandfather's knee, who had played it often for his daughter.

After removing the violin from its case, he plucked the strings and adjusted the pegs to tune it. The melancholy notes rose, sweet and pure from the instrument under his skilled fingers. He closed his eyes and soaked in the sound. Music flowed through his veins as life-giving as blood, the part of his mother's people he had inherited, and it tugged at his heart.

Finishing the requested song, he started another more lively tune. As a child, he'd seen his mother dance to it, twirling in her colorful skirts, so full of joy, the men clapping their hands as they gazed upon her with wonder. She'd been happy then, before *he* came back.

When her eyes began to glaze once more, Oliver struggled to hold her to the present. "Would you like to go for a walk? It's cold, but the air might do you good."

But it was too late; she'd gone back to the place where she found peace. He removed the bottle from the table, tempted to pour it out, but slipped it in his coat pocket, hoping to keep it from her as long as he could.

He turned toward Miss Evers. "You may go home if you like. I'll pay your full day's wages." Their unusual arrangement consisted of Miss Evers arriving in the morning and leaving when Oliver returned home. It suited both Oliver's meager funds and Miss Evers' desire to spend the evenings with her aging mother.

Truth be told, he had hired her as more than a tutor for Tori. But his hope that Miss Evers would provide companionship to his mother and monitor her use of the mind numbing drug had been dashed early into their agreement. If anything, Oliver suspected Miss Evers encouraged his mother's reliance on the painkiller.

Perhaps submitting an advert for her replacement would be in order. Lady Denby popped unbidden into his mind at the thought of advertising a position. *Drat!* Why did his thoughts constantly return to her?

He plopped down on the sofa, hung his head, and ran his hands through his dark hair.

"You need a haircut, Ollie. It's growing past your ears."

He glanced up into Tori's adoring face, the one bright light in his dreary world. "Do I?" He struck a pose even Brummell would envy. "I understand longer hair on gentlemen is all the fashion."

Girlish giggles erupted from her, the sound like music to his ears.

For all his protests about society, Tori deserved to fit in

somewhere—not be stuck in between worlds as he was. He'd continue to lie about her parentage if he had to. She would secure a suitable marriage if it killed him.

He cringed with shame—both from his heritage and from his disgust at being ashamed. His mother's people were proud, vibrant, rich in culture and tradition. They had been a part of his life once, before Tori had been born. Yet he didn't truly belong to them any more than he belonged to the upper class of his father. Adrift, alone, he had no place in either world.

Perhaps Harry had the right of it. For Tori's sake, he needed to mingle in society. At best, he would remain on the fringe, but association with landed gentry and genteel people would improve Tori's prospects.

He forced his best smile. "And I must be fashionable, Tori, because His Grace has invited me to a ball."

CHAPTER 6—MATCHMAKING FRIENDS

C amilla set aside her teacup and picked up the post from the silver tray. With the winter Season evidently in full swing, the number of invitations had increased daily. As she browsed through the selection, she paused at one particular item. The distinctive seal pictured a stag risen on hindquarters and pawing the air, a crown perched upon its head—the Duke of Ashton's crest.

Eagerly breaking through the wax, she scanned the invitation written in Margaret's precise and delicate hand. *A ball.* A ripple of excitement coursed through her. *Had Margaret mentioned it?* It would be the first they'd hosted since their marriage, and Camilla expected it to be a grand affair. A postscript at the bottom piqued her curiosity.

P.S. Wear your loveliest gown and prepare a selection to sing. I have a surprise planned. ~M

Although Camilla loved her friend, an uncomfortable prickling ran up her spine at the last sentence. Margaret's marriage to the unconventional duke had unleashed a mischievousness in her friend

Camilla hadn't seen since they were girls—the idea both heartening and frightening. No telling what mayhem this *surprise* would unleash.

She made up her mind to visit Margaret later that very morning. Camilla didn't usually perform at a ball, but she went through her music nonetheless, selecting a particularly difficult aria. Next to her selection another piece caught her attention, one that spoke to her mood of late. After a moment's hesitation, she plucked it out of the stack as well.

She arrived at Margaret's townhouse late morning, and Burrows, the butler, escorted her into the drawing room. Harry bent over Margaret sitting on the sofa. His hand caressed her face, and he pressed his lips to hers.

Camilla's steps halted. A slight jealousy tinged her embarrassment. How she missed those touches of affection.

Burrows gave a tiny cough, then announced, "Lady Denby, Your Graces."

Harry straightened from his position, a sheepish grin spreading across his face, and Margaret's cheeks pinkened. Camilla's arrival had obviously interrupted a private moment between the newlyweds.

Burrows seemed unfazed. "Tea, Your Graces?"

"None for me," Harry said. "I'm off to the clinic. Please have my carriage brought around."

He squeezed Margaret's hand. "Here's hoping I don't have to send Somersby home again today. I'd like to leave the clinic on time."

Concern twisted in Camilla's stomach. "Is he ill?" The words flew out of her mouth before she could pull them back.

Harry's eyebrows rose, and he studied her with a physician's interest. "No. Why do you ask?"

Camilla struggled to find an acceptable answer. Her eyes flitted to Margaret, who seemed particularly amused. "No reason, I simply wondered."

"Hmm," Harry said then turned back to his wife. "Have a pleasant visit." He strode past Camilla and gave her an all-knowing smile.

Margaret appeared ready to break out in a fit of giggles.

"What has possessed you, Maggie?" Camilla settled next to her friend, reining in her annoyance.

"I'm simply wondering why you're suddenly concerned about Dr. Somersby. When we spoke a few days ago, it seemed you detested the man."

"I do. He's an oaf." She brushed at an imaginary crease in the soft fabric of her gown. "However, I'm not heartless. I do have compassion for the sick."

As a footman brought the tray with tea, Margaret's lips pressed together in a tight-lipped smile, no doubt holding in those giggles.

Camilla delivered her famous disapproving stare, then changed the subject. "I've come to ask about the surprise you intend to spring on everyone at this ball you're hosting."

"Well, it wouldn't be a surprise if I told you."

"But you can tell *me*, I'm your closest friend."

The laugh Margaret obviously struggled to contain broke free. "Don't try that trick on me, Cam." She laughed again when Camilla made a pouting face. "That won't work either."

"Well, I'm glad at least one of us is happy."

Instantly, Margaret grew serious and reached for Camilla's hand. "I'm sorry. Is something wrong? Why are you unhappy?"

Camilla's chest constricted, the guilt of upsetting her friend weighing heavily. "I'm not unhappy . . . exactly."

The sigh whooshed from her, louder than she expected. "Our conversation a few days ago won't leave me. I'm wondering if perhaps you're right. The sight of you and Harry so happy and in love makes me miss having someone of my own. No, don't apologize," she said, catching Margaret's reaction to her words. "Of course, I'm thrilled for the both of you . . . well the three of you." Her eyes drifted to Margaret's abdomen. "But it has made me reconsider remarriage."

"But Cam, that's wonderful. And it makes the surprise I have planned even more perfect." The mischievous glint reappeared in Margaret's eyes, and, although thrilled at the lightness in her friend's demeanor after years of being crushed by George, Camilla's uneasiness grew.

"Are you certain you won't tell me?"

"No. So you might as well give up."

Conversation turned to other topics as they savored their tea. Margaret shared the news that Manny, the young street urchin she and Harry had adopted, had progressed in his studies and was reading and writing rather proficiently, the pride in her eyes shining brightly.

"You're a natural mother, Maggie. I wish I could make such strides with Philip."

"How *is* Pockets faring?"

"Still resistant to his new name. However, he's become very fond of my father." She took a fortifying sip of her tea, wishing it were something stronger. "So I suppose I should be grateful for that much."

Camilla had agreed to care for the boy as her ward, but struggled to make the connection with him that Margaret had made with Manny. Would she have had the same difficulty with a child of her own? A memory surfaced, dampening her spirits yet again.

Thank goodness for Margaret's sharp sense of observation, for she distracted Camilla's maudlin thoughts. "Did you hear about Lord Trentwith?"

Camilla shook her head, now eager for some gossip.

"Harry said he's looking for a new wife."

"Already? Funny how quickly men recover from the loss of a spouse."

"Oh, dear, I meant to cheer you, not add to your sadness. I only thought that . . . well, he's certainly not ancient and still rather good looking."

"Are you suggesting a match with me?"

Margaret lifted her shoulder. "Why not? He's titled, wealthy . . . handsome." Margaret grinned. "He'll be invited to the ball."

"Then I'll be sure to stay clear of him."

At that, Margaret chuckled, as if only she possessed some information that would make Camilla's statement impossible.

THE MORNING HAD BEEN RATHER UNEVENTFUL, AND OLIVER breathed a sigh of relief that he'd avoided Harry's disapproval so far.

A girl of about fourteen stared moon-faced at him as he bandaged a laceration on her hand.

"The doctors 'ere are so 'andsome," she said, much to Oliver's consternation. "The other doctor said 'e was married." She glanced at his hand as he fastened the ends of the cloth bandage. "I don't see no ring on you."

And here he'd managed to go through the morning being civil to his patients. He pulled in a calming breath. "Simply because you don't see a ring means nothing."

The girl was relentless. "Well, are you?"

"Keep that clean," he said, ignoring her question. "If it starts to ooze or develops a foul smell, return here immediately. And be more careful helping your mother in the kitchen."

Oliver shook his head as the girl jumped off the treatment bench, giggling as she made her way outside.

"Was that Lizzie Johnson?" Harry asked as he poked his head in the treatment room.

"I didn't ask her name."

The heavy sigh Harry exhaled indicated Oliver had once again disappointed his employer. "Oliver, it's important we get to know the patients so we can identify patterns in their physical ailments. Plus, it builds a rapport with them. I thought we discussed this."

Oliver leaned against the treatment table and raked a hand through his hair. "We did. I apologize. The girl made me nervous. Kept asking me personal questions."

Harry laughed. "That's Lizzie then. Perhaps I should speak to her mother. I'm concerned she's injuring herself simply to seek treatment here. I had to convince her I was happily married."

Oliver turned and gathered the supplies he'd used to treat Lizzie. "Maybe I'll concoct a wife of my own."

"Or get a real one."

Oliver snapped his head toward Harry and gave it a slow shake. "Oh, no. You may have been taken in by a woman's wiles, but I have no such intention. My life is perfectly fine as it is."

Harry just grinned.

"What?" Oliver spat the question.

"Well, in my expert opinion as a physician, the love of a good woman might be a perfect remedy to your malady. You've been on edge for the past month."

Burring his lips, Oliver snorted a laugh. "I don't have to marry one to *improve my mood*. There are plenty of women who would be happy to oblige."

Harry leaned against the doorframe, crossing his arms over his chest. "That's fine for simple physical relief, but I'm talking about the connection on a deeper level with someone who shares your hopes, your dreams."

"Spoken like a man newly wed. I appreciate your concern, truly. But what you and Margaret have is rare." Oliver pointed a pair of scissors at Harry. "Plus, you're of the same class, so you had no obstacles to overcome."

Harry's eyebrow quirked and his arms dropped to his side. "No obstacles? Is that what you think?"

Shame crept up Oliver's neck. Harry had told him of the difficult path to his and Margaret's happiness—an orchestrated compromise almost leading to an unwanted marriage of Harry to another woman. Not to mention Margaret's kidnapping. "I apologize. I simply meant you had no *class* obstacles."

With narrowed eyes, Harry seemed to study him, as if he were a specimen under a microscope.

"Is there a woman of another class who interests you? One you believe to be out of reach?"

"No," Oliver said, turning away from Harry's observant gaze. "I simply meant it as an example."

A hand clasped his shoulder. "Because if there is, my friend, I'd advise you to rethink that as an obstacle. Not all women—or men—are so prejudiced as to only consider members of their own class. You must consider the person—the woman herself."

And that was precisely the problem.

CHAPTER 7—MASQUERADE

C amilla stood before the mirror as her lady's maid fastened the
necklace at her throat. The ruby-red gown she'd ordered from
the modiste for the occasion fell in elegant folds over her body. A
daring color choice the modiste had said, but Camilla's decision to
stop sharing Hugh's grave demanded attire to match her new
outlook. She needed to feel alive. What better color than blood red,
the symbol of life.

A week before the ball, a package had arrived from Margaret.
Excitement bubbled as she opened it, revealing an intricately
decorated mask. The note said *For the ball. Please wear it as you arrive.*
As she ran her fingers over the cream-colored face dotted with red
stones around the eyes and edges, Camilla wondered if every mask
would be identical or if each would be specifically designed for its
wearer. Might that be how Margaret would tell her guests apart?

Whatever it might be, the additional thrill of anonymity
solidified Camilla's resolution to begin in earnest to seek a new
husband. What better way to assess each candidate when she had
no fear of being identified. The only drawback to her plan was she
wouldn't be able to identify the gentleman either. Ah, but she had
an idea for that. Camilla was nothing if she wasn't adept at finding

solutions. If a certain gentleman proved interesting enough and in turn exhibited sufficient interest in her, she would suggest they meet somewhere private and reveal themselves.

Her heart raced as her carriage traveled the short distance to the duke and duchess's residence in Mayfair. A fleeting worry surfaced that she had pinned too much hope on one evening, but she brushed it aside as the carriage came to a stop in front of the stately home. She slipped on her mask and made her way to the entrance.

As planned, she had arrived fashionably late. Burrows, Harry and Margaret's butler, greeted her at the door and checked her invitation. "My lady. Allow me to take your wrap." He slipped her cloak from her shoulders, folding it neatly in his arms. "The guests are upstairs in the ballroom. Due to the nature of the ball, no one is being announced by name."

The chatter of voices increased in volume as Camilla ascended the staircase. Soft music played, enough to provide a lovely atmosphere but low enough to allow conversation. As she stepped toward the entrance, a footman stood at attention.

When he stopped her, she was certain she must have misunderstood Burrows, but the footman pivoted and said as he addressed the room, "Ladies and gentlemen, a lady."

Everyone turned in greeting, acknowledging her arrival. Her supposition that each mask would be different proved true. Masks of various, vibrant colors and designs adorned the faces of the guests. Some were brief half masks covering only the area around the eyes, while others like hers extended down the nose and cheeks, leaving only the mouth exposed.

As she took in the scene, a man approached, weaving his way through the crowd. Tall, blond, wearing an unadorned half mask of simple black, he smiled and bowed upon reaching her. "My lady, welcome. Please make yourself at home. I hope you enjoy the festivities."

She couldn't contain her smile. "Ashton?" she whispered his name.

"Since you've already guessed my identity, Harry will suffice." He grinned. "Maggie wasn't very creative with my mask."

"It suits you. Simple and elegant, as befits a duke who's also a physician. But the way you greeted me gave you away, I'm afraid."

"True," he said, laughing. "I thought the idea of a masquerade was rather silly, but I'd do anything to make my wife happy." He held out his arms in supplication. "So, here I am. I'm afraid I also have an advantage as Maggie described your mask in detail, Lady Denby. She said we must be able to identify you for your performance this evening. But rest assured, only she and I know who you are."

He led her into the room, and Camilla marveled at the various colors and styles of masks. Most were ornate, but some appeared simpler. She wondered if there were clues to the wearer's identities hidden in the styles and decorations. Ashton's certainly fit his personality.

When they approached a small group of people, a woman with raven hair turned in her direction. It had to be Maggie. Like her husband, she also wore a half mask, but hers was silver edged with sapphires. It matched her marvelous silver gown trimmed with a sapphire ribbon. Camilla remembered a gown Maggie had worn with the same colors, but in reverse. A strong suspicion arose of some symbolism for the couple.

"Welcome," Margaret said, taking hold of Camilla's hands. "Isn't this exciting!" Joy radiated from her friend's smile, proving that expectant mothers truly glowed.

She wrapped her arm around Camilla's waist and leaned in to whisper, "There are a number of eligible gentlemen here."

Camilla regretted confessing her intentions to her friend. "But how will I know who is eligible and who isn't?"

"That's simple," Margaret said, as if it were a silly question. "All eligible gentlemen are wearing a blue mask."

"And eligible ladies?"

"Oh, no. All the ladies' masks vary. The gentlemen have no idea if a lady is eligible."

"Isn't that . . . risky if not dangerous."

Margaret laughed. "A bit of danger adds to the spice. But my thought was to give the women power to decide whether or not to pursue a liaison."

Harry tugged his wife close to his side. "My wife is devious, but wise."

Camilla wasn't so certain about the second part. "And have you communicated that to all the eligible ladies?"

"Of course. Didn't you read your invitation?"

Camilla blinked. *What?* She forced her mind back, trying to remember the words on the card, but shook her head. "I did but I don't remember anything about that."

"And here I thought I was so clever." Margaret sighed. "It said, *To find your heart so true, look for the men with masks of blue.*"

Camilla laughed. "Maggie, you're no Keats."

"Shh, don't use my name. Remember we're simply a lady or my lady this evening, and the men are simply a lord or my lord."

Camilla glanced around the room. "Is everyone here of the peerage?"

"Not everyone," Harry said. "But all shall be treated as such in my home."

"Now, go mingle," Margaret said, giving Camilla a gentle nudge into the crowd. "Over there is a gentleman with a blue mask."

As she walked away, Camilla heard Harry say to his wife, "I hope you know what you're doing."

Camilla hoped so, too.

※

A WEEK BEFORE THE BALL, OLIVER HAD RECEIVED A PACKAGE. INSIDE rested a sleek, blue half mask with a single, brilliant diamond-like stone by the left eye opening. Next to it lay a note that read *For the ball. Please wear it as you arrive.* Harry had mentioned something about a surprise, but Oliver had not expected a masquerade. Contrary to making him uncomfortable, the prospect of the anonymity the mask provided lessened his anxiety over the occasion.

In addition to the mask, the package also contained an expensive, but elegant waistcoat of sapphire blue, threaded with silver lines. Oliver ran his fingers down the silky fabric. Tucked inside was another note, written in a different hand. *This waistcoat brought me luck, perhaps it will do the same for you. Knowing your pride, consider it a loan, not a gift. ~Harry*

Much to the delight of his tailor, Oliver did purchase a new tailcoat and trousers for the occasion. As he dressed for the evening, he appreciated the man's workmanship. The coat, perfectly tailored to his body, fit snugly yet allowed for ease of movement. It was a vast improvement over his normally ill-fitting coat he wore at the clinic. The trousers, too, had turned out splendidly, comfortable yet snugly fitting his legs and waist.

He fussed with his neckcloth longer than he ought until his mother poked her head around the door.

"Oliver, would you like help?"

The elation he experienced at her lucidity made the evening a success, no matter what else might lie in wait. "Please. I can tie a simple knot, but I presume more is expected at a ball."

The color in her cheeks and sparkle in her eyes brought memories from long ago, before Tori had been born. It had been hell for nearly two weeks, but his mother had now been free of the laudanum for three weeks, using only willow bark tea to manage her pain. The transformation had been nothing short of miraculous—and Oliver didn't believe in miracles.

His eyes remained on her as she worked with the cravat, and when finished, she patted his chest.

"There. You're more handsome than any gentleman has a right to be." A shadow of sadness flitted across her face but vanished quickly.

He turned toward the mirror, and his jaw fell slack at the image before him. The magic she had worked on his cravat simply amazed him. Intricate folds cascaded from the precise knot at his neck.

"It's perfect, Mother." He kissed her forehead. "Now, I'm already late, so I'd better depart."

As he exited his home, he prepared to walk to the hackney stand several streets away, but stopped short at the carriage waiting outside bearing Harry's ducal seal. The coachman jumped down from his

A DOCTOR FOR LADY DENBY

post. "His Grace instructed me to fetch you," the man said, his tone barely containing his impatience. "I was about to come knock on your door."

"Yes, well . . . I had things to attend to." Heat singed Oliver's ears, even though the temperature had dropped to near freezing. He entered the coach and sat back on the plush seat, trying not to compare it to the cracked, stained seats of most hackneys, but his hands couldn't resist running over the soft velvet. A brick for his feet waited on the floorboard, presumably hot at one time, but the warmth had since leached out.

Before he had more time to ruminate over his untenable situation, the carriage slowed and stopped in front of the elegant home. Oliver had visited once before and felt utterly out of place. He slipped on the mask, hoping it might ease the sensation of being a fish out of water.

Upon entering, he presented his invitation to Harry's butler, Burrows, who took his frayed greatcoat and folded it as if it belonged to the duke himself. Oliver had liked the old gentleman from the first time he had met him.

Burrows directed him to the ballroom upstairs, explaining he would not be announced by name. As he climbed the stairs, Oliver ran his hands down his trouser legs, hoping his palms weren't as sweaty as they seemed.

A footman announced his arrival. "Ladies and gentleman, a lord."

A lord? What the deuce? He leaned in to the footman and whispered, "I'm not a lord."

The man smiled. "My lord, every gentleman here this evening is a lord."

Sweat now dotted his upper lip, but he stepped into the crowded room. People greeted him, the ladies curtsied and men bowed, some waved a flute of champagne in his direction as if toasting his arrival. He had never seen anything like it. What on earth did Harry expect him to do here?

The moment he had decided to turn tail and run for the door, someone tapped him on the arm. He spun a bit too hastily, brushing against the glass in the unsuspecting person's hand and spilling its contents.

"I beg your pardon," Oliver stumbled as the man before him simply smiled.

"You're late," the man with the black half-mask said as he wiped the liquid from his finely tailored coat.

Oliver stared, appalled at the nerve of this man to accuse him of being late—even if he was. "I beg your pardon."

The man smiled again. "You've already said that. Now, come and enjoy the ball. I'm expecting the proceeds will garner a healthy amount for our coffers." He chuckled. "Did you like my play on words?"

"Ha-Harry?"

"Took you long enough." He grabbed Oliver by the arm. "Now, let's get you a drink."

"But how did you know it was me?"

"The waistcoat for one. But also because you looked like you were going to be sick on the footman's feet as you entered."

"That bad?" The muscles in Oliver's neck started to relax.

"Worse," Harry said, and laughing, patted him on the back.

Like a lost child, Oliver stayed by Harry's side as long as possible, listening to the easy conversation of his friend with the other guests and desperately searching for topics of his own to share.

Not sure what he expected, the normalcy of the subjects confused him. Rather than talk of politics and indulgences of a wealthy lifestyle, they shared stories of family life. Oliver supposed it was intended to give hints of their identity, all of which was lost on him as he knew nothing of their lives.

Without warning, Harry excused himself to check on another guest. Oliver's mouth suddenly grew as parched as if he had been deprived of water for days, and he shifted uneasily, uncomfortable with the remaining group.

The orchestra had paused in its entertainment and was now returning. He admired the sheer number of musicians assembled for the gathering as they tuned their instruments. As he perused the string section, his gaze landed upon a striking brunette standing in front of the dais.

The vibrant color of her gown seemed out of place among the muted tones worn by the other women. The rich red against her alabaster skin stirred his blood. As it only exposed her mouth and chin, her mask made it difficult for him to detect her facial features, but her figure was exceptional. Voluptuous, he would say, as his eyes locked on the shockingly low neckline, exposing much of her full breasts. His once dry mouth now watered, and he caught himself licking his lips.

He gave a curt nod to the group around him, excusing himself, and threaded his way through the crowd toward her. A man in a blue mask, much like his, stood by her side, and Oliver hoped she wasn't married.

Now standing in front of her, he struggled for something to say. What had he been thinking?

The orchestra began to play, and he turned to see Harry leading a petite redhead to the dance floor. Oliver summoned his courage.

"Would you care to dance?" he asked the brunette in red. He wished he could see her face to gauge her expression.

"I'd love to." She turned to the man next to her. "Please excuse me."

A familiar ring to her voice and the scent of lilac made him wonder where he might have met her.

CHAPTER 8—STRANGERS IN SHADOWS

Camilla had enjoyed speaking with the gentleman she suspected was Laurence Townsend. His analysis of the latest scientific discovery by Danish physicist Hans Christian Ørsted and his enthusiasm over how electric current affected a magnetic field provided the clues to his identity. She liked Laurence, but there had never been any sparks between them. In addition, he had been enamored with Margaret for years, and she certainly had no desire to play second fiddle to any woman for the affections of a man, even her best friend. No. If and when she gave herself to another man, she would have to be the only woman on his mind. She wouldn't settle for less.

The hair on the back of her neck rose to attention as a tall, dark-haired man approached. His blue half-mask only added to the excitement. He moved like a sleek animal as he crossed the room—strong, powerful, determined. The only thing tentative about him was his slight, half smile. Impeccably dressed, his clothes hugged his body perfectly, and her breath hitched in her throat. *Marvelous.*

"Would you care to dance?" he asked, the purr of his voice adding to the animalistic illusion.

"I'd love to." She made her retreat from Laurence. "Please excuse me."

A thrill she hadn't experienced in years shot up her spine when she placed her hand on the handsome stranger's arm as he led her to the dance floor. The steps of the country dance didn't allow much contact between them, but each time their hands did touch, the energy passing between them was undeniable. What she had interpreted as a tentative smile she now recognized as the perfect mixture of confidence and arrogance. Remarkable eyes as blue as the mask he wore peered at her. The way his lips quirked at one corner sent waves of desire coursing through her.

During one of the longer periods of the dance in which they faced each other he said, "Please tell me that wasn't your husband?"

She would not show all her cards yet. Her own lips curved in a sly smile. She had missed the game and enjoyed playing again. "No. He wasn't my husband."

His deliciously low chuckle sent more shivers up her spine. "Perhaps I should rephrase and be more direct. Are you married?"

"Would it matter to you?"

He stopped in the middle of the dance, perplexing the other couples around them at the disruption to the line's formation. "I don't play games. Yes, it would matter very much. Are you married?"

His boldness reminded her of Hugh at their first meeting. Direct and no nonsense, Hugh had simply said he found her attractive and would like to keep company with her. A bittersweet sense of familiarity flashed in her mind. "No. I am not. Are you?" she asked, knowing the answer, but curious to see if he would be honest.

He flashed her a smile, and her heart sputtered. There, in his left cheek, the most glorious dimple formed. *Oh, my!* The room began to sway, and she reached out, grasping his arm.

The dimple disappeared. "Are you all right?" he asked, concern lacing his voice.

"My apologies. I feel a bit flushed. Perhaps some air?"

"It's February, too cold to step outside. Perhaps a less crowded room?"

She nodded and took his arm, allowing him to lead her from the ballroom. "There's a secluded parlor tucked down the hall." The scandalous nature of her suggestion added to the excitement, and she wondered what he thought about her utter lack of concern for propriety. Yet, he didn't object.

Thankfully, other than a few servants, no one wandered the hallway, and they were able to slip into the room unobserved. Only a few candles on a sideboard provided light, casting the majority of the room in shadow. After depositing her on the settee, he moved to light another candle.

"Don't," she said, and he turned toward her. "It might attract attention."

His mouth quirked up and even in the darkness of the room, the dimple announced its presence.

"Perhaps some brandy?" He motioned to the decanter next to the candles.

"Yes, that would be lovely."

Music sifted in, providing enough atmosphere without being intrusive. It couldn't have been more perfect if she had planned it.

He poured two snifters and moved to sit next to her. "May I?"

"Of course."

As he settled next to her, an almost palpable power emanated from him. This was a man used to getting what he wanted, and a trill of danger crawled up her neck.

She sipped her brandy, savoring its warmth as it slipped down her throat. Eyeing him over the rim of the snifter, she said, "So, my lord, does it distress you to have removed yourself from the excitement in the ballroom to attend to a weak female?"

His answering laugh, hearty and full, filled the room, and the dimple shouted at her as if to say *Look at me! Don't resist.*

Her heart pounded like the timpani of an orchestra.

"On the contrary, I'm grateful. And I have the suspicion you are anything but weak, my lady." He trailed a lazy finger up her forearm, shooting sparks along with it. "Not many unmarried ladies would agree to enter a room alone with a man. Aren't you concerned about scandal?"

Oh, but he is delicious.

"Tell me," he said, pausing to sip his own brandy, "You appear to be familiar with the home. Are you a frequent guest?"

Delicious *and* sneaky. "Why, my lord, is that an attempt to discern my identity?"

He cocked his head, and those crystal blue eyes penetrated her. "Not at all. I would imagine the duke and duchess have entertained a great many guests."

Did he realize his statement gave more away than he had intended? The word *imagine* spoke volumes. However, she chose not to pursue it. "Do you plan on contributing to the duke's clinic? It's a very worthy cause. They do so much good there."

His smile widened, and the dimple deepened. "I already contribute regularly, but yes, I plan to continue to do so."

Delicious, sneaky, and generous. He became more appealing by the moment. "What are your other interests beside assisting the poor? Please tell me you enjoy something other than hunting and gambling?"

"If I were to hunt, it would be to eat, and gambling is a vice I prefer to avoid. I've seen people's lives ruined by it." Another sip of brandy. "I enjoy music."

Behind her mask, her eyebrows rose. "Indeed? To listen or to play?"

"Both. And you? What activities do you find to occupy your day, my lady?"

The seductive tone of his voice more than the innuendo lacing the question heated her face. Her heart gave an odd syncopated beat in her chest. Perhaps as a debutante she would have missed his implication.

His lips quirked, indicating he recognized her comprehension of his intention.

She sipped the brandy, hoping it would cool her. It did not, but she swore she wouldn't give him the satisfaction of knowing how he'd affected her. "I'm involved in several charitable endeavors. I don't believe in being idle. As far as pastimes, I enjoy music as well, especially singing."

"Then we have more in common than the desire to avoid large crowds."

"Although I believe it was you, my lord, who indicated he was glad to be removed from the ballroom, I will admit I prefer more *intimate* gatherings." She smiled inwardly. Two could play at that game.

His chuckle, deep and sensual, erupted. "Such talk from an unmarried woman. What would your overprotective mama think?"

His question, although innocent, saddened her. "My mother passed away six months ago, I'm afraid. I miss her terribly. But I'm fortunate to still have my father."

Rather than tease her about an irate father discovering them, his smile faded and his voice became soothing. "My apologies for my callous remark. Losing a parent is difficult. I agree that you're fortunate to still have your father."

An uncomfortable silence settled on them, and she already missed the playful banter they'd shared.

He shifted, his thigh brushing against hers. "Have you ever wondered what your life would be like if you were born to different circumstances?"

What an unusual question. "Such as?"

"If you were free to do as you wish unencumbered. To choose whom you married . . . loved."

"But I believe I already am."

"Are you?" His eyes drilled into hers, disbelief lacing his voice. "So, if you discovered you had fallen in love with a commoner, there would be no pressure to break off the attachment? No objection from either your father or yourself as to his station and suitability as a husband?"

"Well . . . I . . . I don't believe that's what you asked."

"Isn't it? And if you were a commoner and had fallen in love with an aristocrat, would you be content to live as his mistress while he rears legitimate children with his high-born wife?"

An uncomfortable knot formed in her stomach, and she plucked at an imaginary wrinkle in her gown. "This is an odd conversation."

He swirled his brandy in the snifter, then took a languorous sip.

His tone softened when he said, "I beg your pardon. I merely wonder what it would be like to live in a world where our stations and heritage don't dictate our choices."

"You describe a utopia." She gazed into the amber liquid of her glass, contemplating his words, the thoughts new to her. "But I suppose it would be lovely. There is such a disparity among the classes, and by no fault except a person's birth."

She met his gaze, the depth in those blue eyes searching her very soul. "I suppose the reason for this evening's event has precipitated this desire to wax philosophical."

He blinked. "The clinic, you mean?"

"Well, yes. Helping the less fortunate has prompted your question. What else could it be?"

"Of course, what else."

"We should return to the ballroom," she said, rising.

He sprang to his feet with her. "Perhaps we should make an exit one at a time? For propriety?" The smile returned, the dimple accompanying it, and she realized how much she'd missed it during their more serious discussion.

"You've proven yourself a gentleman, my lord."

"I've enjoyed our conversation. I hope we have the opportunity to meet again, sans masks." No hint of sarcasm rang in his voice.

"Meet me back here at eleven o'clock, and we'll discuss it." She turned to exit the parlor, a restrained smile tugging at her lips.

※

OLIVER WATCHED THE TEMPTRESS'S RETREATING BACK, TRANSFIXED by the sway of her hips. Those dark brown eyes had searched his with an intensity that had nearly unmanned him. Her perfume, somehow familiar, had intoxicated him. So enraptured, he'd completely forgotten he didn't belong to her world. What would she think if he returned as she suggested, then discovered he wasn't really a lord? Did she mean what she said?

The old resentment buried deep within him boiled to the surface, and he cursed his father for the thousandth time. After swallowing the remainder of the brandy, he exited the room, still debating whether to pursue the woman in red.

Upon returning to the ballroom, he discovered the dancing had ceased and people were gathering around Burrows, who appeared rather uncomfortable as he stood on the dais.

"My lords and ladies," the butler announced, clearing his throat. "His Grace, the seventh Duke of Ashton, wishes me to thank you all for coming this evening. As you are aware, his philanthropic endeavor, The Hope Clinic, has been a great success in its service of medical care for the poor. However, he requests that I remind you, providing such service is not without cost, but relies on the generosity of those more fortunate. Any generous donations and pledges may be placed in the available box in the foyer."

Oliver fought a chuckle when Burrows' eyes started to dart to where Harry stood near the front of the dais, and with an almost imperceptible shake of his head, Harry reminded him not to reveal his identity.

"To further aid your spirit of giving, Her Grace, the Duchess of Ashton, has not only provided the opportunity to donate anonymously but also arranged for a special bit of entertainment. We have an honored guest here to sing for us tonight. If you would, my lady, please come forward."

The woman in red approached the dais, and Oliver straightened to attention. When she'd mentioned she sang, he'd presumed, like most well-bred ladies, she'd done so in a parlor for her family and friends. Perhaps she wasn't simply one of these toffs, but a professional entertainer. It might explain her nonchalance about being alone with him in a secluded, darkened room. The eleven o'clock meeting now seemed more enticing.

He expected to be moderately entertained, but from the first note out of her mouth, she enthralled him. *Such a voice.* Clear and pure, she hit each note with precise perfection. Gooseflesh rose on his arms. Lord, but she was magnificent.

Yet more than her voice, her passion in the delivery captivated and intrigued him. She performed the aria "Porgi Amor" from Mozart's *The Marriage of Figaro.* As if everyone in the room had become statues, frozen in place, the sounds of her voice and the accompanying orchestra riveted them all.

In his mind, he translated the Italian. *O love, give me some remedy for my sorrow, for my sighs. Either give me back my darling, or at least let me die.* He shifted, uncomfortable as if he'd intruded on the most private of moments, and her words, so filled with emotion, were as though she'd shared her very soul, connecting with his own. He'd never been so moved in his entire life.

When she finished, the room remained quiet, like the solemn moments following a prayer. Then the applause began, deafening and enthusiastic. His own arms ached from expressing his admiration.

A crowd swarmed her as she stepped from the dais, and he stretched to keep her in his sight. However, his efforts proved useless, and a sea of black coats soon consumed the splash of red of her gown.

"She's magnificent."

Oliver turned toward the male voice, rich with aristocratic haughtiness. The man wore a blue mask not unlike his own. When he met the man's clear blue eyes, a chill ran up his spine. It was as if he gazed on his own visage twenty years in the future. *It couldn't be.* He hadn't seen him in nearly twenty years.

"I wonder if she's married," the man said.

Oliver's jaw tensed. "Why?" He practically growled the question.

A smile played at the man's lips, then broadened, revealing a dimple.

Oliver's gut churned.

"I would think that's obvious. With her figure and voice, any man still breathing would be a fool not to wonder if she were available."

"Don't you care about what she thinks, dreams, her hopes?"

The volume of the man's laugh would have turned heads had the commotion in the ballroom not drowned it out. As quickly as the laugh started, it stopped, and the man reeled back. "Why, you're serious. Bit of a romantic, eh? Well, you're young. Give it time.

You'll soon discover that love only leads to heartache and suffering." He patted Oliver on the shoulder and strode toward the crowd surrounding the nightingale in red.

Oliver had the strongest urge to follow him, but decided to bide his time and wait for the eleven o'clock meeting.

The remainder of the evening, Oliver mingled as best he could and touted the merits of the clinic. As he shared stories of some of his more interesting cases, many expressed surprise at the level of care offered. When pressed about his knowledge, he merely stated he had become familiar with them from his dealings with the duke. More than a few conveyed their intention to leave generous contributions. He'd be able to report to Harry that he'd performed his assigned task.

Nothing more kept him there—except the tantalizing prospect of another meeting with the woman in red, perhaps to learn her identity.

As he departed another group of probable contributors, he noticed her speaking with, what appeared to be, the man who'd also shown interest after her performance. Oliver's steps quickened as he struggled to cross the crowded ballroom, but she slipped through the door and out into the hall.

After a few moments, the man also made his way into the hallway, and Oliver's skin crawled when the clock began to chime the eleven o'clock hour.

Someone grasped him by the arm, and he wanted to shake their hand off and tell them to go to the devil. He must get to her in time.

"Are you leaving without saying goodbye?"

He blinked at the man in the black half-mask. *Harry.*

"How the devil do you know it's me *this* time?"

Harry nodded toward Oliver's, or rather *his* waistcoat.

"Oh, of course," Oliver said, wishing to pull away from his employer and friend. "I'm not leaving just yet, but I do have an urgent appointment."

He imagined Harry's brows rising under his mask.

"Oh?"

"With a woman." Oliver regretted blurting out the truth.

A knowing smile spread across Harry's face. "I told you that waistcoat brings good luck. Be off, then."

Oliver nodded curtly and rushed out of the room toward the parlor.

Voices drifted from the cracked door, and Oliver peered into the room.

His instinct to hurry proved true, because the woman in red faced the man who had followed her.

"So, shall we remove our masks?" she asked.

"That would be delightful," the man said.

The seductive nature with which she removed her mask had his blood surging. The urge swelled to barge in and shout, "No! This is supposed to be my rendezvous." Instead he held his breath.

And his heart, beating like a racing thoroughbred, tumbled to his feet as her mask came off, revealing Lady Camilla Denby.

His mind swam as if fighting the current of the ocean when he had fallen overboard on one of his first voyages as ship's surgeon. It couldn't be. His sweet songbird was *her*? The self-righteous, pompous, prudish, meddling witch?

Could the turn of events become any worse?

The man pulled off his mask, and although his back was to Oliver, Lady Denby's words confirmed his worst suspicion. "Lord Trentwith!"

His father.

CHAPTER 9—NEW LOVE, OLD WOUNDS

O liver completely forgot about his promise to say goodbye to Harry. He raced down the stairs, yanked off his mask, and practically growled at poor Burrows when the man assisted him with his greatcoat.

"I'll have His Grace's carriage brought around to take you home, sir."

"Don't bother." He stormed out of the house and stomped down the street to find a hackney. Icy wind whipped at his coat, left unbuttoned in his haste to leave. Snow swirled in the air, painting the streets in pristine purity.

"Ha!" He choked out a laugh at the fitting juxtaposition for the scene he'd witnessed. His blackguard of a father and the high-and-mighty Lady Denby. Well, devil take it, they deserved each other.

The urge to retch in the street passed as he breathed in the frigid air, but nothing would remove the image from his mind.

He barked out his destination to the hackney driver and climbed in, remembering the soft velvet seats and warm brick at his feet in Harry's carriage. The clip-clop of the horses' hooves against the cobblestone streets along with the gentle rocking of the carriage began to work its soothing magic. By the time he arrived home, his temper had reached a low simmer.

He kicked his boots against the door's stoop outside to remove the snow and, taking a deep breath, stepped into his home.

"Ollie!" Tori jumped up from where she lay curled on the sofa in the darkened parlor.

He channeled his leftover anger to scowl at her. "What are you doing still up? You should have been in bed hours ago."

She gazed at him with the doe-eyed expression he couldn't resist. "Shush. You'll wake Mama. I waited until she was asleep and stole out here. Don't be angry. I wanted to hear about the ball."

He pulled off his greatcoat, shaking off the snow. "There's nothing to tell. There was music, some dancing, a lot of rich people talking about nothing of importance."

"Did you dance? Was she pretty? What was she wearing?"

"Slow down. One question at a time." In truth, he preferred to answer none of them, but he knew she wouldn't capitulate. "Yes, yes, and red."

Tori straightened with interest. "A red dress? Describe it." Her fingers ran over her nightdress as if imagining herself in such finery.

"It was a dress, it was red. I don't notice those things." The image resurfaced, the way the gown draped over her body, the delicate cap sleeves barely covering her white shoulders. How the cream-colored lace ribbon encircled her midriff and accentuated the low cut of the gown's bodice, exposing the tops of her full breasts.

Tori plopped down on the sofa. Her bottom lip stuck out so far he could have used it to lift her from where she sat.

He settled next to her and wrapped an arm around her shoulders. "None of that, poppet. Before too long, you'll have an opportunity to go to a ball and find out for yourself."

Her eyes widened, and even in the dim lighting he could see the whites. "Really, Ollie?" She practically bounced on the cushions.

Such innocence. He would be hard pressed to keep her from experiencing the sordid side of life. "In about eight years, so don't become too eager." He hoped by then he would have managed to develop some rapport with the pretentious *ton* besides Harry. However, a duke as a friend was indeed a good start.

His stomach twisted in a knot of guilt at the thought of using Harry's friendship to his advantage. Yet, as unsavory as they might be, in the social circles of London, such practicalities would be necessary.

"Now, I'm exhausted with all the dancing I was forced to do." He stretched and emitted an exaggerated yawn, then dropped his arm to Tori's side to tickle her. "And you should be in bed."

She burst out in a fit of giggles, tears forming in her eyes. "Stop, Ollie, you know I hate that."

"Then off to bed with you." He rose and followed her to her room, tucking her in. Soon she'd be too old for him to perform such tasks under the guise of her brother.

As she settled in her bed and he closed the door, his heart squeezed for the love of his daughter.

◊◊◊

CAMILLA DREW IN A SHARP BREATH. "LORD TRENTWITH!"

"You seem surprised. From our conversation moments ago, I'd presumed you'd already guessed my identity. Your comments about our mutual love of music when I praised your performance indicated you knew it was I."

She struggled to clear her mind and form the appropriate words to answer him. Her gaze dipped to his blue waistcoat. Something was different. Hadn't it been lined with silver threads? Although attractive, and the same deep sapphire shade, it was adorned with subtle geometric designs at the points. And the dimple. Had she imagined it?

His clear blue eyes narrowed, and he tilted his head. The eyes were definitely the same. "You're concerned I'm too old for you, is that it?"

Like a fool, she fumbled to answer and not insult him. "Well, no, of course not."

"I assure you, I have the stamina of a man half my age." The heart-stopping dimple popped.

The tension in her neck eased, and she breathed a sigh of relief. Perhaps she had been too focused on his nearness and smile to have paid attention to the detail of his waistcoat. She sent him an answering smile.

"I confess, I should have recognized you the moment you began to sing. But I've been absent from these gatherings during my wife's illness and, of course, mourning her death."

"Of course, my condolences," she said, her words lacking sincerity. Hadn't Maggie mentioned Trentwith was already searching for a new wife. She should have known.

He waved it off. "It's been nine months. You've suffered your own loss. How long has it been?"

"Almost nine years. Hugh died at Waterloo."

His eyebrows arched. "A long time to be alone. Much too long for someone so young and vibrant."

"Yes," she whispered. Her mind drifted, barely recognizing the implication of his statement.

"Without being indelicate, may I ask, what *was* your intention of inviting me here?"

She snapped back. "Nothing improper. I merely hoped that since we share mutual interests, we might find each other's company agreeable."

The dimple announced itself as he laughed. "Well, if I may be a *little* indelicate, may I say I'm a bit disappointed, but I whole-heartedly agree that an association would be quite enjoyable. If I may call on you—abiding by the rules of etiquette, of course—shall we see if our attraction has merit?"

An uneasy feeling snaked up her spine, but she ignored it. "Yes. I think that's a splendid idea."

He lifted and kissed the back of her hand, his eyes focused on hers the entire time. "To avoid any unnecessary gossip, I shall leave you. Expect me at eleven tomorrow morning."

As he took his leave, she whispered, "Oh, Hugh, am I doing the right thing? Give me a sign."

A burning sensation encircled her finger where her wedding ring had rested only a few days before.

☙❧

Precisely at eleven, Camilla's butler, Stratton, announced Lord Trentwith's arrival. She'd dressed in a gown of a subtle cornflower-blue trimmed with yellow ribbon and embroidered in a delicate design of lily-of-the-valley at the neckline. It had been one of the first she'd ordered after the mourning period for her mother had ended, something about it promising hope. When her hand had landed on it as she skimmed across the assortment in her wardrobe, it seemed a fitting selection for the day.

Trentwith smiled warmly as he entered the drawing room, and she greeted him with a graceful curtsy. Dressed in a bottle-green tailcoat, ivory waistcoat, and tan trousers, the colors didn't seem to compliment him as had his sapphire waistcoat from the prior evening.

He was, however, impeccably groomed, his hair styled in the latest fashion, and his cravat tied in endless intricate folds, much as she remembered during their conversation prior to her performance. In the light of day, fine strands of gray mingled with the dark black of his hair. Perhaps she had not noticed due to the dim candlelight in the parlor the night before. Yet the sensation something was amiss niggled at her and accompanied the unease that had crept through her the night before.

"It's bitterly cold outside today. Perhaps we might remain indoors?" he asked. "However, if that seems inappropriate or you feel uncomfortable, we can postpone to a time when the weather is more accommodating."

His consideration touched her, and although tempted to accept his gracious offer to bow out of their visit, the hopeful look on his face nudged aside the modicum of guilt at disappointing him.

"Nonsense. We'll simply leave the door open, and I'll have Philip join us." She nodded to Stratton, indicating he should fetch her ward.

She commended herself on the brilliant tactic. Not only would the boy's presence ensure propriety, it would also give her an opportunity to assess how Trentwith interacted with the lad.

Trentwith raised an eyebrow. "Philip? A family member I've not met?"

In answer to his question, running feet echoed noisily down the hall. She chuckled to herself, marveling how such a small boy could make such a clatter.

"Oi, your ladyship, you wanted me?" The blond boy grinned as he raced into the room, practically falling at her feet.

Trentwith's eyebrows rose even more, almost reaching his hairline.

"Lord Trentwith, I'd like to present my ward, Philip, although he's still getting used to his new name."

"And what, pray tell, was his name before?" Trentwith eyes narrowed on the boy as if assessing a worn-out workhorse.

"Pockets, your lordship. 'Er ladyship didn't like my name, but I says it's a right good name, it is."

"*Philip*," Camilla said, "is one of the orphan boys Ashton saved from that odious man Coodibilis."

"Oh, yes, I read about that. Didn't he and the duchess take another one of them under their wing?"

"Manny," Pockets said. "'E's my friend." He pushed out his bottom lip. "And they didn't make 'im change 'is name."

"Many of the boys scattered when Coodibilis was arrested. Ashton is still trying to locate them. Pockets needed a home, so I'm looking after him."

"I see. Well, it's a pleasure to meet you, young man." Trentwith extended his hand to the boy.

Pockets gave it a vigorous shake.

The brief flash of distaste on Trentwith's face disappeared so quickly, Camilla wondered if she'd imagined it.

She got Pockets settled with some foolscap and charcoals, having discovered the boy had a knack for sketching. Then she and Trentwith took their seats.

Trentwith's eyes skated over the boy, then met hers. Something bittersweet shone in them, and her heart warmed.

"A son should be a man's pride and joy," he said.

"You and your wife never had children?"

The sadness in his eyes nearly broke her heart. She understood that grief.

"No. She wasn't able to bear children."

"Hugh and I were married for such a brief period, and he left for the wars so soon, we hardly had a chance." She sighed heavily, remembering the devastation that she'd not been blessed with a child to console her in her grief.

How had the conversation turned so maudlin?

As she struggled to salvage the conversation, Stratton appeared and handed her a letter, providing a perfect excuse to end the visit.

❦

OLIVER CALLED IN THE NEXT PATIENT, AN ELDERLY WOMAN WHO reminded him of his grandmother. Guilt heated his neck at his negligence as a grandson. He hadn't seen her since Christmas, and he promised himself he'd visit her again soon.

His mind had been wandering all morning, usually landing on Lady Denby, the vision of loveliness in red. Would she make an appearance at the clinic? If so, would she recognize him, or did she truly believe Trentwith had been the man with whom she made such a profound connection in the dimly lit parlor?

Different scenarios played in his mind. In one, he'd be charming, leaving subtle hints as to his identity. In another, he would parry each insult with a thrust of his own. Try as he might, he hadn't been able to push her from his thoughts.

He forced his attention back to his patient. Bent with age, the woman had to have been in great pain, but she hardly complained when he'd tested her stiff joints.

"Is the willow bark tea helping, Mrs. Curtis?" he asked.

"Oh, I have my good days and bad days," she said, barely

stifling a moan as he extended her elbow. "It does help some, but what you gave me the last time is almost gone."

He patted her hand. "I'll get you more before you leave." After listening to her heart, which was blessedly strong and regular, he sat patiently while she entertained him with stories of her grandchildren. He'd learned early in his time at the clinic that some of the older patients simply wanted someone to provide an ear.

As he left to gather the willow bark from the area where they kept the medicinal supplies, Harry stopped him. "Oliver, I've received word from home that Margaret's unwell."

"Go, Harry. I'll take care of the patients."

Harry nodded. "Yes, I know you will. I don't know how long I'll be gone." Harry paused as if considering something. "I promised Lord Harcourt I'd stop by later this morning. Margaret loves him like a father. Would you mind stopping by and bringing him some St. John's wort? Ever since his wife passed away, he's not himself. I'm growing concerned."

"Not at all. Consider it done."

Harry wrote down some instructions and where Harcourt lived. "Thank you, Oliver."

Oliver placed his hand on Harry's arm. "Send word if you need me for anything." He hoped Harry understood the unspoken words that he prayed for Margaret and the baby.

Harry nodded, grabbed his bag, and left.

After giving Mrs. Curtis the willow bark, Oliver walked her out of the clinic. Much to the detriment of his wandering mind, things had been quiet that morning, and only Mr. Dawes remained. Oliver flipped the sign on the door to *Closed*. He tended to Mr. Dawes, providing a poultice for the man's hacking cough, and sent him on his way.

At twenty after eleven, Oliver boarded a hackney to Lord Harcourt's townhouse. He didn't relish treating an aristocrat, but easing Harry's mind took precedence over his own prejudices. He decided to make it brief. Give the man the medicine, provide an examination in short order, then leave to head back to the clinic.

There's a saying about best laid plans.

Oliver descended the hackney and gazed up at the imposing townhouse. Not as elegant as Harry's residence, which was no surprise considering Harry's title as duke, yet Oliver fought the impending inferiority as he strode up the steps and reached for the knocker.

A wizened ghost of a man answered the door. *Do all butlers look as if they've lived a century?* Oliver coughed, clearing his tightening throat. "Good morning. I'm Dr. Somersby. His Grace, the Duke of Ashton, asked me to call on Lord Harcourt and bring him some medicine."

The door opened, and the butler stood aside, allowing Oliver to enter. "Follow me," he said.

He led Oliver up a flight of stairs, the man's steps as slow as a Galapagos tortoise. Oliver had seen one during his tenure on *The Destiny* when they anchored off the coast of one of the islands. The man's wrinkled skin only served to make the image clearer, and Oliver fought the chuckle forming in his chest.

The moment Oliver entered the room, he donned his mask. Not a plague mask or the elegant blue mask he'd worn the evening before, but an invisible one, the type of mask he wore whenever he dealt with people unlike himself.

When working as a ship's surgeon, he'd occasionally worn a mask when the captain invited him to dine, or when he ventured ashore and partook of the pleasures available. The masks varied depending on the situation and location.

He'd even worn a mask during his interactions with Harry. Although at times, he'd come dangerously close to being himself. Harry had that effect on him.

The most difficult mask for him was the one of brother to Tori. That mask scorched his skin and clawed at his insides as if it were made of spiked, hot iron. That mask was a lie.

Today he wore his professional mask, that of a compassionate physician. At least it was one of the more *comfortable* masks—one he could wear and forget he had on.

"Dr. Somersby, my lord," the butler announced and motioned Oliver toward his employer.

Oliver strode toward the man slumped in a chair in front of a marble fireplace. The fire within, apparently untended, had dwindled to embers, leaving the room chilled. Harcourt didn't rise or look up in greeting as most well-bred men did. His eyes remained focused on the gray ashes of the fire as they emitted sporadic red sparks promising life.

"Sir?" Oliver squatted before him. With the mask now a part of him, compassion flowed within for the husk of a man in front of him. "His Grace had to return home for an urgent matter. He requested I stop by to see you and bring you something to ease your anxiety."

In slow motion, the man's brown eyes lifted from the fire to meet Oliver's. "Ashton's not coming?"

"No, sir. His wife is unwell." Oliver wasn't sure if he should have conveyed that bit of news, but Harry had mentioned Harcourt was like a father to Margaret.

Like flames of a dying fire that suddenly burst to life, Harcourt's gaze sharpened, and he straightened in his chair. "Margaret's ill? Is it the baby?"

"I don't know, sir. His Grace is with her. I'm here to take care of you." He pulled out his stethoscope. "May I take your pulse and listen to your heart?"

"Who are you again?"

"Dr. Somersby. I'm a physician at the clinic."

"Oh, yes. Of course." The focus in the man's eyes dimmed again as he drifted back to wherever his mind had been upon Oliver's arrival.

"Your heart is strong," Oliver said, but received no response. He reached for the man's wrist to take his pulse and found his hands were cold.

"Why haven't your servants tended to the fire? You're obviously chilled." Oliver pulled the poker from the stand and stirred the fire to life, then threw on two more logs.

When he turned around, Harcourt's gaze had refocused, and he was watching Oliver intently. Oliver recognized the pain in the man's eyes, he'd seen it often enough in his mother's. He pulled the

St. John's wort from his bag. "If you make a tea from this and drink it several times a day, it will help your mood. Steep several teaspoons in boiling water. You may add honey as a sweetener if you like, as it can be bitter."

"I have laudanum from my private physician," Harcourt said. "Ashton told me to stop taking it, but . . ."

Oliver gestured to a nearby chair. "May I?"

Harcourt nodded, and Oliver took a seat, preparing himself to have the same conversation he'd had with his mother. "Sir, laudanum has addictive properties. It may briefly . . . numb things, but you'll find you need to increase the dosage to achieve the same . . . effect. I concur with Ashton. I've personally seen the harm it can do."

"You?" Harcourt cocked his head.

"Not me, my mother. Have you taken laudanum today?"

"Yes, earlier this morning."

"His Grace said you've recently lost your wife. Grief is a natural process. It takes time to recover, but you can't stop living yourself."

Harcourt turned away, staring again into the fire that now blazed brightly and generated heat for the cold room. "Hmph, you sound like my daughter."

"A wise woman, I would say. Do you talk to your daughter about how you're feeling?"

He shook his head. "She has her own grief to deal with. She doesn't need to worry about me."

As he had with Mrs. Curtis, Oliver desired to offer a physician's willing ear. But more so, the grief borne from lost love shining in the man's eyes touched Oliver. It reminded him of his mother. An effective course of therapy often involved speaking of the missing piece of the mourner's heart. "Tell me about your wife. What was she like?"

Harcourt pointed above the fireplace. "Beautiful."

Oliver lifted his gaze to the portrait of a stunning woman with chestnut brown hair and warm brown eyes. Her enigmatic smile reminded him of the *Mona Lisa*. She looked *familiar*. "Beautiful indeed, sir. You were a lucky man. But what was her temperament, her interests? Tell me about *her*."

As if a spell had been lifted, Harcourt brightened. "Being around her was like walking outside on a spring morning when the sun came out after a sudden shower. Everyone adored her. With a word, she would turn your most mundane day into a celebration. She was a wonderful wife and mother."

He sighed, deep and heavy, then a smile crept across his face. "Once, when we were first married, we attended a ball and I'd spent too long in the card room." His eyes met Oliver's and a distinct twinkle appeared. "I do love cards. She marched into the room and gave me a serious dressing-down in front of the other gentlemen. She said, 'Robert, if you don't get up from that table and come into the ballroom and dance with me this very instant, when you're not looking, I shall fill your trousers with ants.'"

Oliver broke out in laughter, natural and heartfelt. "And what did you do?"

"Well, I looked at my cards, a certain winner, I might add, then I laid them on the table, got up, and went into the ballroom. I would have been a fool to say no to Georgiana. She was just the woman to follow through on that threat."

He laughed. "Of course, for several months, I had to endure severe harassment from the other gentlemen who'd been at the table. Lord Easton suggested I should just surrender my trousers to my wife since it was she who obviously wore them."

Oliver laughed so hard, tears formed in his eyes. "She sounds like she was a force of nature."

Harcourt nodded. "She was, and our daughter is just like her."

A woman after my own heart.

Harcourt's mood seemed to have lifted. The man apparently needed to share his memories to help him cope with his grief.

"I like you, Somersby," he said.

Oliver was about to suggest that Harcourt find another man to talk to on a regular basis when the sound of running footsteps drew his attention to the door.

A young boy rushed into the room and threw himself into Harcourt's arms. "Oi, Poppy, we 'eard you was feeling sad again."

Oliver couldn't restrain his grin, not only at the lad's exuberance but also at the way Harcourt's eyes lit up when the child climbed onto his knee and hugged him. Yet Oliver struggled with the disconnect between the boy's use of the affectionate term and his manner of speech.

Additional scuffling sounded from the hall, and Oliver recognized the labored footsteps of the butler. Expecting the boy's mother to be announced, he turned toward the door, an eager smile on his face.

The aged butler appeared in the doorway, followed by none other than the high-and-mighty Lady Denby.

Oliver jumped to attention, struggling to find the mask he needed to face her.

CHAPTER 10—REMOVING MASKS

When Camilla had received a message from Holmes, her father's butler, stating her father was again in low spirits, she'd made a polite apology to Lord Trentwith and left immediately, bringing Pockets. The boy's presence always cheered her father more than a strong tonic.

Now face to face with Dr. Somersby, she questioned the wisdom of her mission. The shock of his dimpled smile slammed into her as if she'd been run over by a carriage and four. Her gaze darted to his crystal blue eyes. *It couldn't be.*

Confusion swirled in her mind, but she fought to maintain her composure, focusing on the present. "What are *you* doing here?" She hissed the words at him and immediately regretted her sharp tone.

The man befuddled her to the point she'd forgotten her manners, and she made a feeble attempt to soften her words. "I thought Ashton was coming to see Father."

Dr. Somersby threw his stethoscope back in his bag and snapped it shut, a bit too forcefully perhaps. "Lady Denby." He attempted a weak bow. "He was called home. Her Grace is unwell."

Icy fingers snaked up her spine. "It's not the baby, is it?"

He narrowed those striking blue eyes and said through gritted teeth, "Why does everyone believe I'm privy to what's going on in a duke's household? I'm a lowly physician. I've simply come to deliver medicine to Lord Harcourt, and since I've done that, I'll be on my way."

"Must you go so soon, doctor?" her father asked, his gaze darting between Dr. Somersby and her.

Her father's question puzzled her. He wanted Somersby to stay? He'd always complained that his personal physician seemed more interested in his money than his health. More often than not, her father was grateful the man's visits were brief. Yet now he wished to prolong Somersby's. It was most curious.

"Please don't leave because of me, doctor." She turned toward the butler who straightened his bent body as best he could. "Holmes, please have the cook prepare tea. And biscuits for Philip, too."

Dr. Somersby shifted on his feet. The adorable dimpled grin had vanished, replaced by a glare.

"Forgive my manners," her father said, sliding Pockets off his lap so he could stand. "Dr. Somersby, may I present my daughter, Lady Camilla Denby."

"We've met," they answered in unison, causing Pockets to break out in a fit of giggles.

She motioned to the chair beside him, then took a seat on the sofa. Pockets made himself comfortable on her father's lap as soon as he sat back down.

Dr. Somersby lowered his large body into the chair across from her father, his attention now on the boy before him. "I'm Dr. Somersby, but you can call me Oliver. It's good to meet you, Philip." He shook the boy's hand.

As expected, the boy wrinkled his nose and crossed his arms over his chest. "That's what 'er ladyship calls me. My name is Pockets." He gave a firm nod of his head as if to reinforce his pronouncement.

She sighed, recognizing the futility of trying to change his name. Even *she* thought of him as Pockets. "I fear I'm fighting a losing battle."

"Then perhaps it's best to surrender and minimize your losses," Dr. Somersby said. "There are more important things to worry about in rearing a child than a nickname."

"Perhaps you're right."

His head jerked slightly, and he blinked. "You're agreeing with me?"

She fought the smile curling her lips. "I suppose I am."

His brow furrowed as he studied her, his eyes full of questions.

She imagined a series of cogs turning inside his head.

"I beg your pardon, I was under the impression you weren't married." A muscle in his jaw flexed.

The accusation alone would have convinced her of his identity, but that glorious dimple she'd witnessed as she entered the room had confirmed it. Everything fell into place. His odd question about wondering what life would be like if she were born in different circumstances. Of contributing to the clinic regularly. All the clues were there. She simply hadn't seen them because she believed she'd spoken with someone of the peerage.

Unease pricked her like tiny needles under her skin with the realization she'd mistaken Lord Trentwith for the man with whom she'd had so profound a connection. Heat rushed to her face under his judgment, the enormity of the situation rendering her speechless.

"My daughter is a widow. Hugh died at Waterloo."

She said a silent prayer of thanks to her father.

Dr. Somersby's eyes shot from her father to her. "My condolences." He tilted his head, his attractiveness growing tenfold. "I'm curious. I gather Pockets isn't your son, but he called your father Poppy."

Pockets hugged her father, and a bittersweet twinge squeezed her heart. How she would have loved to have given him a grandson.

"Poppy said I could."

"Pockets," she said, deliberately meeting the boy's eyes, "is my ward."

The boy beamed, and his tiny chest puffed out, obviously relishing his victory.

"Ah," Dr. Somersby said, his eyes widening. "One of the orphan boys His Grace discovered. Of course. I've met Manny." He grinned at her, the expression so genuine it melted her heart. "From what I've heard and seen myself, I'd say you'd better count your silver daily."

Her father ruffled the boy's hair and laughed, the sound so glorious to her ears she wanted to jump up and shout *huzzah*. "I've found my pocket watch missing on numerous occasions."

"But I always give it back. Don't I, Poppy?"

"Yes, you do."

"You seem in fine spirits today, Father. Perhaps Holmes overreacted when he messaged me."

"That man oversteps on a daily basis." Her father shook his head. "If he weren't so old, I'd sack him for his impertinence."

It was all bluster. The butler had been with her family for years, beginning with her grandfather. Her father would never dismiss him.

"But I will admit," her father continued, "that I was feeling a bit under the weather before Dr. Somersby arrived." Warmth exuded from his expression as he nodded toward Dr. Somersby.

Desperate to hold on to the impression of Dr. Somersby as an odious oaf, she offered an explanation. "He said he brought some medicine. Perhaps that has accounted for your lightened spirits."

"He did, but I haven't taken it yet. No, we simply enjoyed a heartfelt conversation," her father said.

Everything she had presumed flipped on its head.

"As much as I enjoyed visiting you, Lord Harcourt, I really must return to the clinic. You're in good company now with your daughter and Pockets." Dr. Somersby rose and gave the boy's blond hair a tousle.

Pockets tilted his head as if studying Dr. Somersby. "You kinda look like that Lord Tentworm bloke, but you're nicer."

Dr. Somersby's brows raised, his head turning toward Camilla. "Lord Tentworm?"

Heat rushed up her neck to her face. "Lord Trentwith, Pockets." She turned to her father to avoid Dr. Somersby's penetrating scrutiny. "Lord Trentwith was paying a call when I received Holmes's message."

"Oh?" Her father's eyes widened.

Dr. Somersby coughed and fidgeted as if uncomfortable. "It appears you have family matters to discuss, and I'm intruding."

"Will you come again?" Her father's words seemed so hopeful. She half expected him to reach for Dr. Somersby's coat sleeve in much the way Pockets would reach for her skirts to restrain her.

"If you like. Send word if the St. John's wort seems to help, and I'll bring more. Now if you will all excuse me."

He strode out of the room, and she found herself bounding to her feet and rushing out to stop him. "Dr. Somersby, might I have a word?"

In the hallway, he stopped and turned toward her. "What is it? I really must get back."

Now that she faced him, she struggled to find the words. "I believe I owe you an apology. It's come to my attention that I've been undeservedly harsh with you. I find I've been mistaken." *About so many things.*

He bowed gracefully. "Think nothing of it, my lady."

He turned again, and she reached out, grasping his arm. His gaze drifted down to where her hand rested on his sleeve, then rose to meet her own.

"Dr. Somersby. I wanted to ask you . . . are you . . ." She swallowed hard before continuing. "Were you at Ashton's ball last evening?"

"I was. What of it?"

"Might we have . . . spoken privately at one point in the evening?"

A dark brow lifted. "Privately? I doubt it, although I suppose it's possible. I conversed with a number of women. Why?"

With those simple words, the door she cracked open to let him in slammed shut. The bitter lump she swallowed did not contain her pride. "No reason. I thought perhaps I recognized you."

"That would have been difficult, would it not, since everyone wore masks?"

"Of course. I'm sorry. Thank you for coming to see my father. Your visit seemed to make a difference."

He nodded, his expression softening. "I like him. He's a good man. He misses your mother. It helps him to talk about her, but that might be too painful for you. I simply listened. Now, I really must be off."

"Of course."

As he turned the final time, she forced down a tiny bit of her pride and said, "Were you wearing a sapphire waistcoat lined with silver threading?"

His footsteps faltered, but he recovered and continued on without answering, taking her hope with him.

OLIVER KEPT HIS TEMPER IN CHECK ALL THE WAY TO THE HACKNEY stand. He refused to give her the satisfaction of knowing she affected him so viscerally.

He'd tried to put her from his mind the entire evening after he'd returned home from the ball. But the image of her with his father taunted him and prevented him from sleeping. He hadn't expected to see her again so soon.

No, the *last* thing he'd expected was for her to have taken an orphan under her wing. He struggled to reconcile the overbearing shrew with the compassionate and affectionate woman who was willing to take on the commitment of a lost boy. Could he have misjudged her?

And she'd been widowed at a young age. She couldn't have been much more than twenty when her husband died. Why hadn't she remarried . . . and why did he care?

He ground his teeth. Any additional encounters with her and they'd be stumps before long. Her attempt to tell him she recognized him as the man with whom she'd had that intimate conversation was genuine, and he all but slapped her in the face. A nasty taste filled his mouth.

He sat back against the worn seat of the hackney carriage,

exhaling loudly, and convinced himself it was for the best. He knew how things ended when a woman invaded his mind to distraction—badly. He'd been down that road before, and he'd prefer not to repeat it.

But Lord, they had so much in common, and although he'd never admit it to anyone—even himself—it frightened him. Their love of music, their strong-willed personalities, their fragile bereft parents, their attempt at veiled parenthood, their undeniable attraction to each other.

However, those things mattered little when one great divide remained. And that particular chasm was too great to cross. Even if they found a way to bridge the gap, such passion would consume them both, leaving nothing but a pile of ash.

No, it was best to end it before it even began, and let it wither and die a silent death.

He arrived back at the clinic to a barrage of patients waiting at the door. As he let them in, he said a silent prayer of thanks he'd at least be occupied the remainder of the day.

By evening, he'd managed to exhaust himself. He locked up and decided to walk instead of taking a coach. The brisk winter air whipped at the edges of his greatcoat, and snowflakes drifted down, covering his hat and shoulders.

Although his head told him to go home, his feet took him in the opposite direction. An hour later he stood in front of Harry's residence in Mayfair.

Soft lights illuminated the windows, and his hands, almost frozen from the cold, ached to reach toward them for their warmth. Before he realized it, he was knocking on the door.

Burrows' eyes widened as he greeted him. "Dr. Somersby. Is His Grace expecting you?"

Of course he isn't. Oliver shuffled his feet, ashamed to intrude, especially in such a trying time with Margaret ill. "No. I wanted to stop by and inquire about Her Grace."

Burrows opened the door and beckoned him inside. "Come in and warm yourself, sir. It's bitterly cold out there and you look positively blue."

Snow fell to the floor from Oliver's hat and coat, and if it annoyed Burrows, he didn't let on. Instead, he took the items from Oliver, folding the coat as gently as he had the evening before and laying it on a bench by the door. "His and Her Grace are in the parlor. Follow me."

Oliver breathed a relieved sigh that Margaret at least wasn't bedridden. As he climbed the stairs, memories of the night before with Lady Denby rushed back. Would he ever be able to be in this house again without the image flooding his mind of her in that red gown, singing like an angel, sharing dreams in a dimly lit room, her alluring scent tickling his nose, then having the memory tainted by the intrusion of his father?

Sounds of children's laughter drifted out into the hallway as he approached the parlor. Had they taken in another child besides Manny?

His gut clenched as Burrows announced him and he caught sight of the profile of the woman seated across from Harry and Margaret. His gaze darted to the boys playing knucklebones on the floor at their feet, the blond head of Pockets bobbing excitedly with each bounce of the ball.

Before he could turn tail and run, Harry rose in greeting, and the woman he'd tried desperately to put out of his mind turned, her eyes wide.

"I'm sorry to intrude. I didn't realize you had guests," he blurted. "I can't stay. I came to see how Her Grace was faring."

"Nonsense," Harry said. "Camilla is family, as are you. Besides, you look frozen. How long have you been outside? I swear your lips are blue." He directed his attention to Burrows. "Some fresh tea, please, Burrows. Ours is growing cold."

Burrows bowed and left. Oliver wished he could attach himself to the old man's coattails and be pulled from the room and his embarrassment.

He inclined his head toward the woman driving him mad. "Lady Denby," he said, his own voice sounding like the growl of a dog. "Your Grace." He bowed, his voice softening in greeting to Margaret. "I trust you're feeling better?"

"A simple dizzy spell. Burrows and Flora overreacted and sent word to Harry." She turned toward her husband, her affection for him written clearly on her face. "He rushed home unnecessarily. For a physician, he worries needlessly." She smiled warmly at Oliver. "Please make him promise to return to the clinic tomorrow. He completely interrupted my lessons with Manny."

The boys glanced up and Pockets grinned. "I know you! You were at Poppy's today."

As Pockets' back was turned, with deft fingers, Manny stole two of the game's stones.

Oliver took a seat in the chair farthest from Lady Denby. "Don't turn your back on Manny, Pockets. He's cheating."

"Whaa?" Pockets spun back around and the boys began wrestling over the purloined stones, their rambunctious laughter filling the room with life.

"Oh, dear," Margaret said. "Harry, stop them. They'll hurt each other."

Harry rolled his eyes, the barely contained smile tugging at his lips. "They're boys, Maggie. Let them sort it out for themselves."

"Why must every act of misbehavior be attributed to their sex?" Margaret asked, sending a pleading look to Camilla.

"Don't enlist my help," Camilla said. "I agree with Harry."

Oliver blinked. "You do?"

His heart rapped against his chest when she sent a wide smile his way.

"Well, of course. But I would argue, it's not only boys who like to rough and tumble. It's simply that girls are told early on it's not appropriate for a lady." A sly gleam shone in her eyes as she turned toward Margaret. "Did you forget that summer when I hid your favorite doll?"

Both Harry and Oliver straightened in their seats and turned their attention to Margaret as the boys continued their wrestling. "I must hear this," Harry said.

Oliver agreed.

"Oh, no," Margaret hid her face in her hands. "Please, don't."

Camilla grinned. "Maggie was eight, and I was eleven. I was

staying at Woodstone Hall"—she turned toward Oliver as if to explain—"Maggie's country home for the summer. Maggie had a new doll she refused to share when we played. While she was sleeping, I crept into her room and took it."

"Perhaps the boys shouldn't be listening to this," Margaret said.

Harry laughed. "They're not, and even if they were, I doubt they'd need ideas for stealing. Go on, Cam."

Cam?

"Maggie was frantic trying to find that doll. I hid it in the stables and unfortunately, one of the horses . . . well, let's just say, the doll required thorough cleaning."

Margaret laughed, waving a hand in front of her face. "Oh, the smell was horrendous."

Although enjoying the story, Oliver was confused. "I'm not following the connection with rough-housing."

"Because I'm not finished. I'd thought it was forgotten and she had forgiven me. But the sneaky thing waited, lulling me into a false sense of security. We'd taken a stroll down to the lake on their estate, and as I sat reading, she pushed me into the water."

Oliver laughed. But as the image of Camilla soaking wet coalesced in his mind, he had a hard time picturing the girl instead of the woman, and his amusement shifted to something more heated.

"Oh, that's not the end of it," Margaret said, clearly remembering the incident with as much delight as Camilla. "Cam floundered in the water, begging for my help. She was a splendid swimmer, so I should have known better. But like a fool, I reached out to assist her, and she grabbed my arm and pulled me in with her. We must have thrashed about in the water for ten minutes before we pulled ourselves out. Soaked to the skin, we threw ourselves on the ground in fits of giggles."

"If my memory serves, we both were sent to bed without our supper," Camilla said, wiping the tears of laughter from her eyes.

Oliver stared at her. Who was this carefree and vibrant woman before him? The truth hammered him. This was Lady Camilla Denby without her mask. His heart thumped in an erratic beat.

Unbidden, his hand rose to cover his chest and massage the not quite unpleasant twinge away.

"Oliver?"

He turned his gaze from—the now intoxicating—Lady Denby to find Harry's questioning eyes.

"Are you feeling ill?" Harry asked. Something about the glint of humor in his employer's face told him Harry understood exactly what was happening.

"Long day," Oliver said. He expected a snide remark or witty retort from Lady Denby, insulting his terse answer, but when he turned back to her, her lips curved in a tiny smile.

"Of course," Harry said. "Camilla told us how helpful you were with her father. Thank you again for stopping by to see him."

"It was my pleasure," he said, truthfully. "It does concern me that his private physician prescribed laudanum."

"I concur," Harry said. "I'll check on him in a day or so."

"Harry, if you don't mind, could Dr. Somersby visit him?"

Oliver blinked, a strange mix of confusion and pride eddying in his mind.

Silence filled the room. The walls seemed to close in as all eyes turned toward him. The boys had stopped their wrestling and sat wide-eyed listening to the conversation.

"I suppose that's up to Oliver," Harry said, pointedly looking at him.

Camilla's warm, brown eyes bore through him. "It's just . . . well, Father appeared so much better after your visit. He told me how much he liked you." Pink crept across her cheeks, the effect most attractive. "I'm sorry, Harry, of course he likes you, too."

An uncomfortable itching sensation manifested around his collar, and he resisted the urge to reach up and run his finger around his cravat. "I'd be happy to, Lady Denby," he said, hoping to be done with it and excuse himself to go home—where he should have gone in the first place.

He rose, eager to remove himself from the awkwardness of the situation. "If you'll excuse me, I didn't intend to stay."

Burrows entered with the tray of hot tea.

"But the tea," Margaret said. "At least warm yourself before you leave."

He dutifully sat down, not as much out of respect for her station, but for her as a person. Harry sent him a look of gratitude.

"Allow me to pour, Maggie. You rest." Camilla poured the tea and handed a cup to each of them.

When she passed the cup and saucer to Oliver, their fingers brushed, and a warmth from more than the tea raced up his arm. His eyes darted to hers, catching the darkening of her cheeks. "Thank you," he mumbled.

"Did you take a hackney here?" Harry asked.

Oliver shook his head. "I walked."

The cup in Harry's hand clattered against the saucer, and his blond eyebrows nearly reached his scalp. "From the clinic? Are you mad? No wonder you were frozen when you arrived. I'll have Burrows bring my carriage around to take you home."

"If I may," Camilla interjected. "I'd be happy to share my carriage with Dr. Somersby. We should be leaving soon as well. I don't want to tire Maggie."

As if paralyzed, Oliver's jaw fell slack at the idea of sharing a coach with Lady Denby. *Close your mouth, you dolt.* Recovering, he said, "I couldn't impose. I'm certain it's not on your way."

"Nonsense. I insist. It's the least I can do for your kindness to my father. Don't argue. You won't win." Her lips tipped up in a half smile, drawing his eyes to them.

Only the desire to capture her mouth with his outweighed the impulse to run his tongue over his own lips. He suppressed both and struggled for a sufficient reason to decline her offer.

"It wouldn't be proper as we're both unmarried." The fact now rooted in his mind to distraction.

"Pockets will be with us. And what can you possibly do in a carriage?" she asked, as if to dare him.

I can think of many things.

A soft cough came from Harry and Margaret's direction, but Oliver remained unsure which of them had emitted it. The realization hit him like a punch to his face. Lord help him, he could deny her nothing. "Very well."

Harry called Burrows to have Camilla's carriage pulled around, and after finishing their tea, they bade goodbye to their hosts.

As Burrows helped them with their wraps, Oliver cringed when her gaze traveled over his frayed greatcoat. What would she think?

Once boarded, he sat in the plush seat across from her and the boy. Silence permeated the compartment, the only sounds the clip-clop of the horses' hooves and clicking wheels against the cobblestone streets. The sweet smell of her lilac fragrance filled his nostrils, and he breathed deeply.

Pockets snuggled against Camilla's side, his eyelids drooping as the rocking motion lulled him to sleep. The boy had to be no older than five or six, and Oliver wondered how his young mind had been affected by the harsh life he'd experienced before being rescued by Harry.

"You've done a good thing taking him in," he said.

Her gaze bolted up to meet his. She ran a gentle hand across the child's blond head. "I've benefited more from him than he has from me. He's taught me patience and the meaning of unconditional love."

Oliver arched a brow. "You didn't have patience before?"

Her lilting laugh bounced through the small enclosure, music to his ears. "You of all people should know the answer to that."

She grew serious as she continued to stroke the boy's hair. "May I call you Oliver?"

The sound of his name on her lips pleased him more than he cared to admit. "If you like."

"Oliver, I fear we got off on the wrong foot. I should like to set things right and begin again, if possible."

An invisible hand squeezed inside his chest. "To what end, my lady?"

She blinked, her head jerking back as if hit by a frigid blast of air. "I . . . I . . . simply thought we could be friends."

Friends—not what he had in mind. "We hardly move in the same social circles, my lady."

"Won't you call me Camilla?"

Blast her. The woman set his teeth on edge.

She hesitated again, opening her mouth and closing it several times. Then she squared her shoulders as if preparing for a fight. "I thought we had a . . . connection. I believed you felt it, too. Something . . ." She stared out the window into the darkness.

Although he tried to stop himself, he couldn't help asking, "Something what?"

Her gaze drifted back to his, her eyes heated, defrosting the chill in the night air. "Something special."

When she sucked in her bottom lip, the urge to leap across the small space separating them became so strong, he feared he would ravish her right in front of the boy.

Leaning forward, he kept his voice low so as not to wake Pockets sleeping soundly against her side. "Are you suggesting we become lovers? I thought only men of your class sought out the lower-born to fulfill their baser desires. Don't women seek out men from their own class for liaisons?"

Even in the carriage the darkening of her cheeks became obvious, and blast it if he didn't find it alluring.

"I know it was you last evening. The man who danced with me, who shared such tender moments discussing our mutual love of music, of a utopia where people are free from society's constraints."

His jaw clenched tight. "I'll not deny it."

"Then you know such a connection is rare and shouldn't be carelessly dismissed."

He glared at her, hoping to dissuade her from pursuing this impossible dream.

"Oliver," she said, her voice so soft he wondered if it could drown a man. "Please say something."

"What do you want me to say? You're a high-born lady, and I'm a lowly physician."

"That doesn't matter." She shook her head so vehemently, he thought her bonnet would fly off. "In all that matters we're the—"

He held up his hand and bellowed, "Don't say we're the same. We're *not* the same and never will be. I saw you eyeing my tattered coat, my worn boots. I'm not some fancy gentleman who can lavish you with fine clothes and jewels."

Pockets stirred, his eyes opening wide in terror. He placed his hands over his ears and huddled even closer to Camilla, his knees pulled tight to his stomach.

Regret and shame slammed into Oliver as he stared at the frightened boy. Mercifully, the coach jerked to a stop at his home.

"I apologize for my outburst. Now, if you'll excuse me, *my lady*."

He jumped out of the carriage and slammed the door before the coachman could descend to assist. After racing up the stairs, he turned one last time to see Camilla's face peering from the coach window. Shame slithered in his gut.

CHAPTER 11—THE PROPOSITION

Camilla stared out the carriage window. She stroked Pockets' arms in an attempt to console him. What had come over Oliver? His reaction seemed disproportionate to what she intended as a simple request to share each other's company and explore their attraction.

Did he truly believe they were so far apart as to not be able to form an attachment? She wouldn't be the first noble woman to marry a commoner.

Wait? Marry? Where had that thought come from? She brushed it aside.

His words rang in her ears. *Are you suggesting we become lovers?* Her heart pounded at the image of being in his heated embrace, and a familiar, pleasant ache flooded low in her body.

"What was 'e so riled about?" Pockets asked, his little body still shaking.

"I don't know."

Answers to the questions assaulting her became as difficult to pull from her mind as treading through heavy snow. Each step a burden, and each foot leaving a deep imprint. She'd go mad if she continued to dwell on it. Besides, Pockets needed her.

"Don't worry about him. I doubt we'll see much of him from now on." A hollow sadness filled her heart. Why did that thought bother her? "Let's go home."

True to her prediction, over the next two months, Oliver Somersby failed to cross her path—unless you counted her dreams. There, he made an almost nightly appearance, leaving an aching in her heart as well as deep in her body when she awoke.

She continued to accept calls from Lord Trentwith, and something about the man intrigued her but made her proceed with caution. He'd hinted at the possibility of a physical relationship more than once, but she feigned innocence and ignorance at his innuendoes. Inevitably, her mind turned to Oliver and their last encounter. She wondered if their association had continued, would she respond in kind to similar suggestions?

The winter months had given way to spring, Camilla's favorite season of the year. She spent more time in the garden, tending her flowers and working in the rich soil. Pockets loved to assist, usually ending with more dirt on him than in the flower beds themselves.

After ensuring Pockets no longer had dirt on his clothing or his face and hands, she prepared a fragrant bouquet of her favorites for an impromptu visit with her father to check on his state of mind.

He'd improved greatly over the past few months, and she wondered how much of his progress hinged on his visits with Dr. Somersby and how much on the strange tea he drank. Although her father mentioned Oliver's visits, he never went into detail regarding what they discussed.

As usual, Pockets raced ahead of her when Holmes led them up the stairs to the parlor. Before she'd made it halfway up, Pockets barreled back down, grabbing at her skirts.

"It's 'im," he said, his eyes wide as saucers. "'E's not yelling, though."

"Dr. Somersby's here?" she asked, her eyes darting to Holmes, who continued to trudge up the stairs at a snail's pace.

"Yes, madam," the ancient man answered.

The urge to turn around and head straight back home tugged at her. Or was that Pockets pulling on her skirts?

"Are you afraid of him?" she asked the boy.

"No, but I figured you'd want to know since 'e yelled at you somefin' fierce last time."

Her heart gave a little squeeze that the boy considered her feelings. Of course she didn't fear Oliver. The desire to avoid him had nothing to do with fear—or did it? Not fear of the man himself, but the power he held over her perhaps. She squared her shoulders and continued up the stairs, only navigating two before catching up to Holmes. "It will be fine, Pockets. Dr. Somersby has had plenty of time to collect himself."

As they entered the room, Oliver's eyes met hers, and she could have sworn an apology lurked in their clear blue depths. A soft sigh of relief escaped her lips—not for herself, she argued—but for Pockets.

He rose and executed a perfect bow. "Lady Denby." The corners of his mouth twitched, and she willed the smile to appear. "I've only just arrived, but if you prefer I leave so you may visit with your father, I can do so."

"Nonsense," she said, her eyes darting to her father, who smiled warmly. A tingle of joy surged through her at his improvement. What magic did the doctor perform to change his course so dramatically? And could he perform the same wonders on her own melancholia that crept in at night as she lay alone in her bed?

"Dr. Somersby was telling me the most marvelous story," her father said. "Did you know he served as a ship's surgeon before he assumed his position at the clinic?"

"Stories?" Pockets asked as he climbed on her father's lap. He clasped his hands under his chin, his elbows resting on his knees. "I love stories."

Camilla did her best to restrain her enthusiasm, but she, too, loved stories, especially those of adventure. She took her seat and found herself leaning forward. "Please continue."

"The sea raged. Waves crashed over the deck, bringing fish with them. They wriggled and squirmed as the men scurried about grabbing them and throwing them into pails." Oliver, still standing, moved about and, in dramatic fashion, demonstrated to Pockets' delight.

"I fail to see how a horrible storm is a *delightful* tale," Camilla said, scoffing.

"Patience, my lady." Oliver flashed her a smile.

Like the storm he was describing, a wave of desire hit her when the dimple popped, throwing her heart into an erratic rhythm.

"As I was saying. The ship tossed against the strong winds as if it were a toy. Men fell against the railings, their shirts and trousers drenched and pressed against their bodies like a second skin. The boatswain called for the second mate to climb the mast and reef the sails."

"Wha's that mean?" Pockets asked, his mouth hanging open.

"Reef is to fold the sails inward so they don't catch as much of the wind," Oliver explained. "The second mate inched up the mast, his hands slick with rain, trying to grab for purchase"—Oliver made a climbing motion with his hands and feet—"when suddenly a gust blew so hard, he fell into the sea!" His hands thrust outward in a V shape as he made a splashing noise.

Pockets leaned forward so far Camilla thought he might tumble off her father's lap. Yet he wasn't the only one enthralled by both the tale and Oliver's dramatic recounting. Camilla found her own body gravitating toward the center of the room where Oliver paused for effect.

She expected Oliver had added the increased dramatics for Pockets' sake, but his descriptions and enactment were so realistic, she could almost smell the sea spray and taste the salty tang on her tongue.

"Well?" she asked, her voice betraying her impatience.

He answered her with a grin.

Pockets climbed off her father's lap and tugged on Oliver's trouser leg. "Did he . . . drown?"

Something deep inside her ached when Oliver reached down and lifted the boy in his arms. "Like your surrogate mother, you need to learn patience, lad." He touched a forefinger to Pockets' nose, eliciting the boy's giggle. "Now shall I continue?"

Pockets gave a vigorous nod.

"The men gathered at the railing, their caps in their hands in sad tribute as they gazed over to where the second mate had fallen. Then we heard it, soft at first, then growing clearer, louder."

"Wha'?" Pockets whispered the word as if in reverent remembrance for the fallen sailor.

"Singing. Sweet and unearthly, so beautiful it sent chills up my spine. Since then, I've only heard one other voice as beautiful." Oliver's eyes met hers, and she flushed with both pride and something more sensual.

Pockets furrowed his little brow. "The men was singin'?"

"Not the men. A female voice drifted up from the sea."

Camilla snorted her disbelief, and Oliver shot her a quelling glare.

"'Tis true. The winds stilled, and the seas calmed at the sound. When we stared into the waves, now gently lapping against the side of the ship, the second mate's body rose from the depths, lifted by graceful hands. Long locks of red hair flowed around her face, so serene and beautiful. She breathed into the mate's mouth, rousing him. Once he'd regained consciousness, he reached for and clung to the rope the men had lowered. As they pulled him up to the deck, she waved in farewell, and with a flip of her tail, dove back into the sea."

Pockets' mouth hung open, and Camilla feared hers did as well. His story was so preposterous, but told so convincingly, even she wanted to believe it. The pragmatist in her wanted to protest against putting such fanciful notions into Pockets' head, but the romantic in her fought back, remembering what it was like to be a child enamored with fairy tales.

"What a marvelous story," her father said.

"Yes," she whispered. The sight of Oliver holding Pockets as he wove his magical tale was something she would always remember. *He would make such a wonderful father.*

"Well, I should be off and leave you to your visit." He lowered Pockets back to the floor and ruffled his hair. "Be good for your mother."

Her cheeks warmed as Oliver's gaze darted to hers.

She nearly jumped when he asked, "Lady Denby, may I speak with you for a moment?"

Still dumbstruck from his story, she managed to nod, then rose to follow him out of the room. "What is it? Is something wrong with Father? He seems much improved."

"He is. I doubt he'll need the St. John's wort much longer, but it's best to have some on hand for recurrences of the melancholia." He shifted as if uncomfortable. "I wished to speak with you on a personal matter."

"Oh?" A thrill raced up her spine, tickling the hairs on the back of her neck.

"My sister needs a tutor. I've had to dismiss her current governess. Since you're rearing Pockets, I thought perhaps you might know of someone"—his already dark complexion deepened —"affordable. As a physician at the clinic, my wages are fair, but meager."

His question surprised her on many levels. "You have a sister? How old is she?"

"Ten—bright and inquisitive. I'm hoping to find someone who will not only instruct her in the usual subjects but will help with the more . . . social aspects of her education."

She searched her memory. Her knowledge of governesses was minimal. "I'm afraid I can't think of anyone at the moment. I'm following Her Grace's lead with Manny and teaching Pockets myself. With their background, we both feared placing them in a more formal educational setting might be too distressing."

"I see," he said, his mouth turning down at the corners, drawing her attention.

A wild idea crossed her mind. If he agreed perhaps the previous connection between them would be reestablished. "May I suggest something unusual?"

His eyes widened with interest. "Please."

"If you'd allow me, perhaps as a temporary solution, your sister could join Pockets in his lessons." An image of the children learning the social graces together brightened her spirit.

"Although I admire your dedication to the boy, you have your own busy social schedule. I couldn't impose."

"Please allow me. I owe you a debt for my father's improvement. It's the least I can offer until you find someone else suitable."

He twisted as if considering, then shook his head. "I'd prefer someone come to my home. You see, Tori—Victoria—helps look after my mother. Although she's greatly improved, she's suffered much like your father. I hate leaving her alone. I'm afraid I've relied on the tutor to . . . provide company to her as well. Unfortunately, the last woman proved too quick to give in to my mother's requests for laudanum, so I dismissed her."

So much about this man she didn't know—and so much a surprise. Still, she refused to give up. "We could alternate. Pockets and I could come to your home some days and Victoria and your mother could come to mine on others. I have a lovely library, and your mother might enjoy reading or working on her needlework during the lessons."

His eyes narrowed, tiny lines forming around them. "Why?"

His taciturn speech began to grate on her nerves, but she held her tongue, hoping he would expand on his question without prompting.

He remained silent.

"Why what?" she asked, her patience giving out.

"Why would you offer to tutor her yourself, to come to my home, to have my family come to yours?"

Reflex made her back straighten and her chin thrust at him. "I believe I made that clear. I wish to repay a debt." That wasn't the reason at all. Why on earth did she say that?

"I can't afford to pay you much."

"No payment is necessary. Think of it like the clinic. Services offered for those in need."

At his wince, she cringed inside. She'd insulted him. She struggled to redeem herself. "I don't need the money."

And that explanation only served to drive the wedge further between them. He closed his eyes, the muscle in his jaw pulsing. "But I *need* to pay." He ground the words out. "Tori's previous tutor came three times a week and was paid four shillings six pence. I could go up to—"

"That would be fine. I'll leave it to you which days you would like me to come to your home and which they will come to mine."

"I'll discuss it with Tori and with my mother, then I'll write to you to make arrangements." He paused. Pride shone in his blue eyes. "Only until I find a replacement."

"Of course," she said, pulling a card from her reticule and handing it to him. "My address."

Their fingers brushed, and the same tingle of pleasure traveled up her arm.

"I'll leave you to your visit, then." He bowed and headed down the stairs.

So much about him reminded her of Hugh—proud, even arrogant at times—and she sighed at the memory. There was something that bothered her when he spoke of his situation, but she couldn't quite place it. His words *my* mother prickled her mind, but she brushed it aside as a manner of speech and returned to visit her father.

CHAPTER 12—LESSONS

O liver grabbed his hat and coat from the ancient butler and traipsed down the steps of Lord Harcourt's townhouse. Was there no end to the way the woman could get under his skin? *One minute she offers to help and the next she reminds me we're worlds apart.*

"I don't need the money, indeed," he muttered her words.

And to consider him a charity case like the poor unfortunate souls who came through the clinic doors. How dare she!

When she'd arrived at her father's, he'd been relieved she and Pockets were alone. Harry had mentioned that Lord Trentwith—blackguard Trentwith, more like it—had been escorting her around town. It stuck in his craw like a parasite, eating him from the inside out. His father and the woman he . . .. He paused mid-step. The woman he what? Cared for? He shook the notion from his mind. She was nothing to him. And yet . . . how could someone who meant nothing torment him so?

In the past two months, since he'd ridden home in her carriage, he tried in vain to put her from his thoughts. Little things would slip in without warning. How when he strolled down the street, the spring breeze bringing the scent of lilac had him expecting to see her round the corner.

A ridiculous notion. She hardly traveled in the same places as he.

Or the time he'd saved up and taken Tori to an opera, sitting, of course, in the lowest priced seats. Listening to the voice of the coloratura soprano, he'd found himself gazing up at the luxurious boxes, searching for rich chestnut brown hair and knowing the woman on stage was no match for Camilla. Then he'd curse himself for succumbing to such folly.

During his visits to Lord Harcourt, he'd found himself eager for news of her, of stories of her exploits as a child. He pictured her running, with her skirts flying behind her as she raced after a pup, or mastering the reins of a gentle mare. Lord Harcourt never seemed to question Oliver's interest in his daughter. In fact, Oliver could swear the man told those stories to gauge the expression on his face.

And those were only his waking hours. She visited his dreams frequently at night, and he found himself both longing for and dreading sleep, only to wake with a throbbing need.

Now, she would invade yet another area of his life.

Damnation!

He stomped down the street, shaking his head and eliciting glares from people passing by. Although angry with himself for giving in to her proposition, part of him welcomed it. The idea of Tori learning the social graces from an actual aristocratic lady rather than a tutor or governess definitely held appeal. He would suggest they concentrate on that aspect of her lessons.

When he arrived home, both Tori and his mother glanced up, their faces bright and happy. It had been a good day, it appeared.

"Ollie!" Tori threw herself in his arms as she often did upon seeing him.

He kissed the top of her head. "And what mischief did you get into that I should receive so exuberant a greeting?" He grinned, knowing she'd concoct a fanciful tale as she always did. The game they played never grew tiresome.

Her eyes sparkled with mischief as she began her tale. "Well, today, an enormous balloon drifted down in front of the house. You know, the kind with the baskets that hold people."

He nodded, determined to keep a straight face.

"It had stripes of bright, beautiful colors. A man dressed all in red jumped out and motioned for Mama and me to join him."

Oliver withheld his chuckle. It seems she'd inherited his talent for weaving preposterous stories. "And what did you do?"

"We went, of course. It would have been rude to refuse. We rose up so high, all the people looked like ants. We flew to Paris and saw the big cathedral." She twirled in a circle, her arms extended like a bird in flight.

"Notre Dame?"

"Yes, that's it. Then we flew to Germany and saw the mountains. They were covered with snow and so pretty. Mama was frightened, but I wasn't."

Oliver glanced at his mother, who shook her head, a smile playing on her lips.

"You're very brave, Tori. I would have been petrified," he said, managing to keep his tone solemn.

"Then we flew over China and saw the long wall."

"The Great Wall."

Tori crossed her arms over her chest. "Who's telling this story? Will you please stop interrupting?"

"Consider me thoroughly chastised."

She gave a quick jerk of her head. "As I was saying, I wasn't afraid at all, but Mama worried we would fall right out of the sky, so the man in red brought us home in time for tea."

"My, this all happened this morning while I was at the clinic? What a shame to have missed the fun. Do you think he will return?"

With a delicate shrug of her shoulders, she feigned a sad expression. "I doubt it. He said he had many more people to visit."

"Well, I'm very glad he brought you and Mother back home safely. Now, I have news of my own, but I fear it pales in comparison to yours."

Tori's eyes widened and from the corner of his vision, his mother straightened in her chair.

"I've found a temporary replacement for your tutor. Lady Denby has offered to provide instruction until I can hire someone."

"A real lady!" Tori squealed.

His mother rose from her chair and began bustling about. "But we must tidy the house. Oh, dear. What will she think?"

"Both of you, try not to be overzealous. As I said, this is temporary. She's not coming today, Mother, and I don't really care what she thinks. If she finds our living conditions distasteful, so much the better. Perhaps she'll rescind her offer. I felt compelled to accept it. She's Lord Harcourt's daughter, and she insisted on repaying me for attending to her father. It's nothing more than that. She's taken on one of the street urchins His Grace rescued last year, and will include Tori in his lessons."

His mother grasped his hands, her eyes hopeful. "Oliver, think what this means. I knew it was an omen when you acquired the position at the clinic with the duke. It truly has opened doors for you, and now Victoria."

"You're reading more into this, Mother. I've not been accepted into society, but I do hope Tori will be with Lady Denby's guidance."

He turned toward the girl who held his heart. "I expect you to be on your best behavior. I'm going to request that Lady Denby focus on the social graces during your time with her. Now, I must write to make arrangements for the days and places."

His gaze shifted to his mother. "She invited you to her home as well, Mother. So you wouldn't be alone."

"I'm not a child, Oliver. I can manage a few hours by myself."

The truth of her statement warmed his heart. She truly had improved over the last few months since she'd broken free of the laudanum's grip. He flashed her a smile, one he knew she couldn't resist. "Of course you can, but would you like to go? Lady Denby has a fine library. Or would you prefer Tori's first lesson be here?"

Unease crept up his spine at his mother's perceptive gaze, and he braced himself for an inquisition regarding his feelings for the lady. He breathed a sigh of relief at his reprieve when his mother said, "Why don't you allow her to choose? A lady appreciates a man who considers her preferences."

The unsettled sensation returned as his mother smiled at him and added, "And I should be delighted to go and meet her."

He chose not to pursue the gleam in her eye and sat down to write Camilla. The precious piece of foolscap before him became an ink-stained mess as he scratched out and rewrote the salutation and signature numerous times. It had gone from *My Dear Lady Denby* to a simple *Lady Denby*, and *Yours, Oliver* to *Sincerely, Oliver*, then *Respectfully, Oliver*, and finally *Respectfully, Dr. Somersby*. The body fared only slightly better, with every word considered before he copied the final product onto a clean piece of paper, folded, sealed, and addressed it.

With no footman to deliver it and no desire to pay the outrageous price of a shilling and six pence to a hackney driver, he found a boy who could read and gave him directions to Camilla's well-heeled neighborhood. "Look for this house number." He pointed to the address on the letter. "No dillydallying. Go straight there and ask if you should wait for a response. Be back here within two hours, and I'll give you two pence."

The boy took off like a flash of lightning, and Oliver sighed, wondering what quagmire he'd just stumbled into.

❧

CAMILLA HAD BARELY ARRIVED HOME FROM HER FATHER'S WHEN Stratton brought in a letter on a silver tray.

"A boy delivered it, madam. He asked if he should wait for a response."

The letter bore the bold strokes of a man's controlled hand. Neat, but not ornate or embellished. Although sealed, no crest left an imprint in the glob of dried wax.

She opened it, skimming down to the signature. "Yes, please have the boy wait." As Stratton turned to leave, she stopped him. "Stratton, how is he dressed—the boy?"

"Rather shabbily, madam. But he was polite enough."

"Take him to the kitchen and have Cook give him something to eat and drink while he waits."

"Yes, madam."

The contents of the missive were concise.

Lady Denby,

I've spoken with Victoria and my mother, and both are agreeable to your offer. My mother recommended I leave the meeting place of Tori's first lesson to you. Tori is accustomed to having her lessons on Mondays, Wednesdays, and Fridays, if that is convenient. However, considering your busy schedule, she is willing to be available at your disposal. I'll await your answer as to the time and place.

Respectfully,
Dr. Somersby

She wrote her response, crafting each word in the same concise manner as his.

Dr. Somersby,

Unless you object, I suggest we meet at your home to ensure Victoria's comfort for her first lesson. The days mentioned are acceptable. I shall arrive at ten Wednesday morning.

Lady Camilla Denby

Once finished, she rang for the servants. "Have my carriage brought around, Stratton. Tell Langley to take the boy back to Dr. Somersby's residence. If he doesn't remember where it's located, have the boy sit up top to direct him."

Stratton bowed and left her with her thoughts, which remained fixedly on Dr. Oliver Somersby.

She paced the room, now uncertain her offer to assist with his sister's tutoring had been a wise decision. Clearly he wanted as little to do with her as possible, and here she was practically forcing herself on his company.

"Blast!" The unladylike curse flew from her lips. How could one person—one man, to be precise—cause her so much turmoil? It was not to be borne. Surely, she could avoid him for the short time it would require him to find a replacement.

The parlor, so often offering a welcome retreat, now seemed empty and lonely. A portrait of Hugh in his dress uniform sat on the mantle, and she moved toward it.

She sighed and traced a finger over the image of his face. "Oh, Hugh. What should I do?"

❁❁❁

AT PRECISELY NINE THIRTY ON WEDNESDAY MORNING, CAMILLA AND Pockets boarded her carriage for Dr. Somersby's. Pockets stared out the window as they made their way through the busy streets of London.

"Where's Oliver live?" Pockets asked, not removing his gaze from the passing streets.

"Dr. Somersby, Pockets. Remember your manners. And he lives not far from the clinic."

"What's 'is sister like?"

The boy had incessant questions, but Camilla refused to discourage him. His inquisitive mind made him an ideal pupil, and he'd improved greatly over the course of the eight months she'd taken him under her wing.

She smiled patiently. "I don't know. I haven't met her yet. Let's hope she's more agreeable than her brother."

Pockets scratched his head, setting his cap askew. "I like 'im. 'E tells good stories."

"That he does." Her admission did nothing to ease the discomfort welling inside her at the thought of seeing him again. At least at this hour of the day, he'd already be at the clinic.

When the carriage arrived, and Langley had lowered the step so they could descend, she took account of the surroundings. It wasn't as close to the clinic as she initially thought, and the modest neighborhood, although far from wealthy, seemed free from the debris and mass of unwashed bodies that littered the streets of the East End.

She'd only seen his residence at night, and the lack of lighting in the area had served to make it appear drearier than it truly was.

96

Now, in the light of day, the buildings seemed less foreboding. True, the doors needed fresh coats of paint and more than a few had cracks in the bricks' faces, but other than a few defects and imperfections, the buildings exuded a welcoming feel. The pavement and steps leading to each home had been well-swept, and curtains adorned the windows.

She lifted the scroll-shaped iron knocker and gave two sharp raps against the wooden door. Within moments, the door opened, and much to her surprise, Oliver greeted them.

He held his pocket watch. "Right on time. I'd hoped you wouldn't be late as I waited for you before leaving for the clinic."

Opening the door wider, he directed them into a small living area. The space was neat and clean, although sparsely furnished. Green cushions on the sofa had seen wear, and an area on one of the arms had been patched. A tray with a steaming pot of tea sat on a small table with curved legs. No portraits decorated the walls, but a lovely oil landscape adorned the area over the sofa.

"I thought it best if I remain here to introduce you. Lady Denby, Pockets, may I present your pupil, Victoria, and my mother."

The girl, a pixie of a thing with dark raven curls and bright blue eyes, was a much smaller and decidedly more feminine version of Oliver. When Camilla curtsied, she followed suit, only swaying to the side by the smallest margin.

She giggled, her hand raising to her perfectly formed cupid mouth. "Pockets. That's a funny name."

Pockets straightened his diminutive stature and crossed his arms over his chest. "Well, so's Victoria." He rounded off his retort by sticking out his tongue.

Oliver shot Camilla an apologetic glance before reprimanding his sister. "Tori, that was rude. Apologize. Lady Denby, I fear your task will not be easy. It's obvious Tori's instruction in the social graces takes precedence."

A blush covered Victoria's fair complexion. "I apologize. I've never met anyone with the name Pockets before."

"He is rather unique," Camilla said. "And we do *not* stick our tongues out at people, Pockets."

"Sorry," he said, although she doubted his sincerity.

Camilla turned her attention to the woman who waited silently. It was no doubt where Oliver got his dark, good looks. The woman was stunning—exotic. Her deep brown eyes stared at Camilla as she twisted her hands in front of her. Her hair, the same raven color as her son and daughter, was styled simply, but suited her well. Like Oliver, her complexion was swarthy, as if she spent her time in the sun.

"It's a pleasure to meet you, Mrs. Somersby," Camilla said, offering another curtsy.

Oliver's gaze darted to his mother, who appeared discomfited.

"My surname is Heron, but please call me Sabina."

Had she remarried? It would be gauche to ask. Instead, Camilla stumbled her apology. "I beg your pardon." So far introductions had not gone swimmingly. Hopefully the lessons themselves would fare better.

With another glance at his pocket watch, Oliver said, "Now, I must be off to the clinic. Har . . . His Grace allowed me this time to make certain everyone was settled."

As he made his way to the door, Camilla followed and tapped his arm. "I apologize, Dr. Somersby, if I've offended your mother. Is your sister's surname Heron or Somersby?"

He tilted his head, and his blue eyes flashed with annoyance. "Does it matter?"

"As she learns the proper etiquette, yes, it does. I would like to address her appropriately in our lessons."

He broke eye contact and huffed a sigh. "Somersby. My mother prefers to use her maiden name."

"I see," she said, but truly she didn't.

He left, leaving her with more questions. The man was a mystery.

Turning to her pupils, she said, "Let's begin."

※

THE LESSON DID INDEED FARE BETTER THAN THE INTRODUCTIONS. True to Oliver's word, Victoria proved an inquisitive and bright girl. A competition developed between her and Pockets as they completed their writing exercises.

"My penmanship is much neater than yours, Pockets. You have splotches all over your paper." Victoria said, lifting her delicate brows. Her little chin, somewhat pointed, reminded Camilla of an elf, and she raised it as well to emphasize her point.

"Pockets is only six, Miss Somersby," Camilla said, keeping her tone gentle rather than accusatory.

Although the girl did have a point. It wasn't only Pockets' paper that was covered with ink splotches, but he had a smudge on the side of his nose where he had absentmindedly scratched it.

Mrs. Heron obtained a warm cloth and assisted in cleaning his face. "Oliver struggled, too, Pockets. And now his handwriting is as neat as the king's."

Camilla laughed. "I doubt Prinny does any of his own letter writing, but your point is well taken, Mrs. Heron. Practice, Pockets, makes perfect."

"Please call me Sabina, Lady Denby."

"Then you must call me Camilla, but I suggest not in front of the children. Part of their instruction is to address us appropriately."

Sabina flushed. "Forgive me. Perhaps it's best if I leave you alone with the children."

Camilla's own cheeks and ears heated. "Nonsense, this is your home. Perhaps we can make an exception." She turned toward the children. "Provided you both remember to address other adults by their proper titles."

The small blond and black heads nodded in tandem.

To make certain they understood, Camilla asked, "Pockets, how will you address Miss Somersby's mother?"

The boy cocked his head. "Who?" His eyes widened. "Oh, you mean Tori's mama. I'll call her Mrs. Heron, your ladyship."

"Very good. And you, Miss Somersby, how will you address me?"

"Lady Denby." Her blue eyes narrowed. "Why does Pockets call you 'your ladyship'? Aren't you his mama?"

The weight of Tori's words slammed into Camilla, and her gaze sought the boy as he stared at her with wide, questioning eyes. She'd done everything she could as a mother for him. He called her father Poppy, and yet, she hadn't extended the kindness to him to call her Mother.

A nasty taste rose in her throat. She swallowed the lump of guilt and regret. She had admired Margaret's easy acceptance of Manny as Harry's and her adopted son. Although the boy still slipped and called his new parents Harry and Margaret, Camilla had witnessed on more than one occasion where they'd corrected him, reminding him to call them father and mother. Didn't Pockets deserve the same acceptance?

"Yes, I suppose I am. Pockets, if you like, you may call me Mother or Mama."

Wetness rimmed the boy's eyes. He ran to her and hugged her about the knees, burying his face in the folds of her skirts. Sobs followed, his small shoulders shaking as he clung to her.

Camilla was mortified. She'd been taught to avoid such displays of emotion while in public. She glanced over at Oliver's mother.

Understanding shone in the woman's brown eyes, and she nodded encouragingly. "I would say the children weren't the only ones to have learned a lesson today."

Tears welled in Camilla's eyes as well, and soon, they were both crying happy tears.

Like a true mother, Camilla mustered her sternest of expressions and said, "You've smeared snot all over my skirts, Pockets."

He grinned at her. "Sorry, Mama."

The beauty of the word rippled through her, and she wondered why she had waited so long.

"Now," she said, summoning the strength to pull from the boy's grasp. "It's time for our etiquette lesson."

CHAPTER 13—A WILLING PUPIL

O liver worried all morning and into the afternoon, barely able to focus on his patients. At first, his concern rested on his mother and how she would handle having a woman of the aristocracy in their home. Then he shifted to Camilla, fretting over what she would think of their humble residence.

His final concern landed solely on his own shoulders. The thoughts so plagued and occupied his mind, other than the necessary questions for diagnosis, he'd barely spoken when treating his patients. In the afternoon, fear gripped his gut that Harry would once again send him home for the compassion he'd failed to exhibit that morning.

Why the blazes did it even matter? Of course his job mattered, but why worry about what the high-and-mighty Camilla Denby would think?

And yet—he did.

He muttered a curse under his breath for his own foolishness. The woman had him at sixes and sevens. He was a grown man, not some doltish schoolboy, mooning over a girl.

But something about seeing her in his home, interacting with his family, made him yearn for . . . he refused to name. He slammed down his fist on a table in the treatment room.

Harry poked his head in. "Did you drop something?"

Yes, my defenses. "No, I . . . ran into the table."

A blond eyebrow rose as Harry's perceptive gaze studied him. Oliver could swear the man could see inside his skull and the workings of his mind. He would have done well assisting his grandmother with her palm readings.

Obviously not believing Oliver's account, Harry entered and leaned against the offending table. "Should I examine you for injuries?"

Not unless you examine my heart. "No. It's nothing. I'm having a little trouble concentrating. Lady Denby is at my home. She's tutoring Tori."

"That's . . . generous of her. Have you two resolved your differences?"

Oliver turned away from Harry's perceptive gaze and busied himself, straightening an imaginary mess on a neatly organized shelf. "You mean the differences in our class?"

A low chuckle arose behind him. "Perhaps I should have said the apparent dislike you had for one another?"

"I don't . . . dislike her."

"What *are* your feelings?"

Oliver spun around to face him. "Does it matter? She's an aristocrat, and I'm a . . . I'm not. Any possible relationship between us is out of the question. Society frowns upon such couplings, and I'm certain the opinion of the *ton* is of utmost importance to someone like her."

Harry straightened. "Then you don't know her as well as you think you do."

"I don't know her at all."

"Maybe that should change?"

"It's easy for you to say. You don't have those obstacles. You're happily married to a beautiful woman—*of your class.*"

"Is that what you think?" Harry snapped the words, his face

darkening. "That it was *easy* for Margaret and me? Do you forget that Margaret was my sister-in-law? That we had to leave the country to be married? That, even now, we risk everything by loving each other."

Heat crept up Oliver's neck. "I . . . I'd forgotten."

Harry motioned to the chair and like a dutiful and contrite employee, Oliver sat.

Harry drew in a breath, his eyes searching the ceiling, but his expression softening. "When Margaret and I decided to marry, we knew we were taking a tremendous risk. If someone contested the marriage, it could be voided. My cousin Ellis had the most to gain since he would be next in line for the title if my marriage was declared invalid. Before we married, Margaret insisted I visit him to —in effect—throw ourselves on his mercy.

"Fortunately, he was compassionate, having made a love match of his own. He already has the title of earl, so although a dukedom would be an advancement, he took pity on us and assured me he wouldn't file a complaint. But what if something happens to him and his son, his heir, isn't as understanding? Each day we gamble with our futures, our child's future."

Oliver swallowed the lump of shame. "Is it worth it?"

"Bloody well right it is. Every single second I have with her is worth it. If our marriage is contested, I'd still have her, and hopefully—this." He pointed, circling the area of the clinic. "We've discussed it and should anything happen to threaten our child's legitimacy, we would go to America where they don't have such archaic beliefs."

Harry patted Oliver's shoulder. "Love is worth risking everything, Oliver. Don't let anyone tell you otherwise." He smiled. "Now, get back to work. We have patients waiting."

<hr />

LOVE IS WORTH RISKING EVERYTHING. Harry's words reverberated in Oliver's mind, bouncing off the walls in his skull, hammering at his defenses.

103

The assault continued even on his way home. With each step the words came back, like a song stuck in one's mind that won't leave.

Could an aristocratic woman like Lady Denby love a bastard? As though hitting a barricade—or that fragrant lilac barrier of Lady Denby herself—his footsteps halted. *Lady Denby and love?* He shook his head, trying to clear the connection of the words.

People pushed past him, muttering annoyance at his sudden lack of direction. A few turned, sending heated glares along with their curses.

Even if she would accept his illegitimacy, would she be able to overcome his parentage—his heritage? Or would it be a river too wide to cross? Shame crept up his neck, itching like a million insects. How could he expect her to accept who he was when even he denied it?

No. Harry, although well-meaning, never feared for his life because of who he was. Although love may be worth risking everything, it didn't guarantee a happy ending. If he revealed himself to Lady Denby and professed his feelings, the result would be disappointment and rejection—or worse.

Finally reaching his home, his hand rested on the doorknob, steadying himself before entering. *Fool, she is long gone.*

Tori's ever cheerful voice greeted him. "Ollie!" The sound of it alone brightened his day, and a genuine smile found its way to his lips.

Billowed skirts trailing behind her, she launched herself into his arms. "There's so much to tell you. We had such a grand time. I adore Lady Denby."

The innocent declaration tugged at him, twisting his gut. "Don't get too attached, poppet. It's only a temporary arrangement."

He kissed her nose and gave her a gentle nudge toward the living area. "Now, allow me to get inside before you tell me all these grand things."

Pleased to see his mother alert and smiling, he took a seat on the worn sofa and prepared for Tori's onslaught of exuberance. "I'm ready. What did you learn today?"

"We learned to walk properly."

"Forgive my ignorance, but I thought you had learned to walk years ago."

"We walked with books on our heads."

Oliver laughed, envisioning the sight, knowing perfectly well the reason behind such practice. "And here I was under the mistaken impression that the goal was to put the contents of the book inside your head."

"No, silly." Tori gave an exasperated sigh. "It's for balance. Lady Denby said, as a lady, I must glide when I walk as if I'm floating on a cloud." Tori twirled before him, arms outstretched, the skirt of her pretty yellow frock forming a circle around her half boots.

"What else did you learn? Anything inside those books?"

"Oh, yes. We learned about Ancient Greece. About a man called Pla . . . Plate."

"Plato."

"Yes, that's it. It wasn't very exciting, and Pockets started falling asleep."

"Well, I hope *you* had better manners than to sleep through Lady Denby's lessons."

"Of course. I'm not a baby like Pockets." Her eyes grew large, as if she remembered a secret to share. "Lady Denby made him cry."

Unease prickled Oliver's skin, and he struggled to reconcile the woman he'd come to know with what would prompt such a reaction from a child. "What happened? Did she strike him? Was she cruel to him?"

His mother, who had been sitting and listening to the exchange, interjected. "No, it wasn't anything like that. Victoria asked her why Pockets addressed her as your ladyship. Lady Denby seemed taken aback by the question. When she told the boy he could call her mother or mama, he broke down in tears. Soon she was crying herself. It was quite a touching moment."

The image provided the final push into the depths Oliver had resisted all day, and he admitted, if only to himself, that Camilla Denby had most definitely, unequivocally, stolen his heart.

CAMILLA CLAPPED HER HANDS, PROVIDING THE TEMPO, BUT POCKETS continued to stumble awkwardly to the music. He'd trod on poor Victoria's feet numerous times during their lesson.

"Ow. He did it again, Lady Denby." Victoria pushed Pockets away and hopped on one foot.

"Perhaps we should stop for a while," Margaret said, looking up from the pianoforte and giving Camilla an encouraging smile.

More than once during the day's social graces lesson, Camilla had lost her temper with the children. Pockets' propensity for giggling each time he put his arm around Victoria had exasperated Camilla to no end.

She fully admitted her lack of understanding when it came to small boys. Men seemed to have no problem at all placing their arms around a woman. That fact had occupied her mind through the majority of the lesson, the primary image being one in which Oliver held her in his embrace.

"Perhaps you're right. We'll pause for some tea. Victoria, I would like you to pour, and Pockets can practice his sipping." She sent him a stern look. "No slurping."

"Yes, Mama." He returned her glare with an angelic smile.

The address still caused her heart to squeeze, although it had been three weeks since that most embarrassing incident at Oliver's home. Even more than the word itself, the emotion with which he said it caressed her like a soft kiss. She blinked back the tears welling.

"It's a shame Manny couldn't join us," Camilla said as Victoria handed her a delicate bone-china cup, only sloshing a small amount of tea over the rim. "He might demonstrate to Pockets there is nothing worth giggling about when dancing with a young lady."

Margaret chuckled between sips of her tea. "I'm afraid he wouldn't be much help, Cam. I have as much difficulty with him as you do with Pockets. He'd much prefer spending time with Harry at the clinic looking at festering sores than learning the latest dance steps."

She sighed, and Camilla envied the dreamy look in her friend's eyes. "Although, Harry is an excellent influence on him when it comes to how to treat a lady."

A large slurp rose from Pockets' direction.

"Sorry, Mama." He sipped more gently, and Camilla sent him an approving nod.

There had been times in the last week that she'd sworn he did things simply as reasons to call her 'Mother' or 'Mama.'

A soft knock sounded, and Stratton entered. "Dr. Somersby, madam."

Her heart picked up its tempo as Oliver's large body filled the entryway to the music room. They had arranged to have this lesson at her home since he had no piano.

He bowed and delivered that heart-stopping, dimpled smile. Too bad it was directed more toward Margaret than her. "Your Grace, Lady Denby. With Manny helping at the clinic, it seems I was excess weight and dragging down the ship." His tone, light and teasing showed a side of him Camilla wished to see more often.

"Ollie!" Victoria jumped from her seat on the sofa, bumping the table and jostling the tea tray.

Ollie? Cam rolled the nickname around in her mind. She found the sound of it oddly pleasing, the litheness of it a strange juxtaposition to the rigid man she had initially met—and yet, somehow—not.

Not to be outdone by his classmate, Pockets joined her. "Oliver!"

The children launched themselves into his arms, and he hugged them, lifting Pockets high in the air and eliciting another set of giggles.

He would make a wonderful father.

Her breath hitched as the thought invaded her mind once more.

"I'm sorry to interrupt, but it's a long way home, and Har—His Grace suggested I leave early to retrieve Victoria."

"Oliver, you can certainly call him Harry in front of me. No need to be so formal," Margaret said in her usual gracious manner.

"Would you care to join us for tea, Dr. Somersby?" Camilla asked, trying to keep the hopeful tone from her voice. "Victoria is learning to pour."

An dark eyebrow lifted, drawing Camilla's gaze to those incredible blue eyes. "My, she's learning so many things I thought she'd already known how to do. First it's walking and now it's pouring tea."

Pockets snorted a laugh.

Camilla shot him a quelling look.

"Sorry, Mama."

A gentleness softened Oliver's typically strong features as he glanced between her and Pockets, and like his teasing smile, it was another aspect of him she felt privileged to witness.

"Ollie," Victoria said, raising her chin as Camilla had taught her. "There's a proper way to pour. You don't simply slosh it in the cup."

A smile tugged at Camilla's lips, and she gestured toward the teapot. "Why don't you demonstrate, Victoria?"

With care, Victoria poured the tea, careful not to spill a drop, and set the pot back on the tray with the spout facing her. She handed Oliver the cup and saucer, then added a little curtsy for good measure.

Camilla beamed at her. "Excellent, Victoria. Well done."

"I don't see the difference," Oliver said, and proceeded to slurp his tea.

Camilla stared at him with horrified eyes.

Pockets broke out in fits of laughter, and Camilla expected him to begin rolling on the floor.

Oliver's lips curled on one side in a playful half-smile.

The rake! He'd done that on purpose!

Well, she would show him. She picked up her cup and slurped as loudly as possible. Soon all of them were laughing and slurping their tea.

"I'm afraid I'm a bad influence, Lady Denby. I seem to have undone all of your good work for the day." The twinkle in his eyes made it clear he was not sorry in the least.

"There is a way you could make amends, Oliver," Margaret said, still trying to stifle her own laughter.

Oh, no. What is she planning?

"Oh, pray tell, Your Grace. How may I be of service?"

"Well, Pockets is having difficulty with his dance lessons. He seems to find placing his arm around Victoria humorous," Margaret said. "Perhaps you might demonstrate and show him the advantages of learning the art?"

"Ooooh," he said, drawing out the word. "I'm afraid when it comes to boys and placing their arms around the female sex, it takes a little more maturity to appreciate the—what did you say? Advantages." He placed his tea down on the table—quite gracefully, Camilla noted—and stood before Margaret. "But I would be most delighted to demonstrate, Your Grace."

"Oh, not with me. With Camilla."

Camilla shot Margaret an *I'll get even with you* look.

Completely ignoring her, Margaret said, "You see, I must play the piano. Although Camilla has an outstanding voice, she can't play worth a stitch."

"I beg your pardon," Camilla said, laughing at the slight.

"It's true, Cam, and you know it." Margaret tapped a finger to her chin, a strange glint appearing in her violet eyes. "Now, I think a waltz would be a superb choice."

Camilla would most definitely have a *chat* with her later.

Oliver seemed flustered, but turned toward her. "Very well. Lady Denby, may I have the honor." With a gentlemanly bow, he held out his hand to her, and as she slid her fingers across his palm, a shiver of excitement ran up her arm.

"You see, Pockets, it's actually all very normal," he said, slipping an arm around her waist. "You'll appreciate it when you get older. But for now, you must learn the proper steps so you don't injure the lady with your clumsiness when it comes time to woo her."

Woo her?

He smiled, the full force of it knocking Camilla's breath from her lungs.

Damn that dimple.

Her knees buckled, and he gripped her tighter, holding her upright—and smiled wider.

Moving her gaze to anything other than his swoon-producing

smile, she met his eyes, and the intensity in their clear blue depths drilled down to her very soul. Her mind barely registered the triple beat of the music as Margaret began to play.

Sweet notes filled the room as he moved her gracefully across the floor. For a man so large, he moved like a cat—an enormous, powerfully-built cat. She could almost hear him purr as she discreetly ran her hand up the sleeve of his coat, pleased when the muscle beneath it tensed reflexively.

Close enough to breathe in that intoxicating scent of wood, polishing oil, and something masculine and uniquely him, she inhaled deeply. His eyes never left hers as he spun her around the floor, and the hint of seduction shining in them heated her cheeks.

Applause brought her to her senses when the music stopped. Even Pockets clapped his little hands, his face alight as his gaze moved from Oliver to her. She imagined his quick mind formulating a family. Or was that her hope?

"When you finish the dance, Pockets," Oliver said, his deep voice displaying a hint of amusement, "you must bow to your lady, and kiss her hand."

With that, he gave a deep bow, and kissed her fingers, lingering perhaps a bit too long. Was that her imagination as well—or her desire?

"Now, as much as I've enjoyed the tea—and the dance," he said with a wink, "Victoria and I must be off. My mother will be waiting."

"Oh, of course. Please allow me to provide my coach to take you home."

He bristled at her offer. "That's not necessary."

She opened her mouth, ready to insist, but reevaluated and considered his pride. "Forgive me. I only meant as in gratitude for being such a willing participant in our lesson. It would mean so much to me if you would accept that small token of thanks."

The muscle in his jaw pulsed, and he ran a hand across the back of his neck. "Well, it would be more comfortable for Tori. I accept your kindness."

"Good. Next time, please tell your mother that she's most welcome to join us."

He nodded and, after bowing to Margaret and tousling Pockets' hair, he grasped Victoria's hand and exited.

She continued to stare at the empty doorway of the music room.

Only the mischievous tone of Margaret's voice brought her back to the present. "Cam?"

She cursed her friend's perception and prepared for the inquisition.

CHAPTER 14—INVITATIONS

A spark of hope surged in Camilla's heart. Something had definitely changed between her and Oliver during the impromptu dance lesson. The attraction she and Oliver had felt during their brief encounter at the masquerade ball had transformed into an unspoken agreement rather than denial on Oliver's part.

She'd admitted as much to Margaret when she'd questioned Camilla relentlessly. Yet, with each passing day, Camilla cursed the restrictions of her sex as she waited for Oliver to pursue a more intimate acquaintance.

Expectation that Oliver would call upon her dwindled. When two weeks passed without word from him, she took matters into her own hands. Inspired by what she believed a splendid excuse, she sat down at her escritoire. Confidence flowed through her as she put pen to paper and wrote to Oliver, extending a rather forward invitation.

She smiled at her brilliance as she folded and sealed the letter, even sprinkling a little lilac water on the paper for good measure.

The only thing left to do was wait and hope she hadn't misinterpreted the signs of his interest.

WEARY FROM HIS DAY, OLIVER SHRUGGED OFF HIS COAT AND LET HIS body drop to the sofa in the small living area, curious why Tori hadn't bombarded him as she was inclined to do.

The house was blessedly quiet. As he leaned his head against the wall, he closed his eyes, only to be inundated with the persistent voices battling in his head. He hadn't been able to erase Camilla from his thoughts for the past few weeks—ever since he'd held her in his arms for the waltz.

Lady Denby is too far above you.

Ah, but the passion in her dark brown eyes ignites a fire within.

She would never accept your heritage.

With her strength and determination, she could move mountains and slay dragons, even those of your past.

She's toying with you, a plaything she can discard when she's had her fill.

No, there was a connection between us, she admitted as much.

She represents everything you hate!

Not everything. She's caring and—

"Oomph." The weight of Tori as she threw herself into him knocked the air out from his lungs. Had he been so lost in his thoughts he couldn't even hear her approach?

"Ollie!" She kissed his cheek, a gesture he cherished. "You got a letter." She waved the parchment in front of his face.

The scent of lilac tickled his nose, and he straightened in anticipation. "A letter so important you had to disturb my rest?"

"Yes," Tori answered, her voice solemn.

Curious, Oliver plucked the letter from Tori's hand and gazed down, recognizing the imprint on the wax seal.

"Well, are you going to stare at it or read it?" Tori's mouth twitched, obviously struggling to maintain her serious expression. Finally losing the battle, her lips widened in a grin.

Oliver broke the seal, cleared his throat, and read aloud.

"My dear Dr. Somersby.

"The most delightful idea came to me today. The children have worked hard on their lessons, and I believe they deserve a reward for their diligence. I propose we take them on an excursion to Vauxhall Gardens."

Tori gasped and clapped her hands.

Oliver shot her a quelling look as he continued. "Please respond with a day and time that meets your schedule. On the chosen day, I shall arrive for you in my carriage.

"Yours, Lady Camilla Denby."

"Oh, Ollie, can we? Can we?" Tori practically bounced on the sofa next to him.

Oliver's eyes remained glued to the letter, his mind fixating on several choice words and phrases. *My dear. We* take them. *Yours.* He shook himself back to reality and met Tori's hopeful face.

"I don't know if I can spare time away from the clinic." He smiled, hoping to soften her disappointment and, at the same time, avoid the allure of the tempting Lady Denby. "My wages are what buy your pretty frocks and ribbons for your hair." He gave a playful tug on a long, black lock.

"Please." Resorting to her most dangerous weapon, she pouted, her expression reminding him of a sad puppy, and he admitted he was helpless to resist.

"Very well. I'll speak to His Grace about spending some time away from the clinic. At least with the warmer weather, the number of patients seems to have decreased."

Tori threw her arms about his neck, lavishing kisses across his face.

He closed his eyes, wondering what the deuce he'd gotten himself into and how he would control his ever increasing feelings for Lady Camilla Denby.

❦

WHEN CAMILLA HADN'T HEARD BACK FROM OLIVER IMMEDIATELY, she'd almost given up hope and had severe regrets over her impetuous invitation. Several days later, she received word that he accepted her gracious offer and would be available the following Sunday afternoon. Excitement quickly replaced her initial relief.

Pockets slid across the carriage seats, peering from window to window as they rode to collect Oliver and Victoria. Unable to keep the bemused smile from her lips, Camilla marveled at the joy the boy could glean from a simple carriage ride.

Taking a moment from his wide-eyed perusal of the passing scenery, he turned toward her. "Tell me again about the gardens, Mama."

She'd adjusted to the child calling her Mama, but the sound of it and the adoration in his eyes continued to squeeze her heart. "They're very lovely, Pockets. You can practice your identification of various plant species as we stroll along the pathways. If we're lucky, since it's Sunday, perhaps there will be entertainers present. Maybe even jugglers or acrobats."

The boy's mouth formed a perfect little *O*, mimicking his wide eyes.

At times, she grew angry at the mother who had so easily discarded him, wondering how anyone could throw away such a precious gift as a child. Rash though it was, since she had no idea of the reasons for his abandonment and subsequent misuse by the vermin Coodibilis, part of Camilla was grateful as Pockets filled the void in her she hadn't even realized existed.

She'd never been the type of woman who required a family to feel complete. Although unable to pursue many of the opportunities available to men, her involvement with charity work provided purpose and direction. She'd been a silent partner in the clinic, working tirelessly to secure funding. With Margaret's upcoming confinement, her shared duties in that regard had increased tenfold.

However, with Pockets now in her life, she couldn't help but wonder what it would be like to have a man by her side to help rear the boy, and if she were honest, to love and cherish her the way Harry did Margaret.

The carriage pulled to a stop at Oliver's residence.

Before Langley could lower the steps and allow Camilla and Pockets to descend, Victoria bounded out of the modest home, her black curls flying behind her. Oliver appeared, lifting his hands in a "what can you do" gesture.

A giggle burst forth from Camilla's lips, and Pockets turned and grinned at her. The children were like young foals, anxious to run in the fields.

Victoria entered the carriage first, seating herself next to Pockets. Oliver removed his hat, dipping his head as his tall body moved into the compartment and took a seat next to Camilla. He looked exceptionally handsome in his black coat and vibrant blue waistcoat, his neckcloth tied in intricate folds. He'd obviously taken care in his appearance for their excursion, and a shiver of satisfaction slipped up Camilla's spine.

As he settled next to her, and his thigh brushed against hers, a surge of heat replaced the prior shiver. She cast a furtive glance in his direction, catching a flicker of a smile twitch his lips. Then he moved away, taking the delicious heat with him.

Pockets, on the other hand, had scooted as far away from Victoria as humanly possible, practically pressing his little body against the side of the carriage.

Victoria giggled. "Afraid I will bite you, Pockets?"

"No," he muttered and moved a fraction of an inch closer to her.

"Still struggling with dance lessons, lad?" Oliver asked, his deep, throaty chuckle reviving Camilla's tingly skin.

"Girls smell funny," the boy said, wrinkling his nose and giving a sharp nod.

"Oh, I don't know." Oliver leaned over, his face impossibly close to Camilla's hair, and drew in a deep breath. "I find their fragrance rather nice. Lilac, isn't it?"

"Why thank you, Dr. Somersby. And yes, it is."

He tapped the side of his nose. "Doctor's diagnostic tool."

What an intriguing statement. "Truly?" she asked. "Can you diagnose on the scent alone?"

"Perhaps not only on smell, but I've come to recognize certain odors associated with some illnesses. For example, someone suffering from pneumonia has particularly foul breath. And from my time aboard a ship, scurvy could be detected by putrid sweat."

"That's fascinating." She found herself leaning in closer.

He responded in kind, his breath sending small puffs of sweet smelling air her way. "And it's not only illness. Most animals sniff out their mates." He grinned and lowered his voice as it took on a sensual purr. "Even humans."

Heat rose up her neck to her cheeks, and she tore her gaze away from his searching eyes.

Another throaty chuckle followed.

Deciding to shift the focus of the conversation, she turned her attention to Victoria. "That's a lovely frock, Victoria. The color complements your eyes." Too late she realized it was the same color of Oliver's waistcoat, which also matched and made his glorious eyes appear even bluer.

She darted another surreptitious glance his way, only to catch his lips curl in a half-smile. *Why the arrogant—*

"I, for one, detest drab colors in one's clothing," he said. "That is unless it matches my mood. Wouldn't you agree, Lady Denby?" His eyes drifted over her subdued beige gown.

"Sometimes it's a matter of being practical," she said. That and the fact that the lovely spring green gown she'd initially planned to wear had an unfortunate encounter with her morning tea.

His smile widened, exposing that delicious dimple, and her heart thrummed.

"You see, Pockets can become a bit overanxious, and I'm preparing in the event he grabs my skirts with less than clean hands."

"I presume you warned him to keep his hands low. I wouldn't want him to receive a slap to his face." The playful twinkle in Oliver's eyes confirmed his intent to remind her of their first meeting.

"My, it's warm in here." She fanned herself, trying to remove the blush that most assuredly had crept to her cheeks.

He laughed again, soft and low, a sound she admitted she enjoyed immensely.

After descending the carriage and entering the gardens, they strolled along the paths, the children scampering in front of them.

Oliver clasped his hands behind his back, keeping a respectable distance between them, and she tried in vain to shake the disappointment he had not offered his arm.

"I wanted to thank you again for your help with Tori," he said, breaking the comfortable silence between them.

He had been staring ahead, but turned to meet her eyes, his gaze earnest. "Truly. I see the difference in her. Her mind is sharp, but her manners . . . well, they've improved tenfold." He graced her with the sensual chuckle. "She's even taken to correcting me."

"It's no bother. She's been a delight and a good influence on Pockets. He may pretend he doesn't like her, but he anticipates our lessons with great eagerness. Why today, he didn't even grumble when I combed his hair."

"Ah." Oliver nodded and grinned, popping that dimple she loved. "I wondered what was different about him today."

Camilla's gaze drifted to his pursed lips, wondering if they were as soft as they appeared. "There's something else you wish to say?"

"Only that I admire what you're doing for the boy. It's clear he dotes on you."

"I worry, though," she admitted. "A young boy needs a man in his life, someone to instruct him in matters a woman cannot."

The ease of their conversation vanished, and his body stiffened as if she'd slapped him, the muscle in his jaw twitching.

She willed him to look at her, to grace her with another smile, but his eyes remained fixed on the path ahead of them. A long silence stretched between them.

Confused by his reaction, she whispered what she'd hope was an apology. "Did I say something to offend you?"

His chest lifted as he inhaled a deep breath, then exhaled a heavy sigh. He turned toward her, the tenseness of his face softening. "Think nothing of it. I'm sure it wasn't intentional. There are many men who've been reared by their mothers without the aid of a father."

Ahead of them, Pockets and Victoria had stopped to watch a juggler, their eyes wide with wonder and innocence. When had that innocence been taken from Oliver? She'd never asked about his father. Where was he? Was his statement indicative of his own upbringing?

As if sensing her discomfort, he smiled, although it didn't travel to his eyes. "You were speaking of Pockets. Your father is a fine role model. Kind, fair. The boy is fortunate to have him *and you* in his life. Be grateful for that."

Taking his lead, she continued to lighten the mood. "I'm afraid my father spoils him horribly. Pockets needs a firm hand. He can be quite stubborn."

A more genuine smile crossed his lips, warming her heart. "I wonder where he gets that from?" He chuckled, his pointed gaze making his meaning evident.

A warm breeze blew against her face, or was it heating on its own from the intensity of his stare? "I'm sure I don't know to whom you're referring. It most certainly can't be me. I'm one of the most agreeable people you'd have the pleasure of meeting."

His hand flew to his mouth, muffling a snort of laughter. "Hmm, I seem to remember a lady who was adamant about placing an advertisement for a physician when she had no idea how to phrase it to attract the right man."

She huffed an exasperated breath. "Very well. I'll admit I can be somewhat stubborn at times. But"—she wagged a finger at him—"so can you. I'm pleased we've moved past that." She tilted her head. "We have, haven't we?"

An enigmatic smile was his only answer, and he strolled away to join the children.

How could one man be so frustrating and so alluring at the same time?

⚜

THE DAY HAD BEEN ALMOST PERFECT. ALMOST. COMMON COURTESY dictated Oliver offer his arm, yet he'd not permitted himself even that small indulgence. As they walked side by side, the children racing up the path in front of them, it had taken every ounce of strength to keep from touching her, and he'd resorted to clasping his hands at his back.

As they chatted amiably, making small talk and discussing Tori's improvements, the light conversation matched his mood on the warm summer day. He'd forgotten what it was like to breathe fresher air, to enjoy the more pleasing areas of the city, away from the stench and poverty of the East End.

He fought the urge to compare the dichotomy of the city's areas to the differences between Camilla and him. For a brief moment he pushed it from his mind, imagining strolling beside her in this beautiful place as if he belonged as much as she did.

Yes, an almost perfect day.

Until she'd mentioned the need for a father in a boy's life. Without warning, memories of his mother crying for the man who deserted her and her child—who deserted him—surfaced, unbidden, unwanted. How as a young boy, he'd pretended he'd had a father who loved him, taught him the things a boy should know.

His mother had done the best she could. He'd learned the rest on the streets or at the end of another boy's fists at school. Although he'd tried to hide his parentage, it didn't take long for the other boys to learn he was the bastard son of a nobleman. The bullying had been merciless, but he kept it to himself whenever he returned home to visit his mother.

Lady Denby wasn't wrong. A boy *did* need a man in his life, someone to defend him from those who would taunt and ridicule him. Even though Pockets' young life had a dreadful beginning, he was fortunate to have the concern of Lord Harcourt. With luck, he wouldn't hide his face in his pillow at night to muffle his cries of loneliness and abandonment.

As he stood behind the children who watched in awe while a juggler tossed colored balls into the air, he wondered what would happen to Pockets if Camilla remarried. His blood chilled at the thought of Lord Trentwith filling the role that he rightly should have held for Oliver. He shook off the unpleasant thought.

Peals of laughter filled the air around him as the children

delighted in the spectacle before them, and he couldn't help but smile in response.

"A marvelous feat, wouldn't you say, Dr. Somersby?" Camilla said, touching his arm.

Even through her glove and his coat, heat scorched him as if a branding iron had been pressed against his bare skin, and he wondered how hot the fire would burn between them if he let his passions free.

Unable to resist any longer, he slid his hand over hers as it rested on his arm, squeezing her fingers with the lightest of caresses. He cast a quick glance in her direction, noticing how her cheeks darkened.

Oh, yes. She feels it, too.

His mind began to wander, taking pathways best left untrod. Visions of a home, Tori and Pockets playing happily before a blazing hearth. Camilla fussing over her gown in preparation for another soirée while he studied the latest medical journal.

The hole in his heart, aching to be filled, throbbed mercilessly like a phantom limb.

"Dr. Somersby?"

He blinked, startled from his daydream. Camilla stared at him as if expecting an answer to—something.

"Pardon?"

Rather than being annoyed as some women would be, she laughed, the musical sound reminding him of her exceptional vocal gift. "Where were you? From the expression on your face, it must have been somewhere extremely pleasant."

As he gazed into the depths of her dark brown eyes, seeing the warmth, the kindness they held, he couldn't lie to her. "Very pleasant, but I return here, which is also very pleasant."

His answer seemed to have appeased her, and she graced him with a gentle smile, then turned her attention back toward the children.

"I'd like to host a birthday gathering for Pockets. However, I fear my father, although—as you so kindly stated—is an excellent role model, may be a bit out of touch when it comes to entertainment for young boys. Might you assist me?"

Those brown eyes met his again, dragging him under until he could scarcely breathe. "When's his birthday?"

"I have no idea, nor does Pockets. So I suggested he choose a day, and he settled on June nineteenth."

"Any reason he selected that particular day?"

Pink blossomed on her cheeks, making her already healthy complexion even more attractive. "It's also my birthday, and he said by sharing it with me, I would never forget it."

"I doubt you ever would, but it speaks volumes of the harshness he's endured in his young life."

"Yes, it does." Emotion choked her whispered words, and her eyes glistened with unshed tears.

How had he ever thought her cold and haughty? She had so much love for the child—so much love to give.

She cleared her throat, saying more forcefully, "Based on his teeth, we speculate he is around six. Would you agree?"

He nodded, his own emotions creating an unexpected tightness in his throat.

"So will you assist me? I would love for you and Victoria to come. And of course Manny will join us, even though Margaret is close to her confinement and Harry is reluctant to leave her side."

He chuckled. "Indeed. He's been at sixes and sevens at the clinic. I've suggested he remain at home or I would wind up having to treat him along with the rest of our patients."

"He adores her. They will make such wonderful parents." She sighed, the kind of sound one makes when something they've longed for is right outside their grasp. Had she journeyed into the realm of *what if* as well?

"Who do you expect will attend this soirée? I'm not comfortable around a lot of high class people." *One in particular.*

"Only close friends, people who have met and been kind to Pockets. My father, the Weatherbys, and of course Manny, Harry, and Margaret if she's able."

He'd met the Weatherbys, who seemed a decent sort. "What

about Lord Trentwith? I understand he's been escorting you around town." He almost choked on the name.

The rosy blush painted her cheeks again. "He won't be in attendance."

A spark of something bright exploded in his chest, so he pressed further. "Isn't he courting you?"

The color on her face deepened, but her eyes flashed, bringing back the memory of their first encounter. "Would it matter to you?"

He'd almost forgotten her ability to return his jabs blow for blow. "That's not an answer to my question." He turned away, unwilling to meet her knowing gaze. "But to answer yours . . . perhaps."

With a furtive glance from the corner of his eye, he caught her lips tip up.

"I've put him off . . . temporarily, as I explore other possibilities."

Thunderous applause erupted from the crowd gathered around the juggler, disrupting their exchange. But her meaning wasn't lost on him.

The spark that had ignited in his chest now burned bright and he dared to give it a name—hope.

CHAPTER 15—CELEBRATIONS

T he following two weeks, preparation for Pockets' birthday
celebration consumed Camilla. Oliver suggested planning
games for the children and even conceded to her desire to provide
an abundance of sweet treats.

She stayed late after Victoria's lessons with the specific intention
of speaking with Oliver when he returned home from the clinic. He,
in turn, accompanied Victoria to Camilla's before leaving for his
duties at the clinic. It had been a blissful two weeks of civil
conversation and cooperation.

Not to mention the stolen glances and discreet touches of fingers
as she handed him the list of planned activities she'd prepared. Yes,
blissful was an appropriate word.

As she entered the kitchen to check on preparations the day of
the party, the cook shooed her away. "Off with you, my lady.
Stratton does his job well enough. No need to bother yourself."

Years of observing her mother flawlessly manage large parties
had set the standard of measure. The day must be perfect. She
would not accept anything less.

To that end, she dressed in her loveliest day gown, the bright blue reminding her of Oliver's eyes. She preened before the mirror, wondering if Oliver would like it.

"Mama, come on!" Pockets called as he ran into her room and tugged on her skirts. "Manny's here!"

So overflowing with excitement, he'd barely stayed in one spot the entire morning. It had been nothing short of a miracle to convince him to dress and comb his hair.

He grabbed her hand, pulling her forward to greet their guests. When they arrived in the parlor decorated with festive streamers, her eyes widened at the sight of Margaret.

So busy with lessons and the preparations for the party, she hadn't seen her friend in the past three weeks. Margaret's girth had expanded two-fold. "Maggie, you look radiant."

"You're being kind, Cam. What I need from you is honesty. Admit it. I'm as wide as the dome of St. Paul's." She leaned closer and whispered, "Harry's concerned it might be twins."

Harry's head snapped in their direction at the sound of his name.

"Is that a possibility?" Camilla asked.

"I suppose, all things considered," Harry said, no doubt concerned that a set of twins might prove similar to his own situation. How two brothers identical in looks could be so very dissimilar in nature had always puzzled Camilla. Thank goodness Maggie was free of George and now had Harry.

"Alice Weatherby has proven extraordinarily helpful," Margaret said. "She pointed out that the movement she experienced with her twins was nonstop. If there are two babies in here, they're remarkably calm."

Camilla wrapped an arm around Margaret's waist. "I'm so anxious to see the babies. I believe Andrew said this will be their first official outing."

"Are we going to talk about babies all day?" Pockets whined.

"Nah, you're the only baby here that matters today," Manny said, giving his friend an elbow to the ribs accompanied with an enormous grin.

"I'm not a baby. I'm seven today, right, Mama?"

Camilla gazed down, meeting Pocket's bright blue eyes, reminding her of Oliver. Why hadn't she thought about his eye color before? "That's right. But Manny does have a point. Today is your day."

"Yours, too, Mama. I made you something."

With all the excitement and planning around the day, he took the time to do something special for her. His words stunned her. "You did?"

He nodded, his little head bobbing up and down furiously.

A blush spread across Margaret's cheeks. "Oh, Cam, I'm a horrible friend. I'd completely forgotten your birthday."

Camilla patted Margaret's hand. "With everything on your mind, I forgive you." She winked. "But only this once."

Harry pulled a package from behind his back. "We have a gift for you, Pockets, but you must wait to open it until all your guests have arrived. Agreed?"

"For me?" The boy's eyes grew to the size of saucers.

Once they had settled into the parlor, ensuring Margaret had the most comfortable chair with several cushions at her back, they waited for the remainder of their guests.

When her father arrived, Pockets threw himself into his poppy's arms.

"Your gift is outside as it's too large to bring inside," her father announced.

"Manny's papa says I have to wait to open my gifts until everyone is here." He folded his arms across his chest and stuck out his bottom lip.

"It's the polite thing to do," her father said, hugging the boy and warming her heart.

After giving her a peck on the cheek, he whispered in her ear, "I have something for you, too."

The Weatherbys arrived next, their three-month-old twin girls, Indira and Eleanor, stealing everyone's attention. Even Pockets seemed fascinated by their tiny hands as they wrapped around his finger.

"How can they eat? They ain't got no teeth," he asked.

"Don't have any teeth," Camilla corrected.

"They drink milk," Manny said as if he were the expert on all things baby. "I've been learning so's I can help when our baby comes."

Manny's speech had improved immensely since Margaret and Harry had taken him in over a year ago, and Camilla hoped Pockets would also continue to make such strides.

"And they'll get teeth soon enough," Alice said, then blushed as she added, "hopefully not too soon."

Surrounded by such loving families, a bittersweet pain surfaced, squeezing Camilla's heart. And although grateful to have such wonderful friends, a part of her yearned to share her life with an adoring husband of her own.

Stratton appeared. "Dr. Somersby and Miss Victoria, my lady."

As if reading her hopeful mind, Oliver strode in, making direct eye contact. Her breath hitched at his dimpled smile.

"Happy birthday, Pockets." Oliver tousled the boy's hair and handed him a package.

"This is the best day ever," Pockets proclaimed, laying the package on the table Camilla had prepared.

Like a stealth animal, Oliver moved toward her and bowed. "And happy birthday to you, Lady Denby." He handed her a small package.

If one's heart could melt, Camilla's was the puddle left after the sun heated a mound of snow. He'd remembered and brought her a gift.

"It's nothing much," he said. "But I didn't want you to be forgotten."

She looked up at him, so overcome with emotion she could barely speak. "May I open it?"

"If you wish, or you can save it to open with your other gifts."

The only other gifts were from her father and Pockets, making this one all the more precious. The fact that three of her favorite men remembered her birthday had been enough to make her day special. She tried not to read too much into the gesture, but her heart had already sprinted toward the conclusion. "I'll open it in private. I don't want to take any attention away from Pockets."

Oliver smiled, glancing over at the excited boy. "I don't think that's possible. You've outdone yourself. He looks ecstatic."

With all the guests assembled, Stratton brought in refreshments, including a large cake. Pockets, of course, had a slice much bigger than his stomach could handle. Chocolate, an especially decadent luxury, coated his face as he grinned in bliss.

"Wha's this?" He held up the coin that had been baked inside.

Camilla would never divulge the secret, but she'd asked Cook to mark the place where the coin was hidden so Pockets would receive the special piece.

"Oh, Pockets, you're quite lucky," Harry said. "That means you will have fortune in your future."

The boy nodded. "I already feel rich."

Camilla glanced over at Oliver, who graced her with a wide smile as he met her gaze. When he took a bite of his cake, he coughed, spitting out the ring hidden inside. It clinked against his plate.

Although she'd asked Cook to include the coin for Pockets, Camilla had no idea the conniving woman had also included a ring signifying marriage.

Victoria clapped her hands, bouncing on her feet. "Oh, Ollie, that means you're going to get married."

"Nonsense, Tori. What if His Grace had received it, or Mr. Weatherby? It's a silly superstition."

Pockets frowned and looked at his coin. "Mine, too?"

Color drained from Oliver's swarthy face. "Of course not, Pockets. I must have been mistaken. How else would the ring know to find someone who wasn't already married? It must be true."

Pockets narrowed his eyes, obviously not completely believing Oliver's sudden change of opinion.

Another piece of her heart drifted over to Oliver for attempting to salvage the situation, especially considering his discomfort in receiving the ring. In an effort to divert Pockets' attention, she said, "Perhaps it's time to open your gifts?"

Her words had the desired effect, and Pockets raced to the table holding his gifts. "Which one first, Mama?"

All heads turned toward her. Only her father, Oliver, Victoria, and Margaret had heard Pockets call her mother before. Alice Weatherby's hand lifted to her breast, and tears welled in her eyes. Harry gave a nod of approval, and Andrew Weatherby grinned.

"Whichever you wish, darling. It's your birthday, your choice."

His hands ran over the packages in an almost reverent motion. As most boys would, she supposed, he stopped on the largest.

"That one's from us," Margaret said.

"You'll like it," Manny added.

With slow, precise movements, as if afraid someone might snatch it away if he were to open it too soon, Pockets peeled away the wrapping, revealing a cricket bat and ball.

"We'll teach you to play," Harry said. "Manny's already becoming quite good."

Manny's chest puffed out from the compliment.

Pockets moved on to the next package which contained a bilboquet from the Weatherbys.

"Perhaps you'll be better at it than I was as a boy," Andrew said. "I'm afraid I'm not coordinated enough."

After giving the cup and ball a few tries, and succeeding to capture the ball once, Pockets moved on to the next package.

"That's from Tori and me," Oliver said. "I hope you like it."

Camilla gasped as Pockets unwrapped a child-sized, perfectly formed violin.

"I can teach you," Oliver said. "Then you can accompany your mother while she sings."

The rest of her heart abandoned her forever, to remain solely in Oliver Somersby's possession.

"Oh, it's too much, Dr. Somersby," she said. "However did you manage it?"

"It was made for me when I was a boy. I've obviously outgrown it, and Tori has no interest in learning. I thought perhaps it would be a way to repay the lessons you've provided to Tori."

The memory of their encounter the night of the masquerade

ball when they shared their mutual love of music resurfaced. His confession that he enjoyed both listening and playing became clear.

"It's most generous." Her eyes met his, the connection between them electric. *Ah, he also remembers.*

Aware all eyes were on her, she refocused. "You have two more, Pockets, one from me and one from Poppy," Camilla reminded her son.

Yes, he truly had become her son. The day had become a day to celebrate her new family as well.

Eagerly picking up the one gift remaining on the table, Pockets opened the rectangular package.

All the joy and exuberance he'd exhibited with each gift left his face as he gazed at the book.

Something like cold porridge sat heavy in Camilla's stomach as she witnessed the disappointment on his face and at her own failure to understand what pleases little boys.

Oliver rose from his seat and took the book from Pockets' hands. "What have you got there?" He made a great show of reading the title. "Oh, this is one of my favorites. *Gulliver's Travels.* You enjoyed my story about the mermaid, so you'll love this one. Your mother chose wisely. It's important to enrich your mind as well as exercise your body."

She mouthed a silent *thank you* in Oliver's direction, and he promptly rewarded her with a smile.

"We shall have to go outside for your gift from me," her father said.

Everyone moved outside to the gardens in the back of the house. Once Harry had settled Margaret into a comfortable chair, the footman brought around the final gift.

Camilla stared at the strange two-wheeled vehicle with a seat in the middle. "What is that contraption? It looks unsafe."

"Don't be ridiculous, Camilla," her father said. "It's a velocipede. Latest thing, jolly good fun."

All the men were exchanging excited nods of approval. *Nodcocks, every last one of them.*

As the footman held the deathly device, Pockets climbed on the seat, his toes barely skimming the ground.

With her hands firmly planted on her hips, Camilla made her argument. "You see, it's too large for him. He'll injure himself."

The sheepish look on her father's face defused her annoyance.

"The way he's growing, he'll reach the ground in no time," Oliver said. "In the interim, perhaps we can offer some assistance."

He moved over toward the odious machine and lifted Pockets off. The tension in Camilla's chest eased only to return in full force when Oliver mounted the hideous hobby-horse. "Climb behind me and grab my waist, Pockets."

Were they all determined to kill themselves?

Oliver pushed off, the velocipede wobbling on shaky wheels. Pockets squealed, whether in elation or fright, Camilla wasn't sure.

Certain he'd tip over, injuring them both, Camilla watched in amazement as Oliver steadied the vehicle and made a complete turn around the garden path.

Victoria and Manny clapped their hands, insisting on their turn on the appalling apparatus.

After depositing Pockets safely back to her, Oliver said, "Well done, Lord Harcourt. I do believe your gift has topped them all." He shot Camilla a quick glance. "With the exception of that splendid book, of course."

Camilla snorted a laugh, conceding defeat. "Enough. Consider me properly chastised for my ignorance regarding what delights young boys . . . and grown boys as well, it seems."

Each man had a turn on the velocipede, with Harry falling summarily off when he rounded the corner of the path too quickly. Thank goodness he had ridden alone, allowing Manny to ride on his own since his feet managed to reach the ground. Oliver insisted on supervising Victoria, who managed quite well, impressing even Manny with her dexterity and grace.

As they settled to rest and the children took turns with the bilboquet, Oliver took a seat beside her. "You've managed to make this day something Pockets will never forget. I commend you, my lady."

How could she have ever thought him cold and unfeeling?

"Thank you for rescuing me from my utter faux pas of a gift. I should have consulted you, Harry, or my father."

"Nonsense. Reading improves the mind. Your gift complements the others, which improve his body."

"As yours enhances his spirit and soul. Will you truly teach him to play?"

"If he wishes. It hasn't escaped my notice that he seems more interested in the pianoforte than he does in dancing." He stared ahead of him, as if concentrating on the children, but a teasing smile played at his lips. "And since Her Grace mentioned your mediocre skills at the keyboard, I thought I might be of some assistance with his musical education."

Adopting his mischievous tone, she said, "Although I take no offense from your statement, I demand an opportunity to redeem myself."

The delicious chuckle she loved erupted from deep in his chest, sending gooseflesh up her arms. An almost palpable energy sparked between them.

"One can't expect to be proficient in all things. Your voice more than makes up for any other perceived musical deficiency. Besides, as I stated, I'm indebted to you for your assistance with Tori and wish to repay the kindness."

Oh, what a dream it would be to spend every day like this.

After taking a turn with the children at the bilboquet, her father approached with Pockets in tow.

"Pockets reminded me that his birthday wasn't the only one we're celebrating." He beamed as he turned toward the boy. "Go fetch your gift for your mother."

"With her permission, bring mine too, Pockets," Oliver said, then turned a questioning eye toward her.

"Of course. It's on the table by the sofa," she said.

Pockets raced off with all the exuberance of any boy on his birthday.

"He reminds me of you at that age," her father said, discreetly wiping suspicious moisture from his eyes.

"I'll wager she was quite the hoyden, sir," Oliver said, casting a furtive glance her way.

"You have no idea."

Her heart warmed with her father's bellowing laugh. He'd improved tenfold in the last few months, in large part thanks to Oliver.

Pockets returned holding two packages, one more neatly wrapped than the other.

She made a great show of examining the packages while Pockets bounced on impatient feet. "Oh, which shall I open first?"

Pockets pointed to the oddly shaped package tied with a piece of twine. "Mine first, Mama."

"Very well. What might it be?" She tugged at the tightly knotted twine, struggling to untie it.

"I done . . . I did the wrapping myself."

"And a fine job you did," Oliver said. "But I'm afraid your muscle power made it too difficult for your mother." He pulled a pocket knife from his coat. "May I?"

She nodded, and he cut through the twine in a single motion.

As if unwrapping the greatest of treasures—for that's what it was for her—she moved the brown paper aside. Thinner than her smallest finger, an intricately braided and knotted cord in delicate strands of red, blue, and purple burst forth against the tan background of the wrapping.

"Oh, Pockets. It's lovely."

"I made it myself. Well, Tori and Oliver helped me some. Tori got me the threads and taught me to braid, and Oliver helped tie the knots. You wear it around your wrist."

"Whenever did you have time?" She marveled at the colorful bracelet.

"Tori showed me when you and Tori's mama had tea."

"When you were supposed to be practicing your handwriting?" She tried to force a disapproving scowl but failed.

"Yes, but Tori said it was for a good reason. Then I worked on it at night. I left it with Tori for Oliver to help with the knots."

"I shouldn't countenance such deceptive practices," she said. Her lips twitched upward, betraying her words.

"Mine goes with it," Oliver said, pointing to the more neatly wrapped package Pockets had retrieved.

With shaking fingers, she tugged at the silky red ribbon securing the lovely cream paper. When had she been this excited about a gift? Nestled within the folds of the paper, an oval pendant rested. A small silver loop protruded from the top, presumably to fasten onto a chain. Carved intricately into the face of the pearlescent charm, a mermaid perched on an outcropping of rocks.

"It's beautiful."

"A siren for the siren of song," Oliver said.

Camilla choked back the tears at the perfect gift.

"May I?" he asked, holding out his hand.

She placed the charm in his outstretched palm.

"It's scrimshaw," he said. "I used to watch the sailors work their magic on whale's teeth and bones. It's a crime what's done to those poor creatures. This is made from a simple sea shell, a poor imitation of ivory from a poor physician." He slipped the charm onto the bracelet Pockets had fashioned, then tied it to her wrist.

A tear broke free and trickled down her cheek, and he brushed it away with his thumb.

"You don't like it?" Genuine concern laced his voice.

"It's perfect."

"It would appear we're all of like mind," her father said, handing her his gift.

Opening it, she found a necklace, the locket bearing a miniature likeness of her mother.

The tears could no longer be contained, and she flung herself into her father's arms. "Thank you, Father."

"Me, too." Pockets hugged her skirts, and she bent to embrace him as well, kissing his cheeks.

"Thank you, Pockets. I love it."

Without a thought, she turned toward Oliver and threw her arms about him, his heady masculine scent teasing her nose. "Thank you for making my birthday one I'll never forget."

A delicate cough sounded from behind her, and she turned to find Margaret watching intently.

"Yes, well," her father clapped his hands together. "What say you, Dr. Somersby, shall we teach this young lad how to play cricket?"

As the men and boys gathered on the lawn, Margaret whispered to Camilla, "It would appear you no longer find Dr. Somersby disagreeable."

Camilla stared down at the mermaid, a tiny smile curling her lips. "It would appear so."

CHAPTER 16—NEW BEGINNINGS

As if Oliver didn't have enough reasons to like Lord Harcourt, the man's diplomatic handling in getting his daughter and her would-be suitor out of a delicate situation was nothing short of miraculous. Not that Oliver minded having Camilla throw her arms around him. It had taken everything in him not to pull her closer and kiss her senseless. Thank God one of them retained a semblance of sanity.

More shocking though was the fact that Oliver dared to entertain the notion of being Camilla's suitor. All those months ago when she'd suggested they explore their connection, he'd believed it an impossible dream. The mere idea of it so preposterous, he'd raged in anger. Now, a glimmer of hope taunted and lured him much like the siren adorning his meager gift.

The pressing question remained—could he trust her, or would he continue to deceive her about his heritage? And if she discovered it, would he be dashed against the rocks of love and destroy himself —destroy her?

Manny called, waking him from his daydreaming. "Oi, Dr. Somersby, you going to play or watch the clouds?"

Immersed in the cricket game, it became easy to imagine

himself part of their world. A world where both dukes and street urchins gathered in camaraderie and acceptance. But would they accept a Romani, or to them—a gypsy? Each time he heard the word, he yearned to spit the nasty taste of it out, and he bore the blood. What would they say if they knew? Would he lose his position, any hope of securing a place in society and an acceptable marriage for Tori? Would he lose the dream of a union with Camilla forever?

No, they'd never accept him.

His gaze drifted over to where Camilla chatted with Margaret, and his heart broke for what could never be.

At bat, Harry good-naturedly jeered him as Oliver bowled the ball.

"Harry! Come quickly, it's the baby!" Camilla's voice rang out, bringing the cricket game to a halt.

With lightning speed, Harry raced up to the terrace where Camilla and Alice Weatherby gathered around Margaret. Oliver ran behind him, followed by the boys, Andrew Weatherby, and Lord Harcourt.

"Stop fussing," Margaret said. "It's simply a little—" She clutched her abdomen, her face contorted in pain. "A little twinge."

Harry pulled out his pocket watch, eyes darting between it and Margaret's face. Seconds ticked past, and he crouched before her. "It's more than a little twinge. How long have you been experiencing these pains?"

Sweat beaded Margaret's forehead and upper lip. "It started this morning, but I didn't want to say anything. I'd heard about some women having false pains, and the baby isn't due for another month. Besides, Manny was so looking forward to Pockets' birthday. I didn't want to disappoint the boys. Or you, Cam."

"You goose," Camilla said, the worried tone in her voice softening her admonishment.

"We could have made a miscalculation," Harry said, his own face paling. "You *have* seemed to grow exceptionally large in the last month."

Margaret shot him a pointed glare.

"Allow me to help you get her to the carriage," Oliver said, moving closer.

Margaret's face contorted with pain, and she clutched at Harry's hand. "Oh, here's another one."

"So soon?" Harry, who always seemed so calm in the face of chaos, appeared to be completely flustered. His head turned toward Camilla. "We may not have time to get her home. Is there somewhere . . ."

"Yes, of course. A bedroom upstairs. Tell me what you need."

Harry lifted Margaret in his arms, stifling a small *Oomph*, and followed Camilla inside.

Oliver followed. "Harry, what can I do?"

"Retrieve my bag from the carriage. I always bring it with me."

Oliver dashed off, swiveling like a mad man in search of a footman to show him where Harry's carriage had been deposited. He'd only delivered a baby twice in his life, having mainly dealt with sailors aboard *The Destiny* and the people at the clinic. Midwives typically handled births. Whether Harry and Margaret had planned to use a midwife seemed a moot point, and with Harry's medical bag in hand, Oliver ran back into the house and up the stairs, searching for the right room.

A maid with an armload of towels hurried down the hall and entered a room where Camilla stood guard. Her eyes locked on Oliver's. Fear shone in them.

"It will be fine. Margaret's a healthy young woman, and Harry's a fine physician," he said, patting her arm and slipping past her into the room.

He placed Harry's medical bag on the bed next to Margaret. "What else can I do?"

Harry took the towels from the maid, then adjusted a blanket over his wife's abdomen and legs. "Will you keep Manny busy? He won't admit it, but I know he's concerned."

Oliver nodded. "If you need any medical assistance, I'll be ready."

Harry grabbed his arm. "Thank you. Margaret and I discussed

it. We'd always planned on having me deliver the baby." He gave a weak grin. "Just not so soon."

As he stepped out of the room, Oliver found Camilla speaking to the maid and a footman.

Tension etched her face as she delivered her instructions with all the command of a ship's captain. "Remain stationed here. If His Grace asks for anything, anyone, don't question it. Do whatever he asks."

With a nod to the servants, he followed Camilla to a downstairs parlor where everyone had gathered.

Before entering, she placed a hand on his forearm. "Promise me Margaret and the baby will survive."

With lies already between them, he loathed adding another, but his desire to assuage her worry softened his words. "Childbirth is a natural process. In this case, the prognosis favors a successful outcome. Harry will see to it."

Everyone rose to their feet upon Oliver and Camilla's entrance, their eyes holding the same questions he'd seen in Camilla's.

He held up his hands, motioning for them to be seated. "Babies take their own time making an appearance. It may be hours before anything happens."

Remembering Harry's request to keep Manny busy and Lord Harcourt's love of cards, Oliver suggested they divide into four teams at two tables and teach the children how to play whist.

In an effort to promote fairness, rather than draw to determine teams, they decided to pair the children with an adult, and Oliver found himself at a table partnered with Manny against Camilla and Tori. Lord Harcourt insisted on Pockets as his partner playing against the Weatherbys. Andrew claimed Alice's preoccupation with the twins made concentrating on her hand difficult, providing enough of a handicap. In thanks, he received a severe stare from his demure wife.

After over a dozen hands, and sufficient gloating by Lord Harcourt and Pockets over their wins, Camilla called for refreshments.

Silence settled on the small group as the clock on the mantle marked the passing minutes.

The twins began fussing, and Camilla and Tori accompanied Alice to an adjacent room. The affection he'd witnessed between his daughter and Camilla added to his growing tumultuous feelings. His heart wasn't the only one at risk.

With the men and boys left to themselves, Lord Harcourt took the opportunity to light a cigar. He blew out a circle of smoke, filling the air with the pungent aroma. "I hated this part. The waiting and not knowing. Although, I'm not sure if I envy Ashton or pity him."

"Yes, I agree." Andrew nodded. "I remember the midwife coming out to announce I had a daughter only to rush back in when Alice began screaming again. It took every ounce of strength not to break down the door and see for myself what was happening."

Oliver could only imagine, not having been present at Tori's birth, a fact he bitterly regretted.

Manny had grown unusually quiet, his eyes increasing in size as he listened to the men's stories. Oliver moved to sit by him, wrapping an arm around his small shoulders and giving them a gentle squeeze. "Her Grace will be fine, Manny. She's strong and so is your little brother or sister. They will need you to be strong for them."

"She's the only mother I know," he said, wiping at his eyes.

An odd twinge, much like a too-tight tourniquet, squeezed Oliver's chest. "And she's blessed to have you. Now, dry your eyes before the ladies return."

Manny gave him a weak smile.

The women returned. The twins had been fed and put to bed in a room supervised by a maid. Pockets, too, had fallen asleep on the settee, and Lord Harcourt covered him with a blanket he'd requested from a servant.

Hushed silence followed as the group did its best not to wake the sleeping boy. The lad had experienced a momentous birthday celebration.

Manny now nestled close to Oliver's side, his eyelids drooping, then jerking awake as he fought drowsiness. Sounds of servants bustling up the staircase, alerted Oliver that Margaret must be close to delivering.

Shortly after the clock chimed the quarter hour of eleven, Harry appeared at the doorway. Shirtsleeves rolled up to his elbows, his coat removed, hair disheveled, the grin on his face relayed the happy news before he uttered the words. "It's a boy!"

Everyone jumped to attention. Manny, being the first to reach him, embraced him, no longer able to hide his tears. "Is Margaret a'righ'?"

"Your mother is fine. She wants to see you." Harry lifted his gaze, as he continued to stroke his adoptive son's head. "All of you."

When everyone moved toward the door, Harry laughed. "Not all at once. She requested to see Manny first, to introduce his new brother, Edmund. We're naming him after Maggie's father."

Before Harry could finish, Manny raced out of the room, his feet pounding against the steps. Andrew thumped good-naturedly on Harry's back, while Lord Harcourt offered him a cigar.

Harry wiped his brow, exhaustion warring with the joy on his face. He turned toward the doorway where Manny had left. "I have an heir! Although he understands he can't inherit, I didn't want to say anything in front of Manny. Margaret has been so concerned about providing me a son. I think she's more relieved it's a boy than the fact the birth is over."

Alice chuckled. "I have my doubts about that, Harry."

As Oliver witnessed the camaraderie, the old sensation of being caught between two worlds crashed over him.

He remembered once, as a small boy, accompanying his mother and grandmother to one of the fine houses in this very part of town. Instructed to stay outside and out of sight, he pressed his nose to the window, peeking in, his eyes wide with wonder at the fine clothes and lavish furnishings.

In his sleep that night, he'd found himself inside that home, eating the decadent treats spread in abundance on silver trays, luxuriating in the warmth of a roaring fire, receiving praise from his proud father.

And although this moment was no dream, it was as much out of his grasp as the specters of his slumber. The ache in his chest now dulled, as if his heart had disappeared, replaced with a heavy hollowness.

Camilla's bright smile faltered as she turned from Harry and looked his way. With a lightness that surprised him, she moved to his side. "What's wrong? You look as if you've seen a ghost."

"Simply tired. It's been an eventful day." He nodded toward Harry, still engulfed by the congratulatory group, and a smile came more naturally than he'd expected. "He will be useless at the clinic for a while."

When she laughed, he breathed a sigh of relief she hadn't misconstrued his words as a slight to Harry.

"More work for you, Dr. Somersby? I'm certain you will handle it with aplomb."

Her compliment pleased him, and the unease of being an outsider passed. "So your opinion of me and my skills as a physician have changed since our first meeting?" A quirk of his lips accompanied his teasing tone.

She touched the scrimshaw charm on her wrist. "I'll admit, I may have made a rather hasty judgment. Will you forgive me?"

"On the condition that you forgive me as well. I recall I may have made my own unkind remarks."

She slid her hand through his arm, the action natural, as if it belonged there. "Now, let's go see the baby."

❦

LIGHTNESS FLOWED THROUGH CAMILLA AS SHE AND OLIVER STRODE into the room where Margaret lay, holding her newborn son. Camilla's own breasts tightened at the soft mew from the babe, the bittersweet ache leading her mind down paths of possibility.

Oliver placed his hand over hers as it rested on his arm and gave it a gentle squeeze.

A quick glance in his direction seemed to convey he understood her thoughts when a somewhat wan smile crossed his lips.

Although still recovering from the birth, Margaret glowed with love as she introduced them to the new heir. "Cam, Oliver, I'd like to introduce Edmund Harrison Radcliffe."

Manny stationed himself like a sentry by her bedside, protecting his baby brother. "'E ain't got much 'air."

"So no shaving yet, I presume," Oliver said, a grin spreading across his face.

Camilla stepped closer for a better look. "He's beautiful, Maggie."

Oliver moved to her side, his hand reaching toward the infant. "He seems a good sized lad."

Edmund wrapped his tiny hand around Oliver's finger.

Maggie gazed adoringly at her son. "Harry says he's larger than most babies he's seen."

She turned her attention to Manny. "Would you give Lady Denby and me a moment alone, Manny?"

With a reluctant nod and his eyes still focused on the baby, Manny strode toward the door. Oliver followed him, the door closing with a soft snick behind them.

Worry pressed the air from Camilla's lungs. "What is it? You seem troubled?"

"It's nothing, I'm sure, but would you do something for me?"

"Of course, anything."

"Would you ask Oliver if he's aware of any possibility Edmund could . . ." Maggie swallowed, tears welling in her eyes.

Careful not to jostle her, Camilla sat next to her friend and took her hand. "Maggie, surely you're not worried something will happen to Edmund?"

Although both Oliver and Harry seemed to think he was large, to Camilla the infant appeared tiny as he nuzzled against Margaret's breast. Tiny and perfect.

"I've heard babies who come early have difficulty thriving." Margaret kissed the top of her son's head.

"Why didn't you ask Harry, or Oliver himself?"

"Because I'm not entirely sure Harry would tell me the truth." Still holding firm to Edmund, she raised a hand to silence Camilla. "Not to deceive me, Cam, to protect me. Although my marriage to

Harry is based on mutual respect and trust, in this matter, I fear he would try to shelter me. As for Oliver, I'm believe he would do the same if I asked him. But if *you* asked him . . ."

Camilla scoffed. "You truly believe he'd be more honest with me? That man holds mysteries so close to his waistcoat they blend into the material."

"I watched you two today, and I have confidence in your . . . shall I be delicate and say methods of persuasion? If you press him and don't let him know I'm the one who has requested the information, I'm certain he'll tell you."

Camilla shook her head in defeat, for she could refuse her friend nothing, and acquiesced. "As you wish."

"There is one more thing I would like you to ask Oliver."

"If it's to marry me, you would be overestimating my powers of persuasion."

As soon as the words left her lips and she registered Margaret's stunned expression, Camilla regretted uttering them.

A wicked smile replaced the shock on Margaret's face. "Well, it wasn't quite what I had in mind, but I find it encouraging that particular thought came to yours."

She shifted the sleeping infant to her other side. "No, it's also about Edmund. I don't want to upset Harry. Would you ask Oliver if it's possible for Edmund to inherit traits from . . . other family members in addition to his parents?"

Oh. An uncomfortable sensation of dropping assaulted Camilla's stomach. "You're concerned the child will be like George?"

The idea that an innocent child would transform into the monster who had been Margaret's first husband and Harry's identical twin brother seemed preposterous, but the seriousness of Margaret's concern shone on her face.

"I'll ask him, but how can such a beautiful child, with two *loving* parents be anything other than good and kind?" She squeezed Margaret's hand, hoping to reassure her. "Fretting over such things can't be good for either of you."

Margaret nodded. "Thank you, Cam."

The baby stirred and gave another soft mew.

"Perhaps I should receive my other visitors quickly. I suddenly feel quite tired."

Camilla laughed. "I would think so. The Weatherbys, Pockets, and my father are eager to see the new heir. If you'd allow it, I think Pockets would like to accompany my father."

Margaret yawned as if to prove her earlier point. "Of course."

As she exited, Camilla said, "I'll advise them to make their visits brief."

When she closed the door behind her, Oliver straightened to attention from where he leaned against the wall. The concern in his eyes and his hand placed on Manny's shoulder affected her more than she cared to admit. The question most likely in his mind remained unspoken.

She smiled warmly at Manny. "Your mother is exhausted. Giving birth is hard work. Perhaps it's best if you allow her to rest for a while after she sees the other visitors? I'll have Stratton prepare a room for you for the night."

"You mean we can't go home?" Manny asked.

"Perhaps in the morning. Why don't we send the others to see the baby then get you settled?"

As Manny led the way back to the parlor, Oliver touched her arm, leaning in to whisper, "It's none of my affair, but you seem troubled."

The quick order with which he'd deduced her concern surprised her—and pleased her. "May I speak with you in private?"

His eyebrow quirked. A flash of something dangerous flitted across his face but vanished just as quickly as he grew serious. "Should we alert Harry?"

"No, I simply wish your opinion as a physician."

Sounds of hushed conversation drifted from the room where the remaining party waited. Oliver reached out, holding Manny back by the shoulder, keeping the boy from racing in and disturbing the tranquil sight.

Harry lounged in a wingback chair, his head resting against the back. Alice's eyelids drooped, her head lying on Andrew's shoulder. But nothing surpassed the view of her father, situated on the sofa with Pockets snuggled under one arm and Victoria under the other, both children fast asleep.

Unable to restrain her sigh, she leaned into Oliver at the picture of peaceful domesticity. His arm snaked around her waist, giving her a gentle squeeze. It would appear he, too, found the image heartwarming.

Oliver's breath tickled her ear as he whispered, "I should get her home."

"You could both stay here." *Oh!* What had she suggested?

His lips quirked, the faint dent of the dimple hinting at an appearance. "A generous offer, but your staff will be busy enough with a duke, duchess, and a newborn to care for. However, you did wish to speak with me, and Tori is in excellent hands with your father for the moment."

Once they joined the rest of the group, Camilla instructed a maid to make up a room for Manny. Harry insisted on staying in the room with Margaret in case she needed him. Andrew and Alice decided to take a quick peek at the baby and then return home.

"Father, would you mind watching after Pockets and Victoria for a few moments? I'd like to have a word with Dr. Somersby."

"Not at all. I'd be delighted. In fact, I fear if I moved they would both protest." He smiled, indicating remaining wedged between the two children was no hardship whatsoever.

Careful to maintain propriety, she led Oliver to a quiet spot in the hallway.

"I've said it before, your father is a good man."

"He is, although I worry he will spoil Pockets horribly."

"You can't spoil someone with love."

What an insightful statement. "Ah, but you can with extravagant gifts."

"The lad's had an eventful birthday." He paused, meeting her eyes directly. "As have you. Now, what is troubling you?"

"Are you aware of Harry's brother, Margaret's first husband?"

"Not particularly. Harry's not one to speak ill of anyone, but he has mentioned Her Grace's marriage to his brother was not pleasant."

"He was a brute of a man. It's still inconceivable that he and Harry were identical twins. No two people could have been more dissimilar. But since they were related, is it at all possible that the child . . . Edmund could have the same temperament as his uncle? From your expertise, speaking as a physician, of course."

His eyes narrowed, studying her. "Are *you* concerned or is Her Grace?"

How easily he saw through her ruse. "Does it matter?"

"I suppose not. Although I can't speak to this medically, I do have my own opinions on the subject based on personal experience."

At the words *personal experience,* her interest piqued.

For a moment, his gaze dulled as if he were lost in another time. "Are you familiar with the concept of tabula rasa?"

"Yes, Aristotle and later Locke, I believe."

He nodded. "I believe many behaviors are learned, not inborn. If our parents or family defines us, it's because of the examples they set. To love, to be respectful, to accept others who are different from ourselves. These things are taught. In the same manner, people have to be taught to hate, to fear others unlike themselves out of ignorance. I don't know what Harry's life was as a boy, but someone of importance must have taught him to be the kind of man he is today. I'm certain he will do the same for Edmund."

His words made sense. She expected no less than logic and reason, but an underlying current of pain threaded through his words.

"You said you base your opinions on your own personal experience."

A muscle in his jaw flexed, and she anticipated he would refuse to pursue her open statement. The fleeting glimpse of sadness crossed his face again.

"As I mentioned earlier, we both admitted we may have made hasty and inaccurate presumptions about each other. I'll admit mine stem from my experiences as a boy. But as a man, I'm learning— slowly—to form new opinions."

"As am I," she answered, gracing him with—what she hoped—was her most alluring smile.

"Now, is anything else concerning you?"

"Only one thing. And as you've seen through my façade, I will be more forthright. Because he was born early, Maggie is concerned for Edmund's health."

"Ah, now *that* I can answer as a physician. If I were to venture a guess, from the size of him, I would say Edmund arrived precisely on time. Harry said they could have miscalculated his expected arrival. He appears robust and no doubt will have the best of care if Harry has any say in the matter."

"That's what I told Maggie, but of course, she worries Harry won't be honest with her if there's a problem."

"Well, now you can reassure her with the professional opinion of another physician."

Emotion gripped her, and without warning, tears formed in her eyes.

A lone drop trickled down her cheek, and he brushed it away with his thumb. "You're exhausted. Now, I should fetch Tori and allow everyone to get some rest. I'll contact you about violin lessons for Pockets."

Reluctant to see him go, she grasped his arm, and leaning up, kissed his cheek. "Thank you, Oliver."

It had been an eventful day indeed. Not the least of which had been the positive turn in her relationship with Oliver.

As he gathered the sleeping Victoria in his arms, she clutched a fist to her heart, hopeful that soon she would win his.

CHAPTER 17—THE LANGUAGE OF MUSIC

T he screech of bow against strings sounded worse than when Camilla's cat had managed to get its tail under the runner of a rocker. Victoria held her hands over her ears. Yet, Camilla forced the smile on her face as Pockets met her gaze, begging for approval.

"How was that, Mama?"

"Much better, Pockets. Dr. Somersby will be proud of your progress when he comes today for your lesson."

Oliver had worked tirelessly with him, insisting the boy had talent. Camilla had yet to experience it. Perhaps patience truly wasn't her strong suit. She'd only hoped Oliver wasn't bamming her about Pockets' potential. The idea of offering false praise did not sit well with her honest nature.

Although the lessons had become somewhat of a torture on her ears, Oliver's demonstrations on his own instrument provided a respite—his gift and love of music evident with each stroke of the bow and press of fingers against strings. It was as if the instrument took on a life of its own under his skilled touch.

Which led to more heated thoughts about that skilled touch.

She smoothed her skirts, careful not to fidget as she anxiously awaited Oliver's arrival. Since Pockets'—and her—eventful birthday, they'd agreed to move the children's lessons to later in the afternoon, which would allow Oliver to spend time with Pockets when he came to collect Victoria. With each visit, the bond between the boy and the man grew, and with each visit, she fell more desperately in love.

At times he would linger as they said their goodbyes, his eyes meeting hers, then drifting to her lips.

She could no longer restrain the smile as Stratton announced his arrival. "Dr. Somersby, madam."

The children raced to greet him, hugging him about the waist.

Oliver sent her a bright smile, rewarding her with the dimple she loved so dearly. "How did the lessons go today? Tori mentioned she looked forward to reading a book from your library." He squeezed his eyes shut. "What was it? Ah, yes, Price and Prejudice."

Camilla laughed, knowing full well he teased her. "*Pride and Prejudice*, Dr. Somersby. Mr. Darcy has pride, often acting as if he's superior to others, and Miss Elizabeth Bennet makes too quick a judgment and forms a prejudice against him."

He winked at her. "Such characters sound most unbelievable. Where does this Miss Austen come up with such fanciful ideas?"

"Ah, so you *do* know the book?"

"Merely because Tori mentioned it. Although now that I think about it, I do know a certain party who may have made a harsh judgment too quickly and another who may be a wee bit prideful."

"But the question, Dr. Somersby, is who is which?"

He laughed, the sound so pleasant to her ears and a reminder of the true reason for his visit.

"Have you been practicing?" Oliver asked the boy, still clinging to his coat sleeve.

The boy's blond head bobbed excitedly.

"Very well. Allow me a moment to tune my instrument, and we'll begin our lesson."

Oliver moved over to Camilla and set down his violin case. She breathed in his enticing woody scent as he leaned close and whispered, "Hold out your hand."

Unsure what he intended, a shiver of excitement traveled from her toes to her neck. When she offered her hand, he turned it palm side up and placed two fairly soft, but also prickly, objects on it, then closed her fingers around his gift. "Fluffs of cotton, for your ears. It will help muffle the sound. I'm wearing some myself."

Her gaze darted to the side of his head, and to her surprise, tiny fibers stuck out from his ears, his longish hair covering most of it.

"Don't push it in too far, though," he said.

As he tuned his violin and assisted Pockets tuning his own, Camilla twisted in her seat away from view and gently placed the fluffs in her ears. It scratched a bit from the fibers, but as he'd promised, it most assuredly muffled the sound. God bless him.

Now, when Pockets' bow screeched across the strings, she smiled and nodded in approval, catching Oliver's playful wink.

She marveled at the patience Oliver had with the boy, encouraging and, when necessary, correcting his grasp of the bow and the bend of his wrist, but always with gentleness and a smile. It made every ear piercing caterwaul worth it.

The lesson ended, and as usual, her reaction was bittersweet—grateful for the reprieve to her ears, but disappointed Oliver would soon leave.

He met her gaze and seemed to read the thoughts in her mind. "Practice is hard work, Pockets, but if you're diligent, you'll soon be playing like this."

With that, he lifted the violin and settled it under his chin. She held her breath, waiting for the magic he would produce.

His eyes lifted to hers. "Would you accompany me in voice? The beautiful aria you sang at the masquerade ball, perhaps?"

She spun around, and pulled the cotton from her ears, then faced him. The notes from his violin so sweet, so pure, she almost missed her cue. They blended as if they had performed together for years. When they finished, the children sat wide-eyed, then bounded to their feet, hands clapping furiously.

"Mama, you sing good."

She smiled and bent down, arms wide, beckoning the boy into them. "I shall sing to you each night if you like. I've forgotten how wonderful it feels." Her eyes raised to meet Oliver's, and she mouthed *thank you.*

Although sung with the same passion and pain, the words of the aria no longer elicited the intense despair she'd experienced with Hugh's death. Now, something bright, something promising, dawned on the horizon. Perhaps, even though Hugh would not return, a new love—a different love, would give her relief from her sorrow.

"Play something happy, Ollie," Tori said.

Once again, Oliver lifted the violin, and closing his eyes, the sounds that spilled from him stole Camilla's breath away. A note of familiarity teased her brain, but she would have sworn she'd never heard anything like it. Joyful with a hint of melancholy in the strands of minor key notes, it touched her deep in her soul.

Tori began spinning around the room, her dress whirling around her feet, and Pockets soon joined her, doing more jumping than dancing. Oliver's fingers flew over the neck of the violin. The bow moved furiously, sending the horsehair flying as pieces broke free from their connection.

It was glorious—life affirming, leaving her with no words to convey her amazement. Even her applause when he finished seemed inadequate. Yet he bowed and smiled graciously at her insufficient praise.

"Where ever did you learn to play like that?" she asked.

He shrugged, his already swarthy complexion darkening. "It's in my blood."

As he turned toward Pockets, she sensed his enigmatic answer would be the only explanation she would receive. But she vowed to pursue it at a later time.

After instruction to Pockets about what to practice, Oliver placed his violin back into the case. "I wondered, Lady Denby. Since we both appreciate the opera, would you accompany me for next Wednesday evening's performance of *The Magic Flute*? If a chaperone is required, I'll secure three seats."

Stunned, she simply stared at him, struggling to form an answer.

Lifting a hand to the back of his head, he sighed, his eyes

leaving hers. "I see I've offended you. I apologize." He snapped the violin's case shut and turned toward the door.

Hurry, you fool. Don't let him leave. "Dr. Somersby, please wait."

He turned, the frown still furrowing his brow.

"You haven't offended me, simply surprised me—pleasantly, I might add. I'd love to accompany you. And since we'll be in a public place, a chaperone seems unnecessary."

The creases between his eyes eased, and his lips curved upward. "The seats are not the best."

About to offer her own box, she held her tongue, knowing full well he'd be offended. "I'm sure they'll be perfect. The sound is the same regardless of the seating, is it not?"

He chuckled. "Not exactly, but I appreciate your understanding." He paused as if considering something. "I have a request."

Nervous tingles jittered up her arms. "What is it?"

"Would you wear the red dress you had on the night of the ball?"

❧

THE EVENING OF THE OPERA, OLIVER FIDGETED BEFORE THE MIRROR as his mother worked her magic with his cravat. He'd dressed in his best coat and trousers as well as the sapphire waistcoat with the silver threading he'd borrowed from Harry. With the extra money he'd earned for providing care to Lord Harcourt, he'd even managed to buy a new pair of boots, polished to a brilliant shine.

"Oliver, stand still or I'll never get this fold perfect. Why are you so nervous?"

"I'm not nervous," he lied. Truth be told, he was as jittery as a schoolboy preparing to steal his first kiss. Might an opportunity present itself this evening to do just that? He pulled in a deep breath, imagining the sweetness of Camilla's lips. No, even if circumstances did prove conducive, he vowed to proceed with caution. Lady Denby was no serving wench. She would not expect such familiarity so early in their courtship.

Wait. Courtship? Yes, if he were honest with himself, the evening would be his first attempt to openly woo said lady. He must be mindful not to botch it.

As their first time together without the guise of lessons for children or visits to ailing fathers, his invitation had taken all his courage to overcome the arguments he'd waged against such an attachment.

You're of different classes.

She stated she doesn't care.

You have nothing to offer her.

She'd been overwhelmed by my birthday gift.

If she discovers your heritage . . .

How long could he keep that secret from her? And what would happen if their feelings developed beyond mere physical attraction to something deeper? Would the knowledge of who he was destroy what they had? He pushed that argument aside, knowing nothing could counter it.

In actuality, for him at least, he'd already fallen hopelessly in love with her. The die had been cast the moment he heard her sing.

"Ollie!" Tori rushed in, hugging him around the waist.

"Victoria, you'll wrinkle Oliver's clothing," his mother admonished none too emphatically as she grinned at her granddaughter.

"I'm sorry." Tori pouted, and as she always did, completely erased any thread of annoyance he might have had with her behavior. "I only wanted to see you and wish you luck."

"It's the opera. Luck against what? Horrible singing?"

She swatted his arm. "No, silly. With Lady Denby. She's very pretty."

His mother raised a dark eyebrow and held up her hands as if to say *I had nothing to do with this.*

"Can't two people who enjoy music share an evening at the opera without there being a romantic motive?"

Tori's grin grew so wide, she displayed every one of her teeth. "I didn't say anything about it being romantic. I simply said Lady Denby was pretty."

Eager to escape Tori's questioning, he capitulated. "And as usual, you see through my failed attempt at nonchalance. But if I don't leave soon, I shall be late in collecting the said pretty lady." He kissed them both goodbye and strolled to the hackney stand.

Seated in the carriage, he closed his eyes, attempting to slow his racing heart. The anticipation of seeing her without children present, of being able to exchange conversation not related to lessons or medical care heightened his senses. The even beat of the horses' hooves against the cobbles, the low thrum of activity and conversation drifting in from the street, the faint lingering smell of soap he'd used to shave, the leather of the carriage seat, all bombarded him as if he'd never experienced them before.

When the carriage jerked to a halt, he descended and, taking a deep breath, gave two sharp raps against the door. If only his hands would stop shaking. Stratton, Camilla's butler, answered with his usual air of indifference. Not as old as Burrows, Harry's butler, or especially Holmes, Lord Harcourt's man, Stratton's relative youth didn't preclude him from maintaining the austere composure that most certainly was a prerequisite for the position. Burrows proved to be the one exception, and Oliver attributed much of that to Harry's own ability to put others at ease.

"Good evening, Dr. Somersby." Stratton's mouth barely moved, his lips in a perpetual straight line. He moved aside and motioned Oliver inside the foyer. "Lady Denby requested you wait here."

Unease twisted Oliver's stomach. He'd never been denied entrance farther into her home before. Had she changed her mind about accompanying him and believed it easier for him to leave if he were closer to the door?

Stratton whispered something to a maid who scurried upstairs, presumably to retrieve Camilla, then left Oliver alone. As he waited, his mind played the cruel trick of imagining what it would be like to live here with her. He pictured her rushing from another room to greet him as he arrived home from the clinic, throwing herself into his embrace and whispering in his ear how much she'd missed him. Then he would gather her in his arms and whisk her upstairs to their bedroom to—

"Dr. Somersby." The musical voice interrupted his thoughts at what most likely was either the best possible time or the worst.

When he lifted his gaze, he understood why she'd requested he wait in the foyer. A vision in red, she floated down the stairs, her brown hair fashioned intricately with delicate tendrils of curls brushing her neck. A smile pulled at his lips as he remembered Tori relaying her first lesson of walking with books on her head. Surely Camilla had excelled at that task when she was but a girl. The lady certainly knew how to make an entrance.

He bowed in greeting. "Lady Denby."

When she reached the bottom of the stairway, she placed her gloved hand in his, the bracelet Pockets had made with Oliver's gift of the scrimshaw pendant adorning her wrist. "Would you mind if we took my carriage?"

The fact she'd considered his feelings, pleased him as much as the fact she wore the simple piece of jewelry. "As you wish." He brought her fingers to his lips. "I only desire your comfort this evening."

The coachman assisted her into the carriage, and Oliver settled in the seat opposite her. With the milder weather, no warm bricks were necessary for their feet, but the soft upholstery and lining of the interior compared to the hired hackney emphasized the difference between them. Yet Oliver refused to allow the thought to ruin the evening.

Her enticing lilac fragrance made his head swim as she spoke excitedly about the upcoming performance, expressing her eagerness to hear the renowned tenor scheduled to appear. It struck him how natural it seemed, as if they had done this a million times before, and yet the excitement between them was palpable. At that moment, he knew he'd never tire of being in her presence.

It might have been the luxurious nature of the carriage or perhaps the desire to remain alone with Camilla for a longer period, but the journey to Covent Garden ended sooner than Oliver wished.

Stately Grecian pillars greeted them as they climbed the few steps to the entrance. Oliver's gaze shifted to the frescos and sculpted art adorning the front of the building, admiring their classic beauty.

As they entered the opera house, throngs of people milled about, the low hum of amiable conversation filling the open area outside the auditorium. She placed her hand on top of his offered forearm as naturally as if it had been designed to rest there.

Lush curtains draped the windows and covered the entranceways to the auditorium. Thousands of candles lit the enormous room, their light flickering in excitement as if mirroring the anticipation of the crowd itself. The opulence of the surroundings never failed to amaze him, although Camilla appeared unaffected. Based on her own home, as well as Lord Harcourt's and Harry's that Oliver had visited, it would be logical that such lavishness would be commonplace to her.

So it surprised him when she said, "I always feel like royalty when I come here." She sent him a bright smile. "I should have worn my tiara." Her following laughter conveyed the teasing nature of her statement.

"It's just as well since I forgot to wear my sash adorned with medals."

She squeezed his forearm, sending a wave of pleasure through him. "Tonight, my prince, we shall remain incognito."

He'd almost forgotten he'd already donned his metaphorical mask.

Anxious to take their seats and be away from the pressing crowd, Oliver stared longingly toward the entrance of the theater. Camilla squeezed his arm, pulling him forward. "Oh, there's Lord and Lady Easton and Lord Montgomery. Let's go and speak with them."

Harry had spoken of Lord Montgomery with fondness, so he braced himself for what he hoped wouldn't be an awkward introduction.

"Lady Denby," the younger gentleman said as they approached. His eyes drifted to Oliver, and his lips quirked in a knowing smile.

"Lord Montgomery, it's a pleasure to see you. May I present Dr. Oliver Somersby. Dr. Somersby, Lord Montgomery and his parents Lord and Lady Easton."

"Ah, yes," the older gentleman, Lord Easton said. "He's the physician working with Ashton at the clinic," he added, directing the explanation toward his wife.

Lady Easton glared at her husband. "I know who he is, Nigel. I'm not as feeble-minded as your mother yet."

Oliver stifled a laugh.

"It's a pleasure, madam. Sir. Lord Montgomery, His Grace speaks highly of you. I understand you were instrumental in the rescue of Her Grace during her ordeal last year."

Lord Montgomery's cheeks darkened. Apparently, Oliver had struck a nerve.

"I played a minor part. Inconsequential, really." Montgomery shifted on his feet. "How is young Pockets, Lady Denby?"

"Growing so quickly I'm unable to keep him in breeches. He adores Ol . . . Dr. Somersby."

Montgomery's eyebrow lifted at Camilla's near faux pas. "If you would excuse me, Lord Nash has arrived, and I have a matter to discuss with him."

Oliver breathed a sigh of relief when Lord and Lady Easton departed as well. "I'll never understand titles. How is it Lord Montgomery isn't also Lord Easton?"

"Well, that would be confusing, wouldn't it?" Camilla answered. As if instructing Pockets and Tori, she explained. "Laurence, Lord Montgomery, is Lord Easton's heir. When his father dies, Laurence will inherit the earldom and the title Lord Easton. The family also holds the title Montgomery, so until he inherits, as the firstborn son, Laurence is Viscount Montgomery."

"I'm still confused."

She smiled as if placating a small child and patted his arm. "Follow my lead."

His eyes scanned the crowd, and precisely what he'd dreaded occurred. Panic seized him, and he willed his legs to move—to escape. Slowly edging his way toward them, Lord Trentwith approached.

CHAPTER 18—THE OPERA

Confusion eddied in Camilla's mind when their easy conversation halted abruptly. The happiness shining in Oliver's eyes vanished as he stared at something behind her. She spun around in search of what had changed his mood. Nothing seemed out of place.

When she turned back, Oliver had disappeared. Further perplexed, she scanned the crowd for his tall frame.

"Lady Denby?"

Like a whirling dervish, she spun again at the deep voice calling her name. "Lord Trentwith." Her hand flew to her chest. "Goodness, you startled me."

"My apologies. You appear to be searching for someone. Has your father accompanied you this evening? If so, perhaps I might prevail upon you both to join me in my box?"

With the hope Oliver would return shortly, she forced a polite smile, formulating a response to Trentwith she hoped would discourage him. "Thank you for your gracious offer. My father isn't here this evening. Dr. Somersby has accompanied me, but he seems to have completely disappeared."

"A foolish man to leave such a beautiful woman alone. Doctor, you say? Is he the chap assisting Ashton at his clinic?"

She brushed aside his flattery, focusing instead on the practical. "He is. Speaking of the clinic, I'd been planning on calling upon you regarding an additional contribution. Her Grace is still recovering and unable to make the calls."

"Yes. I heard. An heir for Ashton, welcome news. I hope mother and son are faring well?"

"Both are doing exceedingly well. Ashton rarely leaves their side."

He chuckled, the sound oddly familiar. "Yes, I've missed taking his blunt at White's. He's a fine fellow, but I believe impending fatherhood had him a bit befuddled at the card table."

"Well, perhaps you'll consider using your winnings as a donation. Now if you will excuse me, I must find Dr. Somersby before the performance begins."

"Of course. I'll look forward to your visit."

Camilla edged her way through the crowds, searching for Oliver's broad shoulders and thick mop of black hair. Locating him at last, she moved toward where he stood in a corner by one of the entrances to the auditorium, practically hidden by a curtain.

He stepped out into the crowd as she approached.

"Why on earth did you disappear?"

"Forgive me. I thought I saw a mouse."

Certain her eyebrows reached her scalp, she stared in disbelief. "A mouse? In this crowd?"

"Something was scurrying across the floor." His eyes glimmered with mischief, and his lips twitched as if holding back a smile. "As genteel ladies such as yourself are often frightened by the wee creatures, I thought it best to try to catch it and set it outside before a panic ensued."

She answered his fanciful tale with an unladylike snort. "And? Did you catch it?"

"No, it must have escaped through a hole in the floorboards."

She leaned in to whisper, catching his masculine scent. "I would understand if you simply admitted to requiring the necessary."

He grinned. "You've discovered my fault, my lady. Too much wine before this evening's performance, I'm afraid." He held out his arm. "Which I believe is about to start. Shall we find our seats?"

Once inside the auditorium, they settled in for the performance. The dimming lights and faint hush of the crowd evoked the sense of anticipation Camilla always loved. The evening's offering of Mozart's "Die Zauberflöte" had always been one of her favorites, her heart tugging at the trials the lovers had to endure for their happiness. Grateful for the low lighting, tears welled in her eyes. But reaching into her reticule to retrieve a handkerchief, she'd discovered she'd forgotten to replenish with a clean one.

Oliver's hand stretched over, low enough to be discreet, holding out his own fresh white cloth.

She cast him a furtive glance, worried he would tease her for her emotional state, but his eyes remained focused on the stage before them. As she plucked the cloth from his hand, he took her fingers in his and gave a gentle squeeze.

When the performance ended and the cacophony of applause had died down, she held out the borrowed handkerchief. "Thank you. What would I have done without you?"

His hand wrapped around hers, closing her fingers over the cloth. "Keep it. You may have need of it later."

About to ask if he intended to make her weep, the sultry look in his eyes froze the words on her lips, and she nodded and tucked it in her reticule.

He stood and stretched his long legs, scanning the upper boxes where most of the beau monde viewed the performance. "Let's wait for the crowds to thin. I'm not anxious for the evening to end and return you home."

The beauty of the evening's music brought her thoughts back to Oliver's own talent. "Oliver," she said, and his gaze drifted back to her. "I've been meaning to ask, you said music was in your blood, but who taught you to play?"

A brief flicker of annoyance flashed in his eyes, but softened. "My grandfather."

"Maternal or paternal?"

"Does it matter?" He snapped the words.

Tamping down her own frustration, she purposely softened her voice. "Why must you become so disagreeable when I ask about your family?"

His gaze darted away, and his shoulders dropped, reminding her of Pockets when he'd pilfered an extra biscuit after she'd told him he could only have one before supper. "I apologize."

As if it were the most natural thing in the world, she reached for his hand, saying softly, "Oliver, I only wish to know more about you —to understand you. I'd hoped this evening would be an opportunity for us to start anew. What we have is special."

A sigh, deep and heavy, accompanied him as he sat back down beside her. Her hand still in his, he turned it over as if examining it, then caressed her fingers, stroking them and sending waves of pleasure up her arm. "I'll not deny it. Yet some things are difficult to share."

"But if they're shared among friends, is it not either doubling the joy or halving the sorrow?"

The quirk of his lips eased the tension coiled in her stomach. When he stroked a thumb across her cheek, she leaned into his touch, her hand instinctively reaching up to cover his, pressing it more firmly against her face.

"And when did you become a philosopher?" he asked, his voice teasing.

"Well, the children and I *have* been discussing Plato and Aristotle."

He laughed and unfortunately removed his hand. "My mother's father taught me on the very violin Pockets now torments."

She answered him with her own laughter. "I thought you said he shows promise."

"Oh, he does. His desire to learn is evident, and he has an ear for music."

"Will you tell me about your grandfather? About learning to play? Is he still alive?"

The distant look in his eyes made a reappearance, and she regretted pressing him, but he recovered and smiled, the dimple faintly winking. "So many questions. To answer one, no, he's no longer alive."

He rose again and held out his hand. "The crowds have thinned, and mention of the children reminds me we should be returning home. Let's save the remaining questions for another day."

She slipped her hand in his, her stomach dropping in disappointment. They'd come so far only to have him shut her out once again. Her patience worn thin, she prayed for strength to hold on and give him the time he needed to trust her.

THE HEAT OF THE EVENING PRESSED IN ON THEM AS THEY ENTERED the confines of the carriage. Grateful for the gentle breeze drifting in from the open windows as the carriage began its journey, Oliver settled back against the cushions, taking a quiet moment to once again admire the woman before him. He pointed to the bracelet on her wrist. "An odd choice for such a formal evening."

The wistful expression on her face as she lovingly fingered the scrimshaw pendant and corded bracelet touched him more than he cared to admit. "No, not odd. It was the perfect choice. It's the one piece of jewelry most dear to my heart. This, and"—she touched the locket adorning her slender neck—"this from my father. I couldn't have asked for more thoughtful birthday gifts."

She tilted her head, providing an even more alluring view of that kissable neck. "When is your birthday? I hope it wasn't recently and I've missed it."

Subjects surrounding his birth had heretofore been areas to avoid. Yet, her innocent question held no hint of improper probing into his parentage. He decided to take it on face value.

"I'll be eight and twenty on October twenty-sixth. So no, you haven't missed it."

"If you could wish for anything in the world as a gift, what would it be?"

This question, not so innocent, could not be answered truthfully.

"For Pockets to stop screeching when he bows the violin." He grinned at her. "So there is still time."

He reached across again, touching his finger to the pendant. "You really do like it?"

"I adore it, but I'm afraid I won't be able to reciprocate with such a perfect gift for you. Your faith in Pockets' ability far exceeds mine. Is there nothing you wish that's more in my power to give?"

Uncertain if it was the dim lighting in the carriage or his own hopeful imagination, her gaze seemed heated, her eyes dusky.

He didn't want to push things too quickly, reminding himself she was an aristocratic lady, not some serving wench. However, he couldn't resist. "Perhaps by then we shall be on such terms as to allow me to steal a kiss?"

The seductive quirk of her lips drew his eyes. "I should pretend shock, but I'm well past debutante game playing. A kiss would most definitely be possible."

They settled into a companionable silence, the clip-clop of the horses' hooves against the cobbles and occasional shouts from people on the streets the only things breaking the hush. Yet, energy charged the air of the carriage compartment as they exchanged furtive but heated glances.

The evening had been almost perfect, and as Oliver sat across from Camilla in her carriage, the thought of spending other nights such as this taunted him like a feather on the breeze—so close he could almost wrap his fingers around it, but each time it wafted out of his grasp. Everything in him wanted to trust her, to tell her about his parentage. Yet how could he when he denied it himself? But perhaps . . .

"You asked about my grandfather."

Her eyes widened. "I did. And you suggested we wait until another day to discuss my queries."

"I appreciate the fact you didn't press." He pulled out his watch, making a show to check the time. "But it seems it is another day."

"You tease." She laughed, the sound bright, conveying she didn't mind in the least.

"My grandfather's skill not only lay in playing but in crafting the instruments as well. He made the violin Pockets uses as well as my own. The music he coaxed from the instrument was like nothing I've heard since. Unearthly, reaching in and touching you here." He placed a palm on his chest. "My paltry talent pales in comparison."

"Then he must have been truly great, for your own skills are exemplary."

"Ah, flattery doesn't become you, my lady. But I accept your praise with humility."

"Might I have heard of him? What was his name?"

"If you're asking if he played in any of the fine opera houses or exhibition halls you patronize, no." The temptation to bare his soul to her pressed on him. But caution prevailed, and he settled on threading bits of information to gauge her reaction. "His name was Milosh Heron."

"Milosh, that's an unusual name."

"No more unusual to him than Camilla is to you. He wasn't born in England." He waited for the expected question.

She remained blessedly silent.

Either relieved or surprised—he wasn't certain—he edged closer to the point of no return, delivering what might be the coup de grâce of their relationship. The bitter taste of anger rose with his words. "He died at the end of a noose."

CHAPTER 19—SEEKING ANSWERS

S peechless. A state Camilla had rarely found herself. Even the steady beat of the horses' hooves seemed to vanish, leaving an unearthly silence in the carriage compartment.

Oliver stared at her stone-faced, blue eyes cold as ice. If she'd thought he had been bamming her as he had about the intruding, opera-loving mouse, she would have been wrong. He was dead serious.

"But what? Why?" She choked on the words.

He returned her question with more silence.

She persisted. "What did he do?"

"Nothing." He spat the word, then waved a hand. "Oh, they accused him of theft, but it was only an excuse. They hanged him for no other reason than who he was."

"Who are *they*? I don't understand." She truly didn't.

Oliver turned away, staring out the carriage window into the darkness. "Does it matter? It's in the past and can't be undone."

He turned back toward her, the coldness in his eyes vanishing as quickly as it had risen. "Forgive me for ruining our evening with such maudlin conversation."

Obviously he desired she not pursue it, so she honored his

unspoken request. Yet why would he broach a subject so horrible in the first place? The man was like the changing weather, blowing hot and cold within the same day.

She searched for a safe topic of conversation. "When you disappeared before the performance, I spoke with Lord Trentwith. He's agreed to make a contribution to the clinic. Has there been any progress securing another physician? Perhaps extra funds might help."

He bristled at the mention of Lord Trentwith, and a slight shiver of satisfaction sent gooseflesh up her arms. However, she'd never been one to play games.

"I assure you, his interest is strictly regarding the clinic. I made it clear you had accompanied me."

His lips twitched. "You think I'm jealous?"

"Aren't you?"

She shifted, uncomfortable under the intensity of his heated gaze.

"No."

Unsure if she should be insulted or relieved, she smiled sweetly. "You're very sure of yourself."

"Sure of your feelings for me. Yes."

Oh. Her cheeks heated from his bold statement. She snorted, brushing it off with a laugh. "Arrogant, I would say."

The carriage slowed, jerking to a halt in front of his residence.

"No. Confident." He slid off his seat and onto the seat beside her. "Now I must say goodnight." He lifted and kissed her gloved hand.

When he moved to rise and leave, she tugged his sleeve, keeping him in place. "One moment."

A dark eyebrow arched, his gaze intrigued. "Yes?"

"I thought, rather than wait until your birthday, perhaps a sampling of your gift might be in order. As a thank you for the lovely evening."

As if her pulse wasn't already racing from the mere grin spreading across his face, the full display of that glorious dimple sent her on the verge of the vapors.

"Why, my lady. How bold." With that, his head dipped, and he paused a mere hair's breadth away, the puff of his breath tickling her lips.

She held her own breath, as her eyelids lowered in anticipation.

All of her dreaming and imagining of this moment paled in comparison as his mouth found hers. A light brush at first, teasing, tasting, and with her response, he deepened the kiss, verging on devouring her. He pulled away too soon, his eyes showing the desire surely reflected in her own.

"Now I truly must go, or it may no longer be but a sample."

She stared out the carriage window at his retreating form, admiring his broad shoulders, trim waist, and long legs, until he disappeared inside. Lifting a hand to her tingling lips, the taste of his still lingering, she emitted a contented sigh. Yes, the kiss had been everything she'd hoped for—and more.

◈◈◈

No additional opportunities arose for stolen kisses during the next several weeks—much to Camilla's dismay. However, they did exchange numerous heated glances, touches of hands, and brushes of thighs when seated next to each other on a settee.

Try as she might to encourage him, Oliver refused to accompany her to the remaining house parties or balls of the Season, instead preferring to share their love of music in private or quiet walks in the park. When she pressed him for the reason he avoided societal gatherings, he'd shake his head, mumbling something about not fitting in.

"But you're perfectly at ease with Harry and Margaret, and as a duke, only a prince or king holds higher rank," she argued.

With a lifted brow, he countered her argument. "Ah, but you must admit that His Grace's unconventionality is hardly indicative of typical society."

"My father? Me? The Weatherbys. Shall I go on?"

At that he grumbled and became surly.

The mystery of Oliver plagued Camilla as she tried to

determine which of his personas portrayed the real man. Further attempts to divine the truth proved fruitless. She preferred the smiling, easy-going man who played with his sister and Pockets almost as much as the man who spoke of a utopia with no class restrictions. Most of all, she loved the man who peered deep into her soul—and didn't flinch.

She drifted back to when they first met and he had made that mysterious trip to the outskirts of London. Instinct told her the encampment held the key to his secrets. With her decision made, she set off for answers. Although her coachman still balked at the order to drive there, the prospect of going during daylight hours seemed to appease him.

Traveling to where she'd first followed Oliver the night back in December, no trace of the camp remained, but she would not be deterred. Several inquiries later, she discovered the group had traveled a short distance to the north, away from the city. With a grumble, Langley climbed back to his post and urged the horses forward.

When they came to a halt, she descended from the carriage and, after an admonition from Langley, strode toward the camp. The atmosphere did indeed appear different in the daylight.

No longer shrouded in the mystery of night, people were bustling about in a seemingly endless wave of activity. Children squealed with excitement as they ran from another boy who wore a blindfold. Women scrubbed laundry at the bordering riverbank, and freshly washed vibrant-colored skirts hung on lines next to the muted color of men's trousers. The same bright colors decorated several wagons. Bender tents filled some of the gaps. Several men chopped wood, and another worked on repairing the wheel of one of the wagons. One word came to mind—life. The camp teemed with it.

The distinct smell from the early morning rain lingered in the air. Her half-boots sunk into the mud, and she lifted the skirts of her pelisse and gown. One of the men chopping wood looked up from his labor, his gaze curious but not threatening. "Are you lost, my lady?"

The entire camp, moments ago full of activity, seemed to grind to a halt.

"Hello," she said. "I'm sorry to intrude. I wondered if you are acquainted with a man named Dr. Oliver Somersby?"

The man's almost black eyes narrowed, and Camilla swallowed under his searching gaze.

"Why do you want to know?"

"I'm a friend," she said, hoping it would convince him she meant no harm. "I understand he comes here, and I wondered if I could speak to whomever he visits."

He cast his gaze to the ground and retreated a step. "We don't want trouble," he said, his voice rising in pitch.

"I assure you, I don't either. I simply would like some information."

Leaning on the handle of the axe, he sighed, as if considering her request. "You'll be wanting to speak with old Eva. That wagon there." He pointed to a brightly painted wagon in the middle of the camp. "She may not talk to you, just so you know."

"I'd like to try. Thank you."

All eyes turned toward her as she made her way up the steps of Eva's wagon.

She knocked, softly at first then, when no one answered, more vigorously.

"I heard you the first time." The woman's voice sounded ancient, and a cough erupted immediately after. A moment later, the door cracked open.

No taller than a child, a cataract haze from age covered the woman's cornflower blue eyes, but her face shone with intelligence as she peered at Camilla. Wisps of wiry, gray hair poked from a kerchief tied around her head. "Well, what do you want? I don't do readings anymore."

"Are you Eva?" She caught herself before adding old as the man had done.

"Yes. Who are you, and what do you want? I'm too close to death to waste time repeating myself."

Camilla jerked back at the woman's words. "Are you ill?" Perhaps that's why Oliver came here.

"Not unless old age is an illness. Do I need to repeat my question again, or are you going to continue questioning me without the courtesy of providing your name?"

"I apologize. My name is Camilla Denby. I'm a friend of Oliver Somersby's."

At that Eva threw open the door, her eyes widening in turn. "Is something wrong? Is he hurt?"

"Oh, no, nothing like that. I . . . I wanted to get to know the people he visits."

Eva's head tilted quizzically. "A friend, you said?" Those inspecting eyes narrowed and raked over Camilla from head to toe. How she could see out of them mystified Camilla. "Perhaps more than a friend, and now you think he's not good enough for you. Is that it? I know your kind, and I'd hoped my grandson would have enough sense to avoid repeating his mother's mistakes." A hint of sadness laced the woman's accusatory tone.

Camilla struggled to comprehend the old woman's words. She opened and closed her mouth, trying to form a response. "Dr. Somersby is your grandson?" Vague words of conversation months ago seeped into her mind—commoner, outcast. When she'd discovered Oliver, not Trentwith, was the man with whom she'd had that conversation at the masked ball, she presumed he meant he wasn't of the peerage—but this? She grasped the side of the wagon for support, but it did little to calm her racing heart.

"This conversation may best be had inside." Eva stepped aside and beckoned Camilla into her wagon.

Still reeling from the discovery of Oliver's heritage, she stepped inside, unsure what she expected. The tiny home on wheels was tidy and clean. A small wooden table and two ladder-back chairs rested in the middle, and a beautiful patchwork quilt in the colors of the rainbow covered a single tiny bed built into an outer wall at the back. A steaming teapot rested on the center of the table, and a cup filled with tea sat in the place before one of the chairs.

Eva gestured for Camilla to sit in one of the sturdy, uncushioned chairs. "You Gadje have incredible timing. Would you care for some tea?"

Perhaps it would help calm her racing thoughts. "That would be most kind if you can spare it."

Eva snorted a laugh, and Camilla regretted what the woman probably viewed as an insult.

"Although we don't have the luxuries you English have, we travelers always have enough to spare for our visitors." She moved with slow, steady steps to a shelf above a workspace and retrieved another cup.

The grace with which her wrinkled, gnarled hands poured the tea could be used as a demonstration to Victoria. *Her granddaughter.*

"I have honey if you like." She held up a container with such a small amount of the sticky sweetener, Camilla knew offering it was nothing short of a sacrifice.

"No, thank you." She smiled, hoping to reinforce her appreciation.

Eva took her seat, lifted her cup and sipped, her cloudy blue eyes never leaving Camilla's face. "So"—she drew the word out—"you're a friend of Oliver's, but you didn't know I'm his grandmother. Why don't you tell me the real reason you're here?"

Camilla forced herself not to squirm under the woman's perceptive stare. She lifted her chin and squared her shoulders. "I'll admit we're not as close as I'd like, and I simply wished to get to know him better. I know he comes here on occasion, perhaps to treat the sick."

"He does what he can when he visits. Some of our people are too stubborn and set in the old ways to accept his help. Others are more wise." She smiled, the lines cracking across her weathered face.

The familiar likeness brought a smile to Camilla's own lips. "Is Sabina your daughter?"

"Yes, she was."

Camilla blinked at the response. "Was? She's still alive. I've met her. She's a lovely woman."

Eva's hand slapped against the table. "She disgraced our people. She's dead to me."

The sadness that accompanied the old woman's last statement nearly broke Camilla's heart. How could a mother turn her back on her own child?

"Why? What did she do that was so horrible that you would disown her?"

"That's not my shame to tell. You should ask her . . . or Oliver."

"But you allow Oliver to visit. You accept him."

"Only because my people remember the child. They don't recognize the man he's become. Like you, they think he comes to offer help with sickness."

A heavy coughing fit followed, forcing tears to Eva's eyes, and Camilla had the urge to thump the old woman's back.

Once she stilled, Eva said, "As you can see, it's easy enough for them to believe he comes to treat me. A good ruse, wouldn't you say?"

"You said you weren't ill, but that cough . . ."

"From enjoying my pipe too much," Eva said. "I promised Oliver I would quit, but at my age, there aren't many pleasures left."

To prove her point, she rose and retrieved an intricately carved pipe and leather pouch from a cabinet. After pressing an unusual looking tobacco into the bowl, she used a slender wooden stick and captured the flame from a candle, lighting the pipe.

Eva took a long draw, her eyes closing, savoring the contents. Long moments passed, and Camilla wondered if the old woman had forgotten she was there. She opened her eyes, and although they were clouded, she appeared to study Camilla. "You said you want to get to know the people Oliver visits, but I think you came here for information. Am I right?"

Although the early rain had cooled the air, Camilla's face heated. The idea of lying to the old woman seemed ill-advised.

A sweet, almost sickly smell filled the tiny space, and Camilla's head began to spin, and her tongue loosened.

"I suppose that's true. He's like the winds, changing at a

moment's notice. I'd hoped to understand why, and if there's anything I can do to help him."

One wiry eyebrow lifted on Eva's face, but she remained silent.

Camilla shifted under the woman's watchful gaze. Struggling to salvage both the visit and the conversation, she plucked up her courage and asked the question plaguing her. "Why does Oliver hate the aristocracy?"

"Is that what he told you?" Her question seemed more curious than doubtful.

"Not in so many words, but he's implied it. What happened?"

Eva took another long draw on her pipe as if contemplating her response. "Oliver carries a heavy weight on his shoulders, as much of his own doing as what's been done to him, to us. His vision has narrowed because of it."

Such a cryptic answer. Camilla resisted the urge to huff in frustration and pulled in a calming breath. The heady smoke only added to her confusion.

As if taking pity on Camilla, Eva added, "Oliver doesn't give his trust easily. Once it's given, it's hard to break. But if broken, it's broken irrevocably."

Again, cryptic—although Camilla could see truth in the old woman's words.

"He told me about his grandfather. Was Milosh your husband?"

Eva's mouth gaped, the lines in her brow deepening. Thankfully, the grasp on her pipe remained secure, otherwise it surely would have dropped to the table before them. "He was. What did Oliver tell you about Milosh?"

"He said his grandfather crafted his violin and taught him to play."

Smoke circled around Eva's head like a halo. The old woman closed her eyes, as if recalling a cherished memory. "He had the gift, as Oliver does. The music he coaxed out of that instrument reached deep inside, touching you here." She pointed to her chest.

"Yes, I've heard Oliver play. It's remarkable."

Reluctant to cause the woman pain, Camilla proceeded in her

questioning with caution. "Oliver told me how he died. I'm so sorry."

An eyebrow quirked, and Camilla squirmed under the woman's scrutiny. "Yes, more than friends it would seem. What exactly did Oliver tell you?"

"That he died at the end of a noose."

"Murdered, you mean. By people like you."

Camilla's head spun, whether from the odd smelling smoke, or Eva's words, she wasn't sure. "I'm sorry? What do you mean?"

"So, Oliver left that out, did he?" Eva grunted. "I'm not surprised. He wouldn't want to upset your delicate sensibilities."

"Will you tell me? I want to understand. Is that why he hates the aristocracy?"

Eva studied her, taking long draws on her pipe. "In part. Oliver was only a boy when it happened, and children are impressionable, no? Milosh, Sabina, and I went to entertain at a party given by the Marquess of Edgerton."

Camilla drew a sharp intake of breath. *Lord Nash's family.*

"You know them?"

"Yes."

"Hmm. Milosh played his violin, Sabina danced, and I gave readings. I was giving a reading in another room when it started—shouting, cursing. I ran from the room, discovering several men holding Milosh by his arms. A boy had accused Milosh of stealing a silver goblet. We are not thieves. Milosh pleaded his innocence, but your people are quick to judge and slow to listen. They tied Milosh's hands and took us back to the camp to do their worst. To set an example, they said."

Pain crossed the old woman's face, the horror of the moment clear. "They made us gather around as they threw a rope up a sturdy branch of a tree. Milosh sat on a horse, proud, brave, his hands still tied behind him. As they placed the noose around his neck, he looked at me and said, 'Don't cry, Eva. You know in your heart what is true.'"

"Was Oliver there?"

Eva nodded. "Sabina had gathered Milosh's violin before they forced us from the house party and brought us back to camp. Milosh told him to never stop playing. That the violin was his legacy, and he gave his instrument to Oliver's care."

"Didn't anyone insist on searching him, for proof, evidence?"

Eva snorted. "What for? They believed the word of the boy, one of their own over ours. That was proof enough for them."

"His name? The boy?"

"Roland."

Nash's older brother. "No wonder Oliver doesn't trust us."

"It would seem you are the exception, at least in part."

"You said Milosh's murder was only part of the reason Oliver dislikes the aristocracy. What is the other part?"

"Ah, now that is something you must ask Oliver, for again, that's not my story to tell."

Sounds from people outside drifted in the silent enclosure as Eva studied her. A pleasant sense of euphoria overtook Camilla, as if she had finished soaking in a luxurious bath of warm water.

"Give me your hand," Eva said, breaking the silence and making Camilla jump.

"I . . . I'm sorry."

Eva held her hand out, palm side up, and wiggled her bent fingers. "Your hand, let me see it."

The smoothness of Camilla's skin against Eva's callused palm reminded her of Oliver's work-worn hand. And although it shouldn't, she felt a sort of shame for her pampered skin.

"Hmm," Eva muttered as fingers pressed against Camilla's palm. "Long life line. Oh, this is interesting." Her gnarled finger pressed deeper into Camilla's skin. "My eyes are no good any longer. Does the line here break and then start again?"

Camilla stared down at where Eva had pressed, confusion clouding her already swimming mind. "Yes."

"The first line is deep but short. You had a love but lost it?"

"Y-yes. My husband was killed at Waterloo." Camilla shook her head, trying to clear it. "I thought you said you didn't do readings any more."

Another coughing fit followed a snorted laugh. Once the coughing had calmed, Eva said, "I don't."

"But—"

"Quiet, girl." She took another draw on her pipe, which Camilla began to think wasn't a good idea. "Now, where was I? Oh, yes. Then, after the break, there is another line, just as deep, but longer. Very long. Another love, perhaps?"

"I . . . I . . . no."

The haze-covered eyes searched hers. "You will. A great love, but fraught with obstacles. Maybe you do and won't admit it?" Her lips tipped in a knowing smile, as if even with her clouded vision she could see into Camilla's heart.

Camilla wrenched her hand away. "I don't believe in that nonsense."

Eva shrugged. "You don't have to believe for it to be true."

The weight of Eva's words settled on Camilla, and an unease coiled within her. She cast a quick glance at her hand, now resting on her lap and hidden under the table, half expecting to see Oliver's face sketched in the lines of her palm.

She sensed the old woman studying her, so she met her gaze directly. "Is there anything else you can tell me about Oliver that will help me understand him?"

The laugh sounded more like a snort and preceded another coughing fit. Camilla began to be seriously concerned about the old woman.

Eva waved a hand, indicating she had recovered. "Oliver once told me that when he met the woman he wanted to marry, he would play a special song for her on his violin—something he composed himself."

"We do share a love for music. I sing."

"Oliver once told me he'd heard a woman who sang with such emotion it was as if she could peer into his soul."

"Did he mention her name?" Camilla prayed her breathy question didn't betray the hopefulness in her heart.

Eva shook her head, her attention locked on Camilla. "He said it was best forgotten as nothing would come of it."

Impossible as it was, Camilla could have sworn a twinkle appeared in the old woman's clouded eyes. Eva pointed a gnarled, boney finger at her. "What do *you* think of him?"

As if put under the old woman's spell, Camilla's tongue loosened. "Frustrating, but charming when he wants to be. Aloof at times, and yet, playful and open with children. Intelligent, but stubborn and close-minded. Wild and unpredictable as an unbroken stallion."

She paused, gauging the old woman's reaction, puzzled at Eva's passive expression. "Handsome with a simmering passion under a controlled exterior. A dichotomy that I've yet to understand."

Eva nodded. "And so you came to me hoping to explain him to you."

"Yes."

After another long draw of her pipe—mercifully not followed by another coughing episode—Eva said, "People are not only one thing. They are many things. What they present often depends on the situation and the people they meet. The fact that you've witnessed these many faces of Oliver tells me he wants you to see him as he truly is, his true nature, his *whole* self, so to speak. He may not admit it, but inside him, he wishes it. The question is, my lady, if after seeing him, knowing him, you can accept his whole self."

Eva patted Camilla's hand. "Give that some thought," she said, as if understanding that the question required some contemplation, and some serious soul searching.

By the time Camilla left Eva, her head was swimming, and she suspected more than their exchange was responsible for the morass in her mind. As she descended the stairs of the wagon, she stumbled, and one of the men standing nearby grabbed her arm.

She should have been outraged, should have pushed the man away in indignation.

Instead, she giggled.

Uncontrollably.

Like a ninny.

The man's dark eyes widened.

She giggled again.

After managing to extricate herself from the man's grasp, she wove her way to her waiting carriage. Wove seemed to be apropos as her feet appeared unable to tread a straight line.

A strange urge to raise and flap her arms accompanied the odd floating sensation.

She giggled again.

Langley stared, his mouth hanging open so far she swore she could see his back teeth.

Raising her arm in what was supposed to be a graceful gesture, she said, "Home, Langley," and accidentally slapped the poor man in the face.

A fleeting moment of horror flashed in her mind before being replaced by more giggling.

"My lady, what has happened?" Langley asked, having recovered from her assault.

"Nothing." She waved her arm again, and Langley reared back, barely avoiding another strike.

He held out his hand to assist her in boarding the carriage, his arm outstretched as far from his body as physically possible.

Once settled into the carriage compartment, she ran her fingers along the velvet cushions, marveling at how soft they were. Why hadn't she noticed that before?

The rhythmic sound of the horses' hooves and gentle rocking of the carriage soon had her nodding off, even though it was only midday.

"My lady?" A concerned voice roused her from her slumber, and she snapped her head up, finding Langley's amused gaze.

"Home already?" She straightened her gown and placed her hand in Langley's as she made her way down the carriage step. Luckily, the surroundings no longer swayed.

CHAPTER 20—DISCOVERIES

Oliver had not only dug the hole he was in, he'd fetched the shovel, climbed in, and covered himself, leaving no escape. His mood shifted as quickly as the weather, each interaction with Camilla leaving him both ecstatic and miserable.

The irony of his situation lodged bitterly in his craw. A maddening need to seek a solution tortured his every waking moment.

He wanted her, utterly, desperately, desiring her more than the life-giving air he breathed. All his pondering, searching for an answer led to one undeniable conclusion. His course of action had been determined from the moment of his birth.

He must tell her the truth.

She'd either failed to recognize or ignored the careful clues he'd provided—the strategically placed word choices, the mention of his mother's *people*, his grandfather's death. On a whim, he'd even played his mother's favorite Romani song for her on his violin.

Yet, she never asked the questions held in her eyes. Perhaps she did know and, like him, feared that giving voice to her suspicions would shatter the fragile world they had built. The cocoon of the unspoken kept them safe within their own sphere, free from judgment, free from prejudice, free from hate.

Wistfully examining the ring prophetically found in Pockets' celebratory cake, he sighed. Marriage. He'd only desired it once before when he'd been young and naïve, trusting what he foolishly believed was love only to discover she had used him. No longer that immature, inexperienced lad, he knew his feelings to be true this time. But would Camilla discard him as quickly as *she* had once she discovered the truth?

Love is worth risking everything. Harry's words bounced in his head, ramming into his skull until he could no longer ignore them.

Finished with his work at the clinic for the day, he boarded a hackney carriage, his destination Camilla's townhouse, ready to face his day of reckoning.

His nerves were so frayed, even his own knock on her door set his teeth on edge. Every sensation became magnified. A refreshing breeze blew, yet his hands remained clammy. The scent of the last late-blooming lilac bush wafted against his nostrils, like the promise of Camilla's soft skin. His mouth grew so dry, his tongue clung to its roof. How he would manage the words he planned to say, he had no idea.

The door opened, and Camilla's butler, Stratton, greeted him with a somber stare. "Dr. Somersby, Lady Denby is not at home."

His heart dropped to the soles of his boots. "Is she expected to return soon?" Oliver cringed at the needy tone of his voice. The man must think him a lovesick fool. Which he was.

A flicker of amusement crossed Stratton's face as the man took pity on him. "She and Lord Harcourt left a short time ago for a walk. I believe in Hyde Park."

"Thank you, Stratton." Relief coursed through him, and Oliver resisted the urge to grab the man's hand and shake it. Instead, he raced down the front steps toward the park.

Throngs of people filled the streets leading to the park, obviously taking advantage of the perfect day. *Perfect day.* Would it be so for him? He threaded his way through the crowds as they ambled along the pathways.

How would he ever find her in this mass of people? Yet, he'd know her anywhere—the curve of her jaw, her graceful movements as she walked, her glorious chestnut hair.

There, on the other side of a tree-covered expanse, she strolled with her arm looped through her father's, the copse of trees hiding then revealing her figure as she moved up the opposite path. No mistaking the bonnet that adorned her lovely head, it had been the one she'd worn during their carriage ride months ago when he'd acted like a buffoon, yelling at her and frightening Pockets. What a fool he'd been.

He raced across the grass-covered expanse, his heart thudding to the beat of his pounding boots. Although Camilla wasn't a young debutante who needed her father's blessing to marry, his heart soared at the fortuitous nature of finding them together. He would seek Lord Harcourt's permission on the spot.

One look at Lord Harcourt's face had him skidding to a halt. He slipped behind a tree, hiding like a coward. Oliver had never witnessed so much as a frown from the man, or heard him raise his voice, yet the anger on Lord Harcourt's face froze him in place.

"Dr. Somersby's a gypsy!" Harcourt bellowed. "This is most disconcerting." He swiped a hand across his face.

How had he found out? Everything began to spin before Oliver, and he grabbed onto the tree trunk for support.

"Father, calm yourself. People will hear you."

Oliver's gaze shot to Camilla. She paled under her father's castigation. Or was it her own disgust at Oliver's heritage? His blood chilled at Harcourt's next words.

"How can I be calm? What were you thinking, Camilla, going to that encampment alone? You could have been robbed, hurt . . . or worse."

Blood pounded in his skull at her betrayal. Why hadn't she asked him directly? Why go behind his back? Anger and pain forced out any semblance of reason from his mind, and his gut churned with the foulness of her deceit, allowing no admission of his own guilt in keeping the truth from her.

When he stepped away from his hiding place, his boot landed on a brittle branch. The subsequent *snap* caught Camilla's attention, and she turned, her eyes widening in horror as they met his.

❦

CAMILLA BLINKED, CLEARING HER VISION. HER HAND DRIFTED TO her throat at Oliver's pained expression.

She swallowed, forcing the miniscule amount of moisture down her dry throat to ease it. Yet, as she called to him, her voice remained raspy. "Oliver. I didn't see you there."

"That's obvious," he spat the words. "Tell me, *Lady Denby*, how long before you were going to tell me of your excursion to discover the truth about me? I'm surprised you didn't hire a Bow Street runner."

"It wasn't like that. I was . . . curious."

"You went behind my back."

She recoiled at the vitriol in his voice. "I was unsure you would be honest."

"And there we have it. You don't trust me. Well, worry no more, *my lady*. I shall trouble you no longer. Please give my regrets to Pockets that I will be unable to continue his lessons. I trust with your connections you'll find a suitable replacement in a trice."

Before she could utter another word, he pivoted on his heel. She lunged forward, calling out to his retreating back. "Wait. Let me explain."

An arm wrapped around her waist, her father's gentle hand staying her. "Camilla, don't. He's angry. Allow him time to calm himself."

She spun on her father with a vengeance. "Allow *him* to calm himself? He's upset because he heard you shouting about who he is."

Her father flinched as if she'd actually struck him. He darted a glance at her, then lowered his gaze to his feet. "I apologize, my darling, but your news took me unawares."

"No wonder he kept this from us. Not out of shame, but out of fear of our reactions. Father, I'm ashamed of you."

"Do you think I care a fig about Dr. Somersby's heritage? I'll admit, a man of gypsy blood is not one I envisioned as a suitor for my daughter, but I respect him. He's a good man."

"Then why such a vehement reaction? I merely sought your advice on how to approach him with my knowledge."

He took a deep breath. "Because, my darling, it's not only your safety that concerns me. There's been talk at White's about clearing the encampment." He paused, his gaze unwavering. "By force."

Her fingers gripped her father's arms with such strength, he winced. "His grandmother."

"Yes. And all the other innocents there." He shook his head as if trying to clear it. "I passed it off as bluster. A few too many glasses of whisky loosen men's tongues—and muddle their capacity to think rationally. Perhaps that's all it is, but I shall keep my ear to the ground for any more rumblings."

"I must go to him and explain."

"In due course. Give him time to collect himself. In the meantime, now that I'm recovered from my own shock at your news, I wish to hear all about your visit with Dr. Somersby's grandmother."

After she relayed her visit with Eva to her father, he bid her farewell and wished her luck with Oliver. She tried the clinic first, only to find it closed. Next she tried his home, but neither Sabina nor Victoria had seen him since the morning. *Where could he be?*

Discouraged, she returned home, knowing Pockets would be worried. He never complained when she'd left him in the care of her servants during her charity work, but each time she returned home, his little face greeted her through one of the front windows. She needed his cheerful, loving smile to lift her heavy heart. As she descended the carriage, she gazed up toward the windows, disappointed to find them Pockets-less.

With an unexpected urgency, she entered her home as Stratton held the door. "Where's Pockets?" Her panicked voice sounded foreign to her own ears.

Her butler had always been a man of utmost composure, a trait she'd always appreciated. Yet, at the moment, even *his* eyes widened. "He's in the kitchen, madam. Cook's making his favorite biscuits."

The muscles in her neck eased.

"Madam, while you were out, Dr. Somersby called. He seemed most eager to find you."

Not any longer. "Thank you, Stratton." With a sigh, she steeled herself for the difficult task of informing Pockets his lessons with Oliver would temporarily cease. She refused to accept things had ended permanently.

She'd only visited the kitchen on rare occasions, preferring to deliver instructions to Cook via Stratton or one of the other servants, but if she'd learned anything in her life, it was not to put off the inevitable. As a child she hated porridge. Her mother would say, "Eat it quickly and be done with it." She marched into the kitchen to find Pockets.

Cook snapped to attention from where she sat, piling biscuits in front of Pockets. "Ma'am. I wasn't expecting you."

Pockets stared up at her, his cheeks full of the half-chewed treats. "'Ello, Mama." His words, muffled from the enormous mouthful, sounded more like *errow, Mawmaw.*

Oh, how would she be able to deliver the news and break his heart?

Cook wiped her hands on her apron, then held out the plate to Camilla. "Ma'am?"

"No, thank you. It appears Pockets has eaten more than enough for both of us."

"He does love my baking, ma'am. I never seen a boy eat so many at one time."

Camilla cast a quick glance at Pockets, who looked a little green around the edges. "Precisely how many has he eaten?"

Cook shot her a sheepish glance. "Oh, let's see, I think that's the third batch out of the oven."

"I don't feel so good," Pockets moaned.

Unsure whether she should laugh or proceed with a severe dressing down of Cook, Pockets decided the matter for her when he doubled over, clutching his stomach, and tumbled onto the floor.

"Quick, Cook, send for Stratton and a footman to help me get Pockets to his bed."

Cook gave a curt nod and raced off as fast as her chubby legs could carry her.

"Silly woman," Camilla murmured while stroking Pocket's forehead. "Don't worry, my little love, you will be fine in no time."

With a prayer that her words were true, she continued to comfort him, concerned that he felt warm to the touch.

Pockets let out a sharp yowl. "My 'ead 'urts, too."

More than an indulgence in biscuits appeared to be the culprit. She forced down the panic rising in her chest and took control.

While Stratton carried Pockets to his room, Camilla penned a hasty note and handed it to the footman. "Take this to the Duke of Ashton's home immediately. Do not leave without either speaking to the duke directly, or inquiring of his whereabouts if he is not there. Do not give up until you locate him and deliver this message."

If only she knew where Oliver was, but Harry would come. She was certain of it.

With another prayer, she hurried up the stairs to Pockets' room to wait for help.

⚜

OLIVER SWALLOWED THE LUMP THE SIZE OF GIBRALTAR LODGED IN his throat, waiting for Harry's response. Slimy shame coiled like snakes in his gut at his partial confession. They hissed the unspoken name *bastard*, accusing Oliver of withholding the truth about his father.

Harry remained motionless, his face unreadable.

Say something. Anything.

Harry rose and poured two glasses of brandy, then handed one to Oliver. After a languorous sip, he said, "It took courage to tell me, but why did you wait so long?"

Oliver savored his own gulp of the beverage, the burn of it as it slid down his throat somehow fitting. "The peerage doesn't look on the Romani with favor. They have hanged people for no other offense than being who they were."

Harry's hazel eyes widened. "You can't believe I would . . ."

"No, of course not. But others, yes. I've seen it myself. If word gets out, my position . . . it's not only the nobility who look down their noses at those with Romani blood. The patients might refuse to have me treat them if they know."

Harry turned the glass in his hand, his eyes focused on the amber liquid it held. "I would never tolerate any mistreatment of you . . . by anyone."

For a moment, Oliver breathed easier. "I did fear you might discharge me."

"So why tell me now?" Harry asked. "What's happened that you've come to me?"

Oliver shook his head. "I wanted you to hear it from me rather than . . . another. I've been discovered by someone close to you."

Harry cocked his head. "Has someone threatened you? Because if they have . . ."

"No."

"Who is it? Perhaps I can intervene?"

"Lady Denby."

"I see."

The expression on Harry's face reminded Oliver of his mother's when, as a boy, he'd scraped his knee or fallen from a horse. He hated the look of pity then, and he hated it now. No longer a child, he neither wanted nor needed anyone to kiss his wounds in an attempt to make them better. The only kissing that would help was now out of reach.

"You said you'd been discovered. You didn't tell her?"

"No. She apparently took it upon herself to visit the encampment outside of the city. She spoke with my grandmother."

"How did she take it?"

Oliver opened his mouth to answer and promptly shut it, realizing he hadn't stayed long enough to find out. "I . . . I don't know for certain. I overheard her speaking to her father about it.

Lord Harcourt was livid. But it doesn't matter. It was folly to believe we could . . ."

The blond brow above Harry's right eye quirked. "Could what? Be together? Have you failed to listen to anything I've said in the last nine months?"

Harry leaned forward, hands still cradling the glass of brandy, forearms resting on his knees. "I never pegged you for a coward, Somersby. Camilla deserves better." He tacked on a muttered, "All things considered."

Oliver's head snapped to attention. "Considering what?"

His body falling against the chair's back, Harry closed his eyes. "Blast. I didn't mean to say that out loud. Edmund has both Maggie and me ragged from lack of sleep. Much to my dismay, she insists we tend to him completely ourselves." A tiny smile crossed his lips. "Although she seems to be reconsidering the merits of a nanny."

He straightened, his eyes now serious and meeting Oliver's gaze directly. "Do you swear not to repeat what I'm about to tell you?"

"I don't relish keeping any more secrets than I already have."

Harry nodded. "I understand, but sharing this knowledge would do no one any good, especially Camilla. However, since you asked, it may provide some guidance in your own decisions."

Harry's nebulous words did nothing to ease the anxiety settling in Oliver's chest.

After rising and pouring himself more brandy, Harry lifted the decanter toward Oliver in offering. Oliver shook his head, which he hoped would remain clear enough to make the decisions Harry mentioned.

"You are aware of Camilla's husband, Hugh Denby?"

"That he died at Waterloo, yes."

"I served with him. Was at his side before he died. Major Denby was awarded a baronetcy posthumously for his valor on the battlefield. When he and Camilla married, Hugh was the son of a moderately wealthy landowner, not part of the aristocracy."

Oliver opened his mouth, but snapped it shut when Harry shot him a disapproving glare.

"Patience. I only share this to let you know Camilla doesn't care about titles, but it's not what's important here. Hugh led a charge, some would argue recklessly. Nevertheless, his regiment emerged victorious but sustained severe casualties. Hugh among them.

"When they pulled him from the battlefield, and I examined him, I was certain I could save his life."

"We all hope for the best, but it's often out of our hands."

Eyes full of suffering from the horrors of war stared back at Oliver. "You wish to console me? To give me comfort believing nothing I could have done would have saved him?" Harry took a large swallow of the amber liquid in his glass as if it would provide the fortitude to continue with his story. "There is no consolation. Hugh chose to die."

Unbidden, Oliver's body straightened in his seat. "But he was mortally wounded."

"Not precisely. A bullet lodged low in his spine, I believe damaging his spinal cord. He couldn't move anything below his waist."

A strange sense of understanding floated over Oliver.

"I removed the bullet. He was strong and otherwise healthy. The prognosis for his survival appeared favorable. What remained uncertain was if he would regain movement in his lower body. He swore he would not return to Camilla as half a man. I tried to reason with him, but he became despondent and begged me to help him write to Camilla in the event he died.

"Exhausted from tending the wounded, I retired to my tent for a brief rest. When I returned to check on him, it was too late. I found the empty bottle of laudanum on the ground by his cot."

Harry drained his glass and sighed. "Who's to say he wouldn't have regained the use of his legs, to have been able to function fully as a man? He never gave himself the chance to find out. I hid the bottle and led everyone to believe he'd died from an infection of the wound. My deception lies heavy on my heart as a physician and haunts me as a friend."

Part of Oliver empathized with Hugh. It would be a bitter tonic to swallow to have Camilla as a wife and not be able to perform his husbandly duty. To be dependent upon her or others for the most basic of functions. "Are you saying he was a coward?"

Harry shook his head. "No, I wouldn't go that far. I can't know what was in his mind. But I will say this. He didn't trust Camilla enough to allow her to make the choice. To give her the opportunity to either accept him as he was, or reject him."

"Perhaps he wouldn't have been able to bear the rejection—the pity—he feared he would see in her eyes, regardless of what she might have said."

"Perhaps. We men put such store in our pride, in our virility. But what of the women we love? Are we to choose for them, to take away that right? Is our pride worth more than risking rejection by those we love?"

Oliver had no answer.

A soft knock at the door saved him from struggling to find one.

Burrows appeared in the doorway. "Your Grace, forgive the interruption. Lady Denby's footman is here. He states it's urgent, and he's been requested not to leave without seeing you personally."

Harry's gaze shot to Oliver's. "Show him in."

The footman entered, his steps faltering upon seeing Oliver. He bowed and handed Harry a letter. "Your Grace, Lady Denby insisted I wait for a response."

Icy fingers trailed up Oliver's spine as Harry read the message, the premonition of dread seeping into his core. "What is it?"

"Pockets has taken ill. She requests me immediately." Harry turned to Burrows who waited by the door. "Have my carriage prepared."

Burrows nodded and left.

Addressing the footman, Harry said, "Tell Lady Denby we're on our way."

The early foreboding took root in Oliver's stomach. "We?"

"You're coming with me." Harry paused, his expression serious. "Unless you, too, put pride before those you love."

CHAPTER 21—BITTER TRUTH

C amilla paced the length of Pockets' bed, her steps halting each time he let out another pitiful moan. He lay curled up in a tight ball, clutching his head.

What's detaining Harry?

Heavy footsteps pounded against the stairs, their pace quick and precise.

Thank God.

"Third bedchamber on the left." Stratton's voice, laced with concern, drifted in from the hallway as he directed Harry.

She spun toward the door, her heart beating like a wild animal against her ribs.

Said heart skipped erratically when Oliver appeared in the doorway, and her hand drifted unbidden to her throat.

He stepped into the room, and her heart slowed marginally as Harry entered behind him.

Oliver gave a curt nod, his eyes not quite meeting her own.

"Tell us exactly what happened," Harry said. "What are his symptoms?"

Both men walked past her, taking opposite positions by Pockets' bedside.

"When I returned home from my . . . walk"—her gaze darted toward Oliver who mercifully retained his attention on Pockets—"I found him in the kitchen eating biscuits. He said he didn't feel well, then clutched his stomach and fell to the floor. He said his head pained him. At the time, he seemed warm to the touch."

Oliver placed a hand against Pockets' forehead, his eyes lifting to Harry's. "He doesn't seem feverish."

"Perhaps the heat from the kitchen," Harry said.

"Pockets." Oliver's soothing voice eased the tension in her neck. "How many biscuits did you eat?"

"I dunno." Pockets moaned again, and the fear inched up Camilla's spine once more. "A lot. They was good."

A slight smile tugged at Oliver's lips. "I'm sure they were delicious, but too many aren't good for you."

Like a dog on a hunt, Harry sniffed the air. "Smell that?" he asked Oliver, then turned toward her. "Did he evacuate his stomach?"

Her eyes riveted to Oliver's face, Harry's question barely registered in her mind. "Pardon?"

"Did he vomit?" Oliver asked.

"Yes." She pointed to the chamber pot on the floor by the table. The sickening, pungent odor lingered, and she fought against the foul taste invading her own mouth.

"Does your stomach still hurt?" Harry asked.

"Some. Mostly my 'ead."

"Indigestion doesn't typically cause head pain," Oliver said, directing his statement to Harry, who nodded in agreement.

"Let's see if you can sit up a bit, Pockets." Harry reached behind the boy, assisting him to a sitting position. As he positioned a pillow behind his head, Harry's eyes widened, and his gaze shot to Oliver. "Feel the back of his head."

"What is it?" Camilla shuddered at the sound of her own voice rising in pitch.

"Pockets, did you hit your head?" Oliver asked.

"I dunno."

The men exchanged worried glances, and Camilla's frayed

nerves reached their limit. "Will someone please tell me what is going on?"

"There's a rather large bump on the back of his head," Oliver said. "Did he fall recently? Within the last day?"

"I . . ." She searched her memory. He'd been playing happily in the garden when she'd left for the walk with her father. A footman had been instructed to watch him during her absence.

With a shaking hand, she reached for the bell, summoning the servants. Stratton appeared almost immediately, obviously hovering nearby. "Yes, madam."

"Fetch Ralph." She directed her gaze to Harry. "A footman watched him while I was out. Perhaps he will have information."

Moments later, Ralph shuffled into the room. His eyes darted nervously from Camilla, to the doctors, then to Pockets. "You asked to see me, ma'am?"

"While under your care, did Pockets injure himself, fall, hit his head in any manner?"

The man winced at the sharpness in her voice, but she did not regret it. Her son's health was at stake.

"I only looked away for a moment, ma'am. It happened so fast. He said he was uninjured."

Camilla's hands curled in tight fists at her side in an attempt to prevent herself from lunging at the man and strangling him.

Oliver stepped between them. "Tell us exactly what happened, every detail, no matter how minor."

"We played cricket for a while, but Stratton called Jasper away, leaving only Master Pockets and me."

"Jasper is another footman," Camilla explained when Oliver's eyes met hers in question.

Sweat beaded Ralph's forehead, and he tugged at his neckcloth. "Master Pockets asked to ride the velocipede." His eyes darted to Camilla's, shame and apology glistening. "I told him no, you had forbidden it, but he begged me, ma'am. No one can resist that boy."

The truth of Ralph's words held no weight at the moment. "Did he fall off that hideous contraption?"

"I only looked away for a moment, ma'am. Maize came out to tell him about Cook's biscuits, and . . . well . . ."

"You let a pretty head turn your attention away from my son!" Camilla shouted, sending Ralph cowering.

Ralph twisted his hands in front of him. "As I said, it was only a moment. The next thing I knew, Master Pockets was lying on the ground. There wasn't any blood, only a small bump. I took him to Cook to see if there was any ice from the ice house to put on it."

Harry bent over Pockets, his thumb and forefinger pulling Pocket's eyelids open wide. "Oliver, come here."

Oliver stood on the other side and performed the same motion on Pockets other eye. "You see that?" Harry asked.

"Yes," Oliver said.

"What?" Camilla all but stomped her foot.

Oliver straightened and faced her. "His pupils are unevenly dilated."

"What does that mean?"

"It can indicate trauma to the brain," Harry said.

As if every bone had vanished from her body, Camilla went limp, and she staggered, reaching for purchase on anything to keep herself upright.

Oliver raced to her side, wrapping a steadying arm around her waist. "Forgive my familiarity." He guided her to a chair.

"Will he . . ." Unable to force the word, she changed to a more positive inquiry. "Recover?"

The men exchanged another infuriating glance, and she wanted to butt their heads together to make them speak.

"Excuse us for a moment," Harry said, then motioned for Oliver to step outside.

The snick of the door closing behind them was like a hammer to her own brain, and she pulled herself from the chair.

Pockets appeared to have drifted off to sleep. Surely that was a good sign? She lifted his tiny hand in hers, bringing it to her lips. She strained to decipher Harry's and Oliver's muffled voices, unable to make out anything of use.

The somber expressions on their faces when they stepped back into the room sent a chill racing up her spine.

"We've discussed it," Harry began. "At this time, we believe the best and safest course of action is to wait and do nothing. Depending on the severity of the blow to his head, he may recover on his own."

She swallowed, forcing down the fear rising in her throat. "And if he doesn't?"

Oliver darted a glance at Harry. "There is a procedure called trepanation we could attempt."

She'd heard of the barbaric process. "You'll drill into his skull?" She forced the words out in a frightened whisper.

Oliver took a tentative step toward her but halted. "Let's pray it doesn't come to that. For the time being, we'll watch him. We need to wake him periodically. Someone should remain at his side at all times for the next day or so."

He turned toward Harry. "With Lady Denby's permission, I'll stay. You should return home to Her Grace and Edmund. You're exhausted."

She hadn't even given Harry a careful glance. Dark circles under his eyes marred his handsome visage. "Forgive me, Harry. My concern for Pockets drove thought for anyone else from my head. Of course Dr. Somersby may stay. Please give Maggie and the baby my love."

After exchanging a few more words with Oliver, using medical jargon she didn't understand, Harry bade them goodbye.

Awkward silence settled between her and Oliver until he broke it. "If one of your footmen could take a message to my mother and Tori, I would be most appreciative."

"Of course," she mumbled like a fool and raced off to retrieve foolscap, ink, and pen.

When she returned, Oliver was speaking softly to Pockets. "Although you feel sleepy, it's important to stay awake. I'll stay with you to keep you company."

"I want Mama." Fear laced Pockets' voice.

"I'm here, my darling. I won't leave you."

Oliver wrote his letter while she sat by Pockets' bedside, stroking his head. As her hand drifted back, the bump at the base of his skull shocked her.

With chairs placed strategically on the opposite sides of Pockets' bed, she and Oliver kept a silent vigil. When the boy's eyes began drooping, Oliver would nudge him gently and tell him tall tales of life aboard a sailing vessel.

They said nothing about what had occurred in Hyde Park, and although Oliver remained polite, she was unable to penetrate the icy wall between them.

They paused only to attend to their own physical needs. Weariness pulled at her, her limbs becoming heavy and numb. Dark shadows stretched across the room as the late summer sun too took its rest. She stirred when Oliver lit candles by the bed, ashamed she had allowed herself to drift asleep.

He placed a hand on her shoulder, whispering softly, "Why don't you go to bed? You're exhausted and not used to bedside vigils. I promise I won't leave him."

The kindness, the affection she'd seen in his eyes the last few months returned, and her heart leapt with hope he'd forgiven her.

"Perhaps for a while. Then I shall relieve you. I'll have a chamber prepared for you."

"No." His smile gave her hope. "It's a bit too early to say for certain, but I believe he's on the mend. His pupils are normal again. He says the pain in his head has lessened, and he's been coherent. I'm allowing him to rest for a while."

They both turned toward the sleeping boy, his little face peaceful. Without warning, the tears she'd fought back fell freely, and she sobbed like a child.

Strong arms wrapped around her, pulling her against his chest, stroking and caressing her back. She'd been so independent, so strong, relying on herself for so long. It was heaven to be the one cared for instead of the caretaker.

He held her for several long minutes, allowing her to be the one to break their embrace. When she pulled back and met his eyes, they changed, as if a curtain had fallen over them, hiding the kindness she'd witnessed.

"Oliver, about us——"

With his thumb, he brushed a tear from her cheek. "Now is not the time. Get some rest. We'll speak in the morning." With that, he turned his back toward her and returned to his seat by Pockets' bedside.

She opened her mouth to argue, but closed it. Yes, morning. In the light of day, when Pockets had fully recovered, all would be made right again.

OLIVER CURSED HIMSELF FOR LETTING HIS GUARD DOWN. PLAGUED by exhaustion himself, Camilla's vulnerability had taken him by surprise. Her love for the orphaned boy clawed away at his defenses, against his arguments that a woman of her class would not accept him. They had much to resolve, but now was not the time. Pockets' well-being still hung in a precarious balance.

He'd spoken the truth to her. The boy had improved, but he'd seen too many times where improvement provided a false hope, only to be dashed away with a sudden turn for the worse. The vigil had not ended. In fact, the darkest hours lay ahead. It would be best if she were not here to witness it.

He vowed he would have a servant wake her should it be necessary to say her goodbyes. Pulling out his pocket watch, he marked the time and continued watching the gentle rise and fall of the boy's chest.

"Oliver. Oliver."

He jerked awake at the call of his name. The slimy shame once again coiled in his gut, but this time for falling asleep.

Pockets stared at him with bright eyes. Color had returned to the boy's face. "I'm hungry."

"Not feeling sick to your stomach?"

"No. Where's Mama?"

"She stepped a way for a moment. She should return soon. How many fingers am I holding up?"

Pockets counted. "One, two, three."

Oliver tousled his hair. "Very good. Headache better?"

Pockets nodded.

Oliver tugged the bell pull and requested a servant fetch Camilla and some tea and toast.

When Camilla rushed in, her dressing gown loosely tied around her, Oliver's breath caught. Her chestnut hair flowed down her back, and although in disarray, he'd never seen anything so beautiful.

"Is he . . ." She halted at the entrance, her gaze landing on Pockets.

"Much improved. I'm confident the worst is over."

Camilla wrapped Pockets in her embrace, tears once again flowing as she kissed the boy's face and hair.

"I've requested a footman bring him a light meal." Oliver placed his stethoscope in his bag and snapped it shut. "Keep all his meals simple for the next day. Toast, perhaps a boiled egg. Nothing heavy, and for the time being, limit his consumption of biscuits." He'd meant the last as a joke, but Pockets' forlorn expression indicated he'd taken it to heart.

"Only for a day or so, to allow your stomach to return to normal."

"Oliver, thank you . . . for everything."

Summoning the strength left in him, Oliver moved toward the door, hoping she'd forgotten about her request to discuss what had happened in the park the previous day.

Before he'd taken two steps, she touched his sleeve. "Might you allow me to explain what you overheard?"

The pleading in her warm, brown eyes drained him of any remaining energy to resist her. "Very well."

A maid brought a tray for Pockets, and Camilla instructed her to stay with the boy and call her if necessary.

Oliver followed her out of the room to a downstairs parlor. He clutched his medical bag so tight, he feared he would break the handle.

She closed the door behind them and, turning to face him, motioned for him to take a seat.

"I'll stand, thank you. Please say your piece so I may leave."

Camilla winced from the sharpness of his words. "You misunderstood the conversation you heard between my father and me."

"I heard clearly enough. You went behind my back, digging around where you had no business to dig. You could have asked me directly."

"Could I? Truly? You're so guarded, Oliver. Like the changing winds, I don't know which version of you to expect from one moment to the next. I want to know you, the real you. I sought answers."

"What sent you to the encampment for those answers?"

Her faced paled, then redness rose up her neck to her cheeks. "One night in December after we first met, I followed you. I believed you had gone there to treat someone. At the time, I had no idea about your heritage."

She twisted her delicate hands. "As we grew closer, I suppose somewhere deep inside I suspected you had a more direct connection to the people there. But I promise you, I meant no harm."

"Yet you told your father? Don't deny that he was outraged over the news. I heard with my own ears."

"He wasn't angry about who you are."

"Wasn't he?" Oliver hissed the words.

"No, you've misunderstood."

"It doesn't matter. What's done is done. Perhaps it's for the best. It would never have worked between us. I don't fit in your world, and you certainly wouldn't fit in mine. It was folly to believe it."

"I don't care who you are." Camilla's voice shook with emotion.

"But *I* care. I've lived a lie for so long, I began to believe it, all the while it festered inside me, eating me like a parasite. It's time I face the truth. We cannot be together."

He stepped toward the door. "I've told Ashton about my heritage, and he was surprisingly understanding. However, I would greatly appreciate it if you would keep this information to yourself and ask your father to do the same. I ask not for myself but for Tori's and my mother's safety. Please respect this decision. I shall darken your doorstep no longer. Now, if you'll excuse me."

Oliver stepped out of the room, then out of the townhouse, leaving his heart inside.

CHAPTER 22—REVELATIONS

C amilla stared at the half-open parlor door, and heaviness settled in her limbs. She grabbed the arm of a wingback chair and allowed her body to fall into its softness, unable to digest Oliver's words.

Surely he didn't mean it? Had he not heard one word of what she'd said? Determined to set things right between them, she'd give him time to realize the happiness he had thrown away.

At the moment, her first priority lay upstairs in the form of a helpless child. With several deep breaths, she wrapped the dressing gown more firmly around herself and, after forcing a cheerful expression, headed upstairs to her son.

The following day, Harry stopped by to examine Pockets, concurring with Oliver's assessment.

"He's lucky. There seem to be no residual effects from his fall. The bump on his head has gone down considerably, and he's in possession of all his faculties. Is he tolerating food?"

"Yes, although he's hinted he's tiring of tea, toast, and soft-boiled eggs."

"A return to a normal meal should be fine. Provide small portions at first, then increase them as needed." Harry tilted his head as if speculating whether to pursue the subject foremost on her mind. "You appear weary, Camilla. Are you sleeping well?"

"Not especially. Perhaps with Pockets on the mend, I shall experience a more restful sleep."

As if reading her mind, he said. "Oliver suffers from the same malady, I'm afraid. His mind seems occupied on other matters unrelated to medical treatments."

She didn't wish Oliver pain, but the fact that he, too, had been tormented by their separation provided a strange sort of vindication of her own distress. Throwing her hands up, she said, "Oh, Harry. I don't know what to do. He's shut me out, refusing to listen to reason. I simply don't understand his concerns."

Uninvited, Harry took a seat as if preparing for a lengthy conversation. "Have you considered that may be the problem? Your inability to see things from his perspective?"

Bristling at his accusation, she straightened, unwilling to accept any responsibility for the rift in her and Oliver's relationship. "*My* inability? I've told him his parentage doesn't matter to me. What more can I do?" Her body collapsed onto the settee as she struggled to come to terms with Harry's allegation.

With a slight shake of his head, Harry heaved a deep sigh. "Indulge me for a moment. What did you think about gypsies before your knowledge of Oliver's heritage?"

When she opened her mouth, he held up a hand. "Before you answer, take a moment and think about my question. Be truthful." His perceptive hazel eyes bore into her, demanding honesty.

An oily uneasiness crept up her spine, circling around her throat, tightening. Her mouth moved but formed no words. How could she admit to Harry she'd believed all the horrible things she'd heard? *Thieves, dirty, conniving, immoral, lazy.* The barrage of negative descriptors flew through her mind. She'd heard them as a child and only half dismissed them as an adult—until Oliver, until she'd met and spoken with Eva and experienced the camp herself. Heat flooded her face.

"Before Oliver, I did not hold them in high regard," she

admitted, although the dilution of her true feelings did not escape Harry's keen observation.

"It's good to feel shame when we realize we've held false perceptions. It's what helps us grow. But put yourself in Oliver's position. It isn't about us, it's about him and his people. There are many who, as you say, do not hold gypsies in high regard. Who threaten their lives. Can you blame him for his distrust of us?"

No, she could not. "Do you believe, given time, he will trust me?"

"We men are proud creatures, some would say to a fault. When Oliver told me of his heritage, I sensed he held something back. Something more difficult to share than his gypsy blood. I didn't press, but an underlying current of shame lay in his words, or should I say those unspoken."

"Do you have any idea what it might be?"

"No, and I didn't press him. Whatever demon lurks within him, he must believe it prevents the two of you from being together. At the moment, I believe it's best we trust that, eventually, he will tell us. Give him time, Camilla."

As difficult as it was, she'd give him time. It's all she had to offer.

❦

For a month, Camilla waited and hoped. The letters she'd written to Oliver had been returned unopened. Hope dwindled, and when she pressed Harry or Margaret, neither had words of comfort to offer her. Harry stated Oliver had thrown himself into his work, conversing little regarding personal matters, and when Harry had broached the subject, Oliver had summarily asked him to mind his own business.

She, too, had decided perhaps work would occupy her enough to temporarily put Oliver out of her mind, although he remained in her heart.

Word of a new physician for the clinic brightened Margaret's spirits. Although never one to complain, she'd shared with Camilla her desire to have Harry remain at home more often now that

Edmund had been born. However, with a new physician, came the need for more funds to provide his wages.

True to her word, Camilla had called upon Lord Trentwith, who pledged a large donation but requested a visit to the clinic to witness his funds in action. She suggested he simply arrange a meeting at the clinic with Harry, but he insisted she accompany him.

Trentwith arrived at her townhouse on a blustery late September morning. Dark storm clouds loomed ominously in the sky, along with a marked shift from the summer heat to autumn's chilly rains. The symbolic nature of the weather—a somehow a fitting accompaniment to the prospect of seeing Oliver again—unsettled her.

Nervous energy pulsed through her during the carriage ride to the clinic. She hadn't seen Oliver since the day he'd walked from her townhouse after Pockets' accident.

Trentwith spoke amiably about returning to his country estate the first of October, intimating he'd remained in London much longer than planned specifically in hopes of resuming an association with her.

"I suppose this Dr. Somersby fellow has usurped any hope I might have of securing an attachment with you. I'm surprised you haven't brought him up to scratch."

Her stomach plummeted at the mention of Oliver's name in conjunction with a marriage proposal.

"Or have I missed something? Has he made an offer?"

"No."

Trentwith's eyes shone with interest. "I shall be anxious to meet him, then. Size up my competition."

"Lord Trentwith, I apologize if I have misled you in my intentions. Although I enjoy your company and appreciate your generosity to the clinic, I'm afraid an attachment between us is out of the question."

Genuine disappointment painted his handsome face. "Pity. I suppose one great love in a lifetime is all we can hope for." He sighed, the sound wistful. "But I believe we would have been an excellent match." Drops of rain beat against the roof of the carriage. He turned and stared out the window the remainder of their journey.

Although relieved she'd finally ended the charade between them, her chest tightened with regret that she'd injured him. She'd never been a flirt or a tease. And to think it had all begun as a case of mistaken identity.

The discomfort threading through her was a fitting penance she supposed, but she braced herself for an even greater pain as they descended the carriage and made their way into the clinic. A soft tinkle from the bell fastened at the door announced their arrival. The handful of people sitting in the small waiting area looked up with interest.

"I say there. Hello, Ashton," Trentwith called, obviously unwilling to be patient for Harry to appear.

Several of the waiting people grumbled in protest.

"He's probably with a patient," she explained in a hushed voice. "And he prefers to be called Dr. Radcliffe while here."

A few minutes later, Harry escorted an older woman into the waiting area. "Come back in a few days if the congestion persists, Mrs. Dawson." He patted the old woman's arm, then catching sight of Camilla and Lord Trentwith, nodded in their direction.

"Lady Denby, Lord Trentwith, what brings you here? In need of medical assistance?" he asked, his lilting tone, teasing.

Trentwith perused the clinic. "Perhaps a brief tour of the facility?"

"Of course, it would be my pleasure." Harry motioned them to follow him, entering an empty treatment room. "We have one more examination room, a small space serving as an office, and of course the waiting area. It's small but efficient."

"Impressive, I must say, Ashton. Oh, forgive me, Dr. Radcliffe. Most impressive indeed. I see my funds are well spent," Trentwith said.

"I'm glad you approve. We're very proud of it and the good we're able to do."

Camilla said a brief prayer that perhaps Oliver would not be present and she would be spared any further pain.

Prayers often go unanswered. As they exited the room, Oliver stepped out of the other treatment room into the narrow hallway.

He lurched to a halt upon seeing them, his eyes first locking on Camilla's, then darting to Trentwith. His swarthy complexion paled as if all blood had drained from his face.

⚜

OLIVER STARED AT HIS FATHER. ANGER BURNED WITHIN HIM, mingling with stabbing pain as his father stared back, no acknowledgment indicated in his eyes.

"I'm sorry," his father said, his tone cool and reserved. "Have we met? You look familiar."

Harry spun around. "Lord Trentwith, this is Dr. Somersby. He's been a great asset to the clinic."

Before Trentwith could respond, Oliver spat the words at his father. "Familiar? I would hope so, since I'm your bastard son."

Camilla gasped, her gaze flitting between the three men but settling on Oliver, her eyes filled with pity.

Trentwith's mouth opened and snapped shut so abruptly Oliver envisioned several chipped teeth.

"It's not possible." Trentwith shook his head. "My son's surname is Heron. Ashton said Somersby."

"I took the name Somersby when my mother's people threw us out."

"Us?" The man appeared genuinely shocked. "Your mother? She's alive?"

"She's alive."

"But . . . the child . . . your mother . . . both died in childbirth." The man apparently couldn't put a complete sentence together.

"I hate to disappoint you. She's very much alive, no thanks to you."

"And the child?" Trentwith asked.

If Oliver hadn't known better, he'd have believed the man truly cared. "Dead." His tone mirrored the word.

"Not Victoria?" Harry asked.

Oliver bit down on his tongue, the metallic taste of blood pooling in his mouth.. He'd had his fill of revelations for the day. His rakehell father didn't deserve to know about Tori. "Victoria isn't his."

Harry touched Oliver's arm. "Perhaps we should all sit down and discuss—"

Oliver jerked out of Harry's grasp as if the man's caring touch scorched through his coat. "There's nothing to discuss. He had his chance . . . twice. You abandoned my mother and your own children. For what? Your precious title? An aristocratic wife? Ashamed of your dalliance with a Romani woman? She was good enough to bed but not marry. Am I right?"

The fury raging inside him blurred his vision, and his head pounded. "I have to get out of here."

He marched into the waiting area toward the door of the clinic, but Camilla grabbed his arm. "Oliver, don't go. You need to calm down." Her soothing voice only intensified his rage. The last thing he wanted was her pity.

He wrenched his arm out of her grasp. "I don't *need* to do anything. And I *don't* take orders from you."

The door stuck briefly as he yanked it open. The tiny bell fell to the floor with a soft tinkle. He stepped outside to the pelting rain, slamming the door behind him.

***

HELPLESSNESS WAS AN UNFAMILIAR FEELING FOR CAMILLA AS SHE studied Trentwith's face. It had gone white as his neckcloth. He staggered as if drunk, and Harry reached around him to provide support, leading him to a chair back in the treatment room.

"I had no idea. You must believe me," Trentwith pleaded, anguish heavy in his gaze. "Sabina's people told me she died in childbirth. The boy . . . his grandmother would rear Oliver. Before he passed away, my father had already arranged to provide for him, money for school, for an education. But it was too painful to see him. He reminded me of his mother."

He hung his head, clutching fistfuls of hair in his hands. "If I had known . . ." His back heaved soundlessly.

Camilla met Harry's eyes, communicating a silent question. *Did you know?*

Trentwith voiced her thoughts. "Ashton, did you know? Did you see her? Is it true?"

Harry shook his head. "Oliver kept his personal life private. He never spoke of his mother."

"I knew," Camilla said. She clarified as Trentwith's head snapped in her direction. "Only that his mother hadn't been well. I met her, his grandmother . . . their people. He never told me who his father was." Regret churned in her stomach. Perhaps if she'd waited for him to confide in her rather than going behind his back, he might have trusted her enough to tell her.

"Sabina's ill?" Trentwith shot out of the chair, and Harry forced him back.

"I don't know much. She was injured in an accident at the silk weavers. That's all I know. She seemed much recovered. As Ashton said, Oliver is secretive."

"My God, what have I done?" He clutched his head in his hands again as his shoulders slumped in defeat.

Camilla straightened, fighting the war waging within her between pity and disgust for the man in front of her. "You abandoned your own flesh and blood."

Trentwith lifted his head, meeting her glare. He started to speak, but obviously thought the better of it. His posture spoke of his resignation. "You're right. And I shall live the rest of my life in penance for it. But I must try to make amends. Lady Denby, will you appeal to him on my behalf?"

Camilla fought back the laugh. "He doesn't listen to me, and he's made it clear he wants nothing more to do with me. You heard him. Oliver is his own man. A complicated and proud man. You'll have to appeal to him yourself. I wish you luck, I truly do."

No longer able to stand idly by, she strode into the waiting area, opened the door to the clinic, and left, hoping to find Oliver and do what she could to ease his pain.

She tried his home first. Neither Tori nor Sabina had seen him. Camilla kept the news of Lord Trentwith to herself; it wasn't hers to tell. Next she tried nearby taverns, where the patrons made lewd remarks as she wove through the crowd seeking information.

The only other place she could think of was the gypsy camp, but the force of the rain had steadily increased, muddying the streets, and gusts of wind shot icy pellets sideways. A carriage would likely become stuck and traveling on horseback would be reckless.

She went home and prayed he had found sanctuary somewhere safe and warm. She paced the floor of the parlor, glancing at the clock on the mantle so often she wondered if the timepiece had stopped.

About to go mad from her frayed nerves, Stratton startled her when he appeared at the entrance of the room. "My lady, Dr. Somersby is here. He is . . . quite drenched, my lady. Should I show him in or send him away?"

Before she could answer, Oliver appeared behind the butler, indeed soaked through to the skin, his black hair plastered against his skull like a cap. A puddle formed at his feet from his dripping clothing. Stratton glared at him, his lips pressed tight and eyes narrowed, looking Oliver over as one might a feral cat.

"It's fine, Stratton. Have someone clean that up later. For the time being, please don't disturb me—no matter what."

The butler gave Oliver another appraising look, then nodded and left, closing the doors behind him.

"You're wringing wet. Come, remove your coat and stand by the fire." Camilla took a step toward him, then froze.

"I don't want this, do you hear me? I don't!" he bellowed.

She shook her head. "What? What are you talking about? What don't you want?"

"Any of this. I don't want to . . . feel this." His face distorted, displaying heart-rending anguish.

"You're hurt and angry. I would be, too."

"I'm not talking about that," he yelled.

The rage in his eyes frightened her. And she wasn't a woman who frightened easily.

"Then what?"

"You. I don't want it, but it's there . . . all the time." He beat his fist against his chest. "Eating at me, torturing me with what I can't have." He turned from her as if he couldn't bear to look at her any longer. His hands gripped the fireplace mantel as if he intended to tear it from the wall, his knuckles white, his head bowed. When his shoulders heaved soundlessly, she remembered the same action from Trentwith a few scant hours before.

She braced herself and stepped forward, touching him lightly on the arm. "Oliver, I can't help you if I don't understand what you're talking about."

He spun around so quickly she stumbled back, losing her balance. He snaked an arm around her waist, pulling her close and steadying her. His crystal blue eyes burned into hers. Why hadn't she noticed the resemblance before? The niggling sensation of familiarity now made perfect sense.

His hooded gaze, heated and dusky, dipped to her lips. What she had taken for rage she now understood as passion. Her fear shifted into something just as powerful.

"You. God help me, I want you. I don't want to want you. I hate what you stand for. The pride, the arrogance, the ability to use people and throw them away as if they were nothing but manure on your shoe."

She tamped down her growing frustration, keeping her voice at an even keel. "I'm a person, Oliver, not an institution."

"But you're part of it, so enmeshed in it you have become it. And I hate it."

"Do you hate Harry?"

He reeled back as if she had struck him. "No, but he's different. He despises the arrogance of society almost as much as I do."

"Yet he's part of it. Why is it different for him?"

When he didn't answer, she pressed on. "And Margaret, do you hate her?"

He shook his head.

"Then why me?"

The anger returned. "Because I don't love *them*. I can separate them. But you . . . I can't separate my feelings for you from my beliefs. You've become like a pestilence in me, and if I don't purge myself from it, it will kill me."

His grip around her waist tightened, and he pulled her flush against him, then tangled his other hand in her hair. Pins fell from her curls, musically tinkling against the marble floor, and the loose strands brushed down, tickling her neck and shoulders.

"I want you," he repeated, then crushed his mouth to hers with a ferocity that took her breath away. He attacked, plundered, pulled back, then captured them again.

The enticing scent of wood and lemon oil mixed with something more primitive created a fragrance uniquely him. Her knees buckled, but he pulled her upright, holding her firm.

He pulled back, his eyes penetrating hers. "Are you afraid?"

Her heart pounded like a galloping thoroughbred. "No."

"You should be." He kissed her again, this time more gently, but still with the hunger of a starving man. "I'm not one of your fancy gentlemen. I don't hold to false promises of honor. If you tell me to leave, I will do as you ask. But if I stay . . ."

The final words, though unspoken, were as crystal clear as his blue eyes.

"I want to feel something other than this numbness or pain. I want to feel alive again," she whispered, turning her face up to his.

"I have nothing to offer you."

"You have yourself. It's all I ask."

CHAPTER 23—SOULS BARED

L ike a man possessed, Oliver trailed hot kisses across her jaw, then down her throat, finding the soft flesh above her collarbone. The heady scent of lilac, so alluring, filled his nostrils. She moaned softly, and his lips twitched in satisfaction.

As ill-advised as it was, his desire compelled him, fogging his already muddled thoughts even more. He should release his hold on her, turn and leave, not looking back.

He tugged the sleeve down on her gown, exposing her shoulder. Running his fingertips over her soft skin, his gaze met hers and found the same passion that raged inside him. Her eyelids drooped, her rosebud mouth swollen from their kisses. Pink abrasions from his scruff of a beard marred her sensitive neck.

With his eyes fixed on hers, he reached behind her, his fingers finding the ties securing her gown. No animal, he needed—wanted —her permission.

"Tell me to leave," he whispered.

Her throat bobbed from the swallow she most likely forced. "No."

A single tug of the ribbon released the top of her gown, and his fingers made quick work of the second at her waist. The gown dropped, hanging loosely at her hips and revealing her chemise and stays. She shifted slightly, and it pooled at her feet.

His eyes roamed over her, taking in the delicate swell of her breasts and curve of her hips. His desire became near unbearable.

As he reached for her breast, she stopped him, and he groaned, expecting to be sent on his way.

Instead, she pulled his coat from his shoulders and down his arms, the wet fabric sticking to the sleeves of his linen shirt. She folded it neatly and draped it over the back of a chair near the fire.

Next she unbuttoned his waistcoat, the slow seductive motions driving him mad, and he wished to rip it from his body. When she removed his shirt, her gaze fell on the scar low on his abdomen, and her fingers traced the red welt with reverence.

"Knife wound," he said, answering her unspoken question, his voice gravelly with need. "Harry stitched me."

She stooped before him and kissed it, her tongue grazing the area by his navel. His arousal twitched in anticipation, and his eyes rolled back in his head when she stroked him over his trousers, her touch exerting the perfect amount of pressure.

He grasped her arms and pulled her upright, hurriedly unlacing and discarding her stays. In one quick motion, he lifted her to straddle his hips and moved toward the sofa.

"The floor," she said, her voice thick with passion.

He blinked, unsure he heard correctly. "The floor? It would be more comfortable—"

"No, the floor. Always wanted to . . ."

He laughed, amazed at how she surprised him. "As you wish, my lady."

Still holding her against him, he lowered them both to the floor, laying her down gently, then covered her with his body.

"You're still wet. Your trousers."

He pulled back. Moisture soaked her chemise as well. With a quick tug, he lifted it over her hips and pulled it over her head, tossing it aside. When he reached for the buttons on his fall, she stayed his hands and deftly slipped each button from its opening, freeing him.

He tugged his trousers down his hips, too impatient to remove his boots.

"Are you certain?" he asked, praying she wouldn't throw him out now.

Her eyes glazed with lust, and her eyelids grew heavy. She reached up and stroked his face, the gentle action a strange juxtaposition to their frenzied passion.

Somehow it slowed him as a tenderness filled his chest from her touch. A pop from the fireplace broke the silence of the room, and his head turned in its direction.

A tiny laugh, as musical as her singing voice, drew his attention back to her. He held her gaze as he tasted her lips, their kisses now tender, slow, and satisfying. She tasted minty, fresh and clean, and succumbing to the moment, he closed his eyes and breathed in her fragrance of lilac.

He wanted nothing more than to enter her, to fill her completely. But although he never claimed to be a gentleman, if he took her without first giving her pleasure, he would be nothing more than an animal.

As he trailed kisses down her throat, he toyed with the delicate nipple of her breast, teasing it with his fingers. The softness of her skin against his rough fingertips enthralled him, but also reminded him of her status—pampered and entitled. *Have I lost my mind?*

The thought fled him as she pulled at his hair and moved his mouth toward her breast.

She arched her back, and his lips curved in satisfaction at her low moans when his fingers teased the soft curls between her thighs.

The way she responded to him, her nails trailing down his back, then moving up to thread through his hair thrilled him. She was uninhibited, wild, free. Not at all the prim and delicate woman he'd expected—and he loved it.

He didn't simply desire her, although he'd never wanted a woman as much. Try as he might to put her out of his mind and bury his feelings so deep as to never be excavated, he'd failed miserably. He adored her, cherished her—loved her. With that admission, internal and private though it may be, something shifted in him. The truth became almost unbearable, because the real truth, the horrible truth was she'd never be his, regardless of their feelings.

He pushed it from his mind and hovered over her, bracing himself on his forearms so as not to crush her with his weight. As he stared into her brown eyes, so dark they appeared black, the passion burning in him became bittersweet, and he vowed he would make this coupling memorable—something he would cherish for the rest of his life.

Leaning down, he brushed her lips with his own, lightly at first but becoming more insistent. She grasped the back of his head, crushing her mouth to his, and their kiss became hot, needy— desperate, and he wasn't certain whose mouth plundered whose.

"Oliver," she whispered, her usually soprano voice now husky with desire.

"Impatient?" He laughed and nudged her nose with his, teasing, playful.

She answered him by lifting her hips and grabbing his buttocks. His proper English lady had become a hellcat. Unable to restrain himself any longer, at her insistence, he plunged into her, leaving him breathless.

The furious pounding of his heart beat in double time to the steady ticking of the clock on the mantel, and as he pressed close to Camilla, her own heart matched his in syncopated rhythm.

As they moved together, her fingers trailed along his back, playing him like the strings of his violin, coaxing sweet music from his soul.

He concentrated, praying he would last long enough for her to find completion. Slightly shifting and balancing on one hand, he lifted her thigh and angled her to the perfect position.

She broke their kiss, throwing her head back and gasping in pleasure. Her eyelids fluttered, and he knew she was close to finding her release.

Nails scraped his back, the brief sting of pain overshadowed by pleasure. With several strong thrusts, he brought her to completion.

She shuddered, her muscles clenching him in sheer ecstasy. His mind so muddled he barely recognized the words she uttered.

"I love you."

And with her declaration, he allowed himself his own release. As clarity returned to his mind, he knew that, lost in her arms, more than a physical joining had transpired between them. Secretly, in his heart, he answered, *I love you, too.*

CRADLED IN HIS ARMS, CAMILLA REMEMBERED HOW MUCH SHE adored the gentle aftermath of lovemaking. Almost as much as the heated passion itself—*almost.* A giggle escaped.

Oliver raised a brow, his serious face focused on hers as if no one else existed in the world. Perhaps at that moment, no one did. "I amuse you?" He trailed a finger down her arm, raising gooseflesh.

"You make me giddy. Like an empty-headed girl."

He rewarded her with that heart-stopping dimple. "And you make me run mad. They should lock me away in Bedlam for what I've done."

Regardless of his smile, her stomach dropped. "Do you regret it?"

"Not for a moment." As if to prove it, he leaned down and captured her mouth in a searing kiss.

The fire popped, and he rose to stir the embers to a full blaze, grabbing a covering from a chair before returning to her.

With tender care, he lowered the covering over her, then lay down, crawling under it beside her. "I must go soon. But for a while longer, I'd like to simply savor this feeling."

Her fingers played with the wiry, black hair on his chest, then flattened to run across the hard planes of his abdomen, drifting lower inch by inch.

His eyes squeezed shut, and he sucked in a shuddering breath and halted her hand. "Temptress. Tell the truth. It was *you* in the sea, luring men to their deaths."

She wanted to laugh, but she forced it down. They needed to discuss more serious matters. "Oliver, will you tell me? What happened with your father and mother—your childhood."

A muscle in his jaw twitched, and he rolled onto his back, pulling his heat away from her.

"Why? It's in the past."

"I want to know, to understand. After what we shared, don't you owe me the truth?"

Silence filled the room, the only sound the fire now roaring and popping, the rain beating against the windows.

She waited.

And waited.

He turned back, pulling her into his arms, into his warmth. "I don't remember much. And of course, what occurred before I was born, I only know what I was told. They met when she was a mere child—fifteen, and he was not much older. My grandmother did readings for the nobility, and she took my mother with her to dance. According to my mother, she met *him* at a house party where she and my grandmother were *entertainment*." He spat the words as if trying to purge the foulness from his mouth.

"They fell in love instantly." He sighed, shaking his head. "I'd discounted such things, but then"—he searched her face—"I met you."

The meaning of his words hung in the air, and her heart beat faster.

"It started as a simple flirtation, but he began seeking her out at the camp. She said they'd sneak off into the woods, sharing their hopes, dreams, and a few kisses."

He paused again, as if straining to draw his courage. "Eventually they shared *more*. When she discovered I was growing inside her, he promised he would marry her. Of course, that was impossible. My mother said his father—"

"Your grandfather."

His eyes bore into hers. "I don't claim him, just as he never claimed me. *His father*, the Earl of Trentwith, visited the camp offering money and support, but made it clear there would be no marriage."

No tears formed in his eyes, only hardness, and her own rage at the injustice dealt them twisted her stomach.

"I love my mother," he said. "But she was blinded by love and an unfailing belief that their love was *different*—that once his father was gone, they would be together."

His Adam's apple bobbed furiously, as if choking down the next words. "He kept returning to the camp, not often, but enough for her—for us—to believe his lies. When I was eight, my mother found herself expecting another child."

Camilla struggled to do the calculations, her mind too muddled with the barrage of information his tale imparted.

"Another Romani woman, who *entertained*," again he spat out the word, "at their parties, informed my mother of his engagement to a noble woman. In her grief, my mother refused to eat. She contracted a sickness, and in her weakened state, she lost the baby. When he appeared at the camp, seeking my mother out, my mother's people told him she had died in childbirth along with the child. But the truth was we had been cast out. They could forgive one indiscretion, but two—never.

"We moved into the poorest section of London, and my mother found work in a silk factory. My grandmother forwarded the money that had been set up in trust for my education by *his* father and then by *him*. I pleaded with my mother to use it to support us, but she refused, insisting I go to a boarding school."

Camilla pulled out of his embrace, leaning on an elbow above him. "Is that when you took the name Somersby?"

He barked the laugh, the sound ugly and harsh. "Yes. In shame of my heritage, fear for my life even." He shook his head as if disgusted with himself.

"But Victoria? She has your name. You said she wasn't Trentwith's daughter. Is Mr. Somersby Victoria's father? Did you take his name when he married your mother?"

"There is no *Mr.* Somersby, only Dr. Somersby. My mother

never married. My very birth made her undesirable. Roma are even more stringent about a woman's virginity than you English."

As if a curtain had been pulled back, revealing the secrets behind it, she understood.

"Victoria is your daughter," she said, as sure of the statement as she was her own name.

He smiled weakly, his hand brushing her cheek. "Yes. Are you shocked?"

"Not shocked. Puzzled perhaps. Why does she believe she's your sister?"

"Have you heard the phrase lesser of two evils?"

"Yes, Erasmus, then Chaucer."

"A learned woman. I knew my heart didn't stand a chance." His smile widened, then disappeared entirely. "At sixteen, I made the rash decision to confront my father and kill him."

She bolted upright. "Oliver, no!"

He pulled her back against his chest, stroking her arms and soothed her with a kiss.

"I went to a pub to drink some courage, but I only wound up drinking myself blind drunk. In my stupor, I told my plan to a serving girl and was stupid enough to mention my father was an earl. She talked me out of my plan and into her bed. In the Romani culture, sex outside of marriage is forbidden. As my first . . . encounter, I believed myself to be in love. I spent one month with her."

He exhaled as if trying to expunge a weight pressing on him internally. "My naiveté was more shameful than my ill-advised plan. When she spoke of having a family together, a strange gleam in her eye chilled me. It seems she was under the false belief that I was a legitimate heir, not a by-blow. But when she learned the truth, she cast me from her bed and her life.

"Nine months later, she showed up on our doorstep, thrusting the babe from her arms into mine, telling me the child was my problem."

A strange mix of pain and love swirled in his eyes. "One look at the tiny child and my heart was forever lost. So helpless, so trusting, so alone. Her own mother abandoning her as if she were nothing but a piece of rubbish to be thrown out into the street."

Empathy gripped Camilla's heart, realizing he too must have felt discarded and unwanted. "You believe she truly is your daughter?"

"How can you doubt it?"

She nodded. "It's true. I remember when I met her I thought she was a female replica of you."

"My mother and I discussed it and decided to rear Tori as her child. I was only seventeen, heading to university. My mother insisted I continue with my studies and pursue my dream of becoming a physician. We agreed it was best for Tori not to know about her mother. We fabricated a Mr. Somersby who died working on the docks. A deceased father seemed preferable to a mother who abandoned her own child."

"But Oliver, how can you stand it? I've seen the love you have for that child. Don't you think she has a right to know she has such a loving and caring father?"

"And lose the only mother she's known?"

"But she wouldn't lose Sabina, she'd still be there to love her and care for her as always."

She paused at the thought rising to her mind. Things had changed between them, but would it be enough? Could she hope for a future with him?

She forged on, praying he would accept what she offered. "If you marry, Victoria could have two loving parents."

He reeled back as if she'd slapped him. "Who would you have me marry?"

She pleaded with her eyes, sensing the moment the meaning of her words dawned on him.

He shot up from where he held her in his arms, grabbing his clothing and dressing in haste. Unintelligible words fell from his lips as he muttered more to himself than to her.

She rose to a sitting position, clutching the covering he'd so gently placed over her to her bare breasts. Time seemed to stretch in front of her, and she wondered if he'd ever turn to look her in the eye.

"Oliver?" she whispered his name.

He stilled, his back toward her. In slow motion, he turned to face her, his eyes distant as if a curtain had closed, separating them again. Breath trapped in her lungs as she waited.

Holding out his hand, he said, "Allow me to assist you in dressing."

With a gentleness breaking her heart, he laced her stays and tied her gown. "I'm afraid I am not much use with hair. My mother and Tori assist each other, but I shall attempt my best."

Finally, his use of *my mother* made sense. All pieces of the puzzle that was Oliver snapped into place, and the pain he'd buried deep within flowed into her as well.

Fingers, skilled in ways she now understood fully, worked her hair into a tidy array, pinning the curls into place. When he finished they lingered, gently stroking the back of them along the curve of her neck.

She turned toward the window to gage her appearance. Rain pelted against the glass, the streams of water marring her reflection.

"Now I must take my leave. I beg your forgiveness for my impetuousness. Please notify me if there are . . . consequences."

Removing his jacket from where it lay across a chair drying by the fire, he pulled it on, then quit the room, the closing snick of the door latch echoing the finality of his words.

CHAPTER 24—
CONFRONTATIONS AND
TRUTH

W hat in God's name had he done? Everything he hated about his father pointed an accusing finger back at him. He was no better than the man who had used his mother and thrown them both away. Guilt and shame slithered in his chest.

The look in Camilla's eyes—first the love, the trust, then the pain—would forever haunt him.

Turn around, you fool. Go back to her. Fall on your knees and beg her to marry you!

"No!"

Heads of people passing by swiveled at his vocal outburst. Like a mad man released from Bedlam, he stood in the pouring rain, his partially dried clothes becoming soaked through once more. He stumbled to the hackney stand and, barking his destination at the driver, climbed into the compartment of the carriage.

He needed time, a clear head, to decide his next step. Her words echoed in his ears, taunting him. *If you marry, Victoria could have two loving parents.*

He fisted handfuls of his hair, willing her proposal to cease its torment.

Home. At home he would find peace.

It seemed there would be no limit to his err in judgment that day. As he stepped into the entrance, shaking off the droplets of rain from his coat, a distinctive male voice drifted out from the parlor. Every nerve in his already frayed system buzzed. His gut hardened, tightening as if encased with bricks.

His pace quickened at the sound of a woman weeping. *If he has hurt her again, I will truly kill him with my bare hands.*

Nothing could have prepared him for the sight that awaited. Seated on the sofa, his mother wept against his father's chest while the man stroked her hair and back, whispering soothing words.

"Shush, my love. All will be well now."

The man's lying promises pierced Oliver like poison-tipped arrows.

"Get out!" Oliver bellowed.

His mother jerked from his father's arms. When she gazed at Oliver, the same slimy shame twisted in him. Her face appeared more radiant than he ever remembered. She sprang from her seat on the sofa. "Oliver, you don't understand."

"I understand well enough. He's here to feed you more lies and empty promises." The vision of Camilla lying on the floor by the fire surfaced, mocking his hypocrisy. He pushed it aside, arguing he had promised her nothing, yet knowing even that was a lie.

So taken aback by his father's presence in his home, he'd failed to notice Tori's absence. "Where is Victoria? Has she witnessed this unholy display of false affection?"

"Now, see here, Oliver," his father bolted from his seat on the sofa. "I will not allow you to speak to your mother in that manner."

"You'll not allow me? How dare you? You abandoned me and my mother, leaving me the sole caretaker of her and my daughter, and now you waltz in as if no time has elapsed."

"*Your* daughter?"

Oliver spun around at the sound of Tori's voice, small and trembling, and his blood chilled.

Her mouth formed a little O, matching her widening eyes. "Wha . . . what do you mean?"

"Tori, let me explain." He reached out to her, but she wriggled out of his grasp and raced off, tears streaming down her face.

Pulled in two directions, Oliver pivoted between Tori's retreating form and his father. The tumultuous nature of the day drained him of all strength, and he cast a pleading glance at his mother.

She placed a calming hand on his arm. "I'll go to her. Stay and speak with Charles. Allow him to explain."

The mere idea of giving his rakehell father the opportunity to explain anything seemed ludicrous. "I should plant you a facer for what you've done."

Trentwith held out his hands to the side in supplication. "Then go ahead if it gives you satisfaction. God knows I deserve it."

Like bees buzzing, the words flitted in Oliver's skull. The man admitted it? Hands fisted at his sides, Oliver could only stare.

"If you're not going to strike me, shall we sit, or do you prefer to stand?" Trentwith asked.

Oliver begrudgingly motioned toward the sofa, then took a seat in a wingback. "Say your piece and get out. At least I'll be able to tell my mother I listened."

Trentwith removed a handkerchief and wiped his brow, his hand shaking. "Very well. I'll not deny that deserting your mother and you was wrong. But Oliver, I loved her. I still love her."

Although he'd suggested they sit, Trentwith rose and paced the floor in front of Oliver. "You don't understand what it was like. Being the heir, the pressure from my father." He turned toward Oliver. "Your grandfather."

"I refuse to claim him as he refused to claim me."

"He regretted it, Oliver. On his deathbed, he told me about the trust he'd established for you . . . for your education. I didn't know it at the time, but he hired people to inquire about you, to gather information, to watch you."

He pulled out a flask and took a drink, then offered it to Oliver, who refused. "When I learned of your mother's second pregnancy, I told my father I planned to marry her. He threatened to cut me off, keeping me a virtual prisoner in my own home. Without my permission, during a party where one of your mother's people came to entertain, he announced my engagement to a viscount's daughter."

His face drawn, Trentwith seemed to have aged ten years in the course of the day. Threads of white spun through his dark hair, and fine lines crinkled around his eyes and mouth. "My wife had a sizeable dowry, and the estate needed funds. I had no choice. It was a loveless marriage, if that makes you feel better."

"It doesn't."

Trentwith nodded. "I have no heirs. Your mother was the one bright spot in my life. When they told me she died in childbirth, the child with her, seeing you became too painful. It was easier to continue to support you through your grandmother. The woman hated me, and I don't blame her, but she took my money."

His bloodshot eyes met Oliver's, and for a fleeting moment, compassion flared in Oliver's chest. "When I tried to correspond through Eva, her responses were cryptic at best. I had no idea you took another name. I don't blame you for hating me, but I'm asking, for your mother's sake, for the love you have for her, to tolerate me, and in time, perhaps forgive me."

"Tolerate you? For what? Do you plan to resume your relationship with my mother? If so, I will fight you with my last breath."

"I've asked her to marry me."

"You what?" Surely he hadn't heard correctly.

"It's true. I'll request a license immediately."

"You would marry a *gypsy*?" The vile name stuck in his throat, but he forced it out. "Subject yourself to gossip and censure? To be shunned by society?"

"I would marry the woman I love. If the *ton* doesn't like it, so be it. I've wasted enough years, wouldn't you say?"

He looked upon his father with new eyes. Who was this man before him? Not the villain who had haunted his nightmares as a child, but a broken, lonely man filled with regrets.

Muscles in Oliver's neck tightened. He would not relinquish the image of the demon who discarded people so carelessly.

"I might suggest the same to you, Oliver. What are your intentions toward Lady Denby?"

"I will not discuss her with you."

"She loves you, you know. I saw it in her eyes at the clinic. Don't toss love aside flippantly."

"As you threw my mother and me away?" He raked a hand through his hair. "This is too much. I must go to Tori and explain."

"My granddaughter. She's lovely, Oliver. You should be proud."

The compliment sat like a stone in Oliver's gut, and without responding, he quit the room in search of Tori.

Mournful sobs greeted him, tearing at his heart as he approached Tori's room. His mother sat on the bed next to the prostrate child, stroking her back and singing a soothing lullaby.

The words that had shaken him from his dreamlike state with Camilla taunted him. He stepped into the room and prepared for the hardest thing he'd ever done.

His mother raised her head, her own eyes rimmed red.

What a hellish day it had been for all of them—and yet the sweetness of love had mingled with the sorrow of his. The joy he'd experienced in his coupling with Camilla somehow overshadowed the grief.

"I haven't said anything. It would be best to come from you," his mother said, rising from the bed.

He nodded and took her place next to his precious daughter.

Tori buried her face in her pillow. "Go away! I don't want to see your face ever again." Her words cut him deeper than the sharpest scalpel, slicing through him into his very soul.

"I will never leave you. No matter what you shout at me. Or how angry you are. No matter how much you may hate me. I will never abandon you."

Tentatively, he held his hand over her, fearful she would jerk away from his touch. Summoning enough courage, he laid it gently against her head, and stroked her hair. "Allow me to explain. I will answer all of your questions truthfully."

With a sob, Tori rolled over to face him. The sadness in her eyes became almost more than he could bear. How much misery had his lies inflicted on those he loved?

"Mother is not my mother?" she asked.

"No. She is your grandmother, and she loves you dearly."

He removed his handkerchief and held it to Tori's nose. "Blow." The memory surfaced of offering his handkerchief to another female he loved, but it would have to wait. He could only handle one crisis at a time.

"Who is my mother? And where is she?"

These questions would prove more difficult. He'd prepared a speech in the event this day would come. One of a fairy tale love that ended in tragedy. But the time for lies had passed. Tori deserved the truth. "Her name was Edith, and I don't know where she is."

Tori watched him expectantly, and he continued. "I was only a lad. I believed myself to be in love, and that she loved me. Perhaps she did. However, I disappointed her, and she ended our . . . association. I didn't know I'd left her with child until she brought you to my door." He gazed into his daughter's eyes, cringing at the pain within and hoping to soften the news. "It was the best gift I've ever received."

"Then why tell me you were my brother?"

"As I said, I was young, unfit to raise a child. Your grandmother offered to rear you as her own, and I was grateful. It meant I could have you in my life, but protect you from knowing the origins of your birth."

"I'm a bastard."

Oliver flinched at the name that had haunted him his entire life. "I could lie and tell you I married your mother, but I won't. But that doesn't mean you are any less wanted."

"And the man downstairs, he's your father?"

With gentle fingers, he tucked a lock of Tori's dark hair behind her ear. "He is."

"Do you hate him?"

How could he answer her question and not condemn himself? "I did. I felt abandoned and unwanted. So I did everything in my power to make sure you always felt cherished and wanted—because you are."

"Will you tell me about my mother?"

He closed his eyes, breathing deeply to calm himself. "What would you like to know?"

"Was she pretty?"

A smile tugged at his lips. "Not as pretty as you."

"As pretty as Lady Denby?"

The odd squeezing sensation in his chest resurfaced. "No. Lady Denby is quite extraordinary."

"Do you love her? Lady Denby?"

What purpose would it serve to admit his feelings? To encourage hope not only in himself, but the one other person he loved more than life. "Does it matter?"

Tori's clear blue eyes searched his. "Yes. Maybe she could be my mother."

Camilla's words echoed again, the words that had him turn tail and run like a coward. *If you married, she could have two loving parents.* The ugly, slimy shame roiled in his chest. Tori deserved better than a coward, as did Camilla. He stroked his daughter's face. "You'd like that, would you?"

"Yes." She chewed her bottom lip, her brow furrowing.

"What else?"

"Are we gypsies? I heard you say it to the man—my grandfather."

"We are Romani. Some people call us gypsies."

"Are they bad?"

"No. They—we—are proud and noble people. But many don't understand, and they hate us for who we are."

"Will you tell me more about them?"

"If you wish. My grandmother—your great-grandmother is a wise woman. Perhaps she will help me decide the best course of action to take with Lady Denby. Would you like to meet her and our people?"

"Oh, yes, please." Her sobbing had ceased, replaced by the familiar, yet somehow different, affection in her gaze.

"I promise never to lie to you again, Tori. Am I forgiven?"

A yawn accompanied her nod. "Yes."

He rose and tucked the blanket around her slim body and shoulders.

As he prepared to leave, she grasped his sleeve. "May I call you Papa, Ollie?"

The name on her sweet lips became a balm to his soul, giving him hope. "I would like that very much, poppet." He bent and placed a light kiss on her forehead. "Now rest."

As he closed the door with a soft snick of the latch, he took a fortifying breath and made his way back to the parlor. Perhaps he should take a lesson of forgiveness and acceptance from his daughter.

CHAPTER 25—MASKS DISCARDED

Numbness drifted through Camilla's body, and she stared at the closed door. Like a spooked horse, Oliver had bolted as if the room had been on fire. He'd completely shut down at the mere suggestion of marriage.

Anger replaced disbelief at his parting words. *Please notify me if there are consequences.* Her hands curled into fists at her side. *How dare he!*

At least he'd had the decency to assist her in dressing. Had she truly become so wanton as to not be concerned what her servants would think of her disarrayed state? The vow to maintain decorum, to be above approach—so easily shattered by the lure of a man—no longer mattered. She strode out of the parlor past Stratton, issuing a curt order to send Rose, her lady's maid, to her room.

In silence, Rose redressed Camilla's hair and helped her into another gown, the unasked questions practically bubbling on her lips.

Camilla dismissed her, sending a prayer of thanksgiving that her servants had proven their loyalty and discretion. Her hand dropped to her abdomen as Oliver's words took root. *Consequences.* Such a horrible word men used for such a sacred and precious thing as life.

Was it possible? Could she be with child?

A painful memory surfaced, so similar to Sabina's tragic past. Although she'd only had five months of married bliss with Hugh before he left for the war, their lovemaking had been active and frequent. When she'd found herself with child, she'd been ecstatic, anxious to write and tell him the news.

Then the letter came, destroying her world. Buried in her grief, she'd lost the baby, wondering if she'd imagined the tiny life within her. No one knew. It was a sorrow she'd never shared with anyone, not even her parents. She'd resigned herself to never experience the joy of having a child, building walls to protect herself against the emotions that still raged raw inside her.

Pockets had chipped through those walls, his own little heart reaching through to touch hers. But as much as she loved him, she hadn't nurtured him with her body, felt him quickening in her womb.

It shouldn't matter—and yet it did.

What would Oliver do if they had created a life together? Surely he wouldn't permit another bastard to be brought into the world, not with the pain he himself endured, and how he had protected Victoria.

She paced the floor beside her bed. If he proposed, would she accept a marriage based solely on obligation? *No!* She would not trap him into an arrangement he did not truly desire. He might grow to resent her and possibly the child.

Yet he doted on Victoria, his love for her clear. Would their child be any different?

"Arghh!" She pulled at her hair, undoing Rose's handiwork.

She must give him time, make him understand no obstacle would be too great for them to face—together. That their love could overcome anything.

But if she could not convince him and she found herself pregnant, she would go away to have the child in secret, raising him or her as a ward like Pockets. A bitter taste rose at the idea she would be forced to deny her own child, driving home the pain Oliver had endured for the past ten years with Victoria.

Determined it would not come to that, she sat at her escritoire to pen a letter, conveying everything she held in her heart. She had never been one to beg, but she would be damned if she'd allow him to toss what they had aside as if it were no more than chaffs of wheat.

The pen poised above the parchment as she struggled to form the words without sounding like a needy child pleading for affection. She still had her pride.

The paper remained as blank as the expression on Oliver's face when he bade her goodbye. Finally scribbling what she hoped presented a clear and logical argument, she folded it, sealed it, and rang for a footman to deliver it.

❧

TWO DAYS PASSED WITHOUT WORD FROM OLIVER. EACH TIME Camilla entered or even walked by the parlor, she envisioned him, standing in front of her, soaked to the skin, burning for her as she had burned for him. His mouth hot and hard on hers, their passion heating the floorboards.

Why did he remain so ominously silent? Had everything she believed about him, about his feelings, been a lie? Even Pockets failed to cheer her, try as he might. And although his playing had indeed improved as Oliver had predicted, each squeak of the violin only stabbed at her heart as if the bow itself pierced her skin, each note reminding her of Oliver's skilled touch.

Her nerves had become so on edge that each time Stratton made an appearance in the doorway, she practically catapulted from her seat in the hope that Oliver would appear behind him. Even the understanding in her butler's perceptive gaze became unbearable as he would shake his head and then announce dinner.

The scrimshaw pendant bearing the siren upon the rocks became a talisman, and her fingers rubbed against its surface so often, she feared she would destroy the image and ruin the one thing Oliver had given her.

No amount of coaxing and pleading from her father or

Margaret was able to lift her from the darkness that engulfed her. Only once before had she been in the depths of such despair. As she gazed at the portrait of Hugh in his dress uniform, a cry of fury rose in her throat. How could life be so cruel to take not one man, but two from her after such a brief span of time together?

A delicate bone china cup bore the brunt of her rage as she picked it up from its resting place on the table and hurled it toward the fireplace.

"Have I come at a bad time?"

She spun toward the deep voice, hope rising in her heart, then crashing and shattering as surely as the broken pieces of porcelain now littering the fireplace hearth.

"Lord Trentwith. I didn't see you."

"Obviously," he said. He darted a glance toward the broken cup and took a step back. "Your butler suggested I announce myself."

He turned toward the hall. "Is the man suddenly fearful of announcing guests?" Sadness shone in his eyes, even though he offered a pleasant smile.

With a quick swipe across her cheek to remove the dampness, she donned the mask of proper English hostess. "Only fearful of disappointing me, I believe. Why are you here?" The question came out more sharply than she'd intended.

His dark brows lifted, indicating her bluntness had not gone unnoticed. "I came to ask for your assistance, but perhaps now is not a good time. I beg your forgiveness for the intrusion."

Sickly shame at her rudeness soured her stomach. Had she thrown out her manners? "I beg your pardon, Lord Trentwith. Please have a seat. How may I be of assistance?" If nothing else, she could gaze on the visage so like her beloved's. How had she not seen it before?

"It's not a small favor. I'd hoped you'd intercede on my behalf with Oliver. His mother and I are to be married, and Oliver wants no part of it. It's breaking Sabina's heart. He will not speak with me, Lady Denby, and has told his mother he will not step foot in my home."

"Can you blame him?" She cringed at her continued bluntness, yet a modicum of satisfaction on Oliver's behalf expanded in her chest.

"No. I cannot." He sighed, the sadness aging him. "It's naïve of me to hope for us to be a family, to live together in my home. Yet I do wish it, to repair the damage I've done."

"I don't know how you think I could help. Oliver won't speak with me either."

The sadness emanating from him, now turned to despair as Trentwith's body seemed to close in on itself. "Then it's much worse than I feared." He shook his head. "His stubbornness and pride surpasses even my own father's."

Pockets' cheerful voice rang through the hall. "Poppy!"

Could this day become any worse? The idea of facing both Oliver's father and her own on the same day, struggling to maintain decorum when all she wanted to do was weep herself to sleep, pushed her close to the breaking point.

With Pockets close behind, her father burst into the room, his face pale. "Have you seen Dr. Somersby?" His eyes darted to Trentwith, his address curt. "I beg your pardon, Trentwith, Stratton failed to tell me my daughter had a caller."

"What is it, Father? You appear distraught."

"Do you remember what I told you I'd overheard at White's? About the gypsy encampment?"

Trentwith bounded to his feet. "What about it?"

Flustered, her father's gaze danced between them, as if seeking permission.

"Father, Lord Trentwith is Oliver's father. Whatever you have to say, you may say in front of him."

As if a strong wind had knocked him over, her father's body fell to the sofa, and, removing his handkerchief, he wiped his brow.

Pockets stared wide-eyed. "Whaaa?"

"Has something happened at the camp?" Camilla attempted to bring the focus back to the reason for her father's visit.

"Lord Cartwright told me his valet said a group of men have planned a raid on the camp, to clear it. Apparently someone claimed the gypsies were taking work away from the townspeople."

Camilla's hand involuntarily lifted to her throat, attempting to stifle the panic surging. "When? Did he say when? We must warn them."

"This evening."

"No!" Trentwith shouted, his eyes now wild. "Sabina said Oliver planned to take Victoria to meet Eva this evening."

"Perhaps they haven't left," Camilla said. "Oliver stays late at the clinic. We may have time to stop them, to warn the others."

Pockets pulled at her skirts. "Mama, will they hurt Tori?"

Trentwith's head spun toward her. "He calls you Mama?"

How dare he question me? "Do you object to a child needing a parent?"

Holding his hands up defensively, Trentwith flinched. "No, of course not. It's simply . . . I can see why Oliver loves you."

Trentwith's words clung to her mind like honey to the comb.

"He said he loves me?" Hope, like the wings of a tiny bird, fluttered faintly in her chest.

"He didn't have to. His face betrays him whenever your name is mentioned. I pleaded with him not to repeat my mistakes. I see my words have fallen on deaf ears." His gaze rose to meet hers. "Perhaps I've misjudged and you do not return his affection? Have you broken his heart, Lady Denby?" No trace of anger or malice lingered in his voice.

"It is I who am left broken-hearted, my lord."

With another tug at her skirts, Pockets brought them back to the matter of utmost importance. "Mama, Tori!"

"We'll find her, Pockets . . . and Oliver. Don't worry."

"I'm coming with you," her father said, rising from the sofa.

"All of us, then," Trentwith said. "My carriage is large enough and has four strong chestnuts."

With a final word to Stratton to detain Oliver on the off chance he should call, they hurried from Camilla's townhouse, heading first to the clinic.

She prayed they would be in time.

❧

Oliver assisted Tori from the hackney carriage and held her hand as they wove their way through the camp to his grandmother's wagon. Curious eyes followed them, some of the women nodding in greeting and recognition, and he tipped his hat in return.

"Ollie, I mean, Papa, is she nice?"

A smile tugged at his lips at the image of his acerbic grandmother, who was tough as leather on the outside but had the softest heart he'd ever known. "She is if she likes you."

Tori's eyes widened. "Will she like me?"

"No," he teased. "She will love you."

"Oh, you." She swatted his arm, then shot him an apologetic glance. "I'm sorry. It's wrong to hit your papa, isn't it?"

"Not if he deserves it. Consider me thoroughly chastised."

The aroma of roasting meat drifted on the early autumn breeze. A rosy glow from the setting sun cast magical shadows over the tents and wagons as people prepared their evening meals.

He tapped on the door to his grandmother's wagon and whispered to Tori, "Call her Mami. It means grandmother in Romani. That will win her over."

The door creaked open, and his grandmother's face brightened, her smile growing even wider upon seeing Tori. "Have you brought a visitor, Oliver?"

He stepped inside, kissing her cheek. "I have, Mami. This is Victoria."

"Pleased to meet you, Mami." Tori performed a perfect curtsy. Camilla would have been proud, and Oliver's heart squeezed at the thought.

"She knows," he said, the brief words conveying volumes.

His grandmother gathered Tori in her arms, hugging her tightly. "I've been waiting for this day, my little one. Your father is a stubborn man. It's taken him long enough. Now, come, come. Our meal is almost ready."

Grateful for the distraction, Oliver mentally rehearsed his prepared speech, withholding his news until the proper time. After playing his grandmother's favorite song on his violin, he placed the instrument aside. Tori had stretched out on his grandmother's bed, her full stomach making her drowsy.

His grandmother retrieved her pipe, filling it with the drug she insisted eased her pain.

"Must you smoke that with Tori present?" His attempt to keep the scolding tone from his voice failed.

She raised a wiry gray brow. "Very well, but you may need to pry me from the chair without it." Rather than light it, she chewed on the stem.

"I'm not so certain your reason for smoking is to relieve the stiffness in your joints."

She answered with a cackling laugh, then narrowed her eyes on him. "Your lady didn't seem to mind when she visited."

He'd hoped to postpone this particular topic of conversation. "She's not my lady."

"And yet, you knew immediately who I meant." Her clouded eyes studied him like a bird of prey preparing to descend upon its evening meal.

"Of course I knew. How many aristocratic ladies have come to your door seeking information about me?"

"For a Gadje, I like her. She has spirit and courage."

Unable to restrain the smile tugging at his lips, he agreed. "She does indeed."

"Enough to withstand pressure from her people?"

Could she? In his mind, Camilla Denby could conquer giants. Hadn't she done so to his unreachable heart?

"You said she's not your lady, but do you wish it?"

The memory of his moment of passion with Camilla raced through his mind. *Yes, I wish it.* "Wishing for something that cannot be is folly, Mami. I've put her out of my mind."

"Your face betrays your feelings, Oliver. Will you allow something as insignificant as class to stand in the way of your happiness?"

"I can't believe you of all people are asking that. After everything that happened with Mother."

"You are not your mother, and Lady Denby is not your father. You have a choice, Oliver. Your mother did not."

He swallowed, preparing himself. "Mami, about that."

She lowered the pipe from her mouth.

"Trentwith has returned. He has asked Mother to marry him."

As if suddenly becoming thirty years younger, she sprang from her seat. "Impossible."

He shook his head. "I would have said the same thing had I not heard him tell me himself." He searched his grandmother's eyes. "I cannot forgive him, but I'm hoping you will forgive her. She misses you."

All the youthful vigor she'd exhibited moments ago dissipated as quickly as morning dew on a hot summer's day. "You think I don't miss her?" Tears welled in her eyes. "When she left, she took a piece of my heart with her."

"You threw her out. Threw me out."

"No." She shook her head, wisps of her hair falling loose from the kerchief on her head. Tears welled in her eyes, and her voice shook with emotion. "It was the way. Not my choice. As a woman, I had little say in the matter."

"And now? As an elder, you have a power over the community."

Silence settled within the confines of the small wagon, and she became pensive. With a groan, she rose, moving toward the bed where Tori rested, and placed her gnarled hand on his daughter's head. "She reminds me of you." She lifted her gaze and waved a hand. "Not only in appearance, but in spirit. She has a Romani heart. I should like to get to know her better."

"As your great-granddaughter or as the daughter of the doctor who visits you?"

He didn't intend to wound with his words, but she flinched nonetheless. She locked eyes with him. "Let us rectify that immediately. Come."

As they descended her wagon to the camp outside, she called one of the men, requesting him to assemble the people. Curious eyes studied Oliver as they waited for the gathering crowd.

"What is it, Eva?" one of the younger men asked, speaking in Romani. "Is this man bothering you?"

"This man, who you all know as a doctor, is my grandson. This is Oliver, Sabina's son. The child who arrived with him is his daughter, Victoria. They are my family."

Hushed murmurs rose from the group as heads bowed together in consultation. One of the elderly men approached, his hand gripping a crooked branch he used as a cane.

He shook his finger at her. "Many are too young to remember, to know, but I do, Eva. Are you asking that we accept them back? To forgive her transgressions? To ignore our traditions, our way of life?"

"I'm asking you to show mercy for my grandson and his daughter. To allow me to see my daughter, even if she is not received back into the community."

A woman as old as Eva pushed her way through the crowd and stood by the old man. "My husband is old and quickly forgets what it was like to be young, and although I'm almost as old, I remember. Why punish someone for following their heart, no matter how foolish it might have been?"

"My mother only wishes to see her own mother. She and my father are to be married."

"A little late," the old man said and received a solid swat to his arm from his wife.

"Let the boy speak."

Oliver hadn't been called a boy in ages. "Although I've yet to forgive him, he insists circumstances prevented him from marrying my mother when she was carrying me. I, too, have made mistakes, have let differences get in the way of not only my happiness, but that of those I love. Is it not time for healing between the Romani and the English?"

A strange rumbling rose in the distance, the sound like continuous thunder. As it grew nearer, angry voices filled the gap of what he recognized now as wagon wheels and horses' hooves.

The crowd before him scattered as people raced to their tents and wagons. His grandmother grasped him by the arms. "Take Victoria and leave at once. This doesn't bode well."

"I won't leave you. I've run away from who I am long enough."

CHAPTER 26—VIOLENCE AT THE CAMP

P iled in Lord Trentwith's carriage, the tiny band tried the clinic first. They rushed in to find Harry escorting the last patient of the day from a treatment room.

"Please tell me Oliver is still here." Camilla's words tumbled out before Harry could even say hello, the panic rising in her throat.

Harry guided the patient, a middle-aged woman, out of the clinic and closed the door behind her. "No. He requested to be dismissed early and left some time ago. Why?"

"We expect an uprising at the gypsy encampment," her father said, filling Harry in on what they knew.

"Perhaps he's still at home," Harry suggested, his voice hopeful, belying the concern on his face.

"We should check," her father said.

"And if he's not. we've wasted valuable time," she argued.

"She's right," Trentwith said. "Perhaps if we divide our forces? Ashton, if you and Harcourt could proceed to Oliver's home, make certain Sabina is safe, Lady Denby and I will head to the encampment."

She gazed at Trentwith in amazement.

"I knew you would insist," Trentwith said, his weak smile reminding her so much of his son.

Her father shook his head. "Camilla, it could be dangerous."

"I'll protect her, Harcourt. I promise on my life."

"We're wasting time." Her forceful reminder snapped the men to attention. "Harry, would you take Pockets with you? Perhaps leave him with Sabina where he'll be safe?"

"Of course. Once we've checked at Oliver's, we'll meet you at the camp," Harry said. "If he's at home, he'll still want to know what's happening."

They boarded their separate carriages, and she prayed they would arrive in time.

The sun, which had drifted low in the sky when they'd set out for the clinic, now disappeared behind the horizon in a shower of reds and purples, and the moon cast ominous shadows through the trees as the carriage made its way out of town.

Camilla's mind drifted back to the night she'd first ventured this way. So much had changed. The man whom she first detested now held her heart, her very soul in his hands.

She couldn't lose another love. She wouldn't.

The carriage slowed and came to a halt, the coachman descending. "I can't get any closer, sir." The man appeared as nervous as Langley had been. She couldn't blame him.

Trentwith assisted her out of the carriage. "Stay close to me. I only wish I had my pistols. If things become violent, return to the carriage immediately."

What good could they do against an angry mob, armed only with their wits and words of reason? Very little. God help them.

Abandoned wagons cluttered the dirt road as they approached the camp. Fire from torches lit the night as men raised their voices in angry shouts.

Panic seized her, and she cast a worried glance toward Trentwith, whose face appeared as hard as steel.

What if they were too late?

CHAOS ERUPTED AROUND OLIVER AS THE ANGRY MOB OF TOWNSFOLK shouted filthy slurs and threats. He pushed his grandmother behind him to shield her, the bile rising in his throat at the hateful words. The mob waved torches toward the tents in menacing arcs.

"Dirty gypsies," one man shouted. "Let's burn the filth. This is our land, and we're taking it back."

Oliver scanned the mob, which comprised both upper class and common working men, none of whom appeared familiar. He held out his hands, in an attempt to calm them. "Be reasonable. We don't mean you any harm. Leave us be."

"Why should we?" a man with one arm said. "You keep stealing what little work we 'ave along with anything else you can get your thievin' 'ands on."

A man in a tattered shirt pushed through the crowd toward Oliver. "I know you! You're the doctor at the clinic. 'Ere treating the filthy savages, doctor? Better check your pockets before you leave."

Cackling laughter followed the insulting remark, pushing Oliver over the edge.

"I'm here because I'm Romani."

The man cocked his head. "You mean you're one of *them*?" He took a threatening step forward.

Straightening to his full height, Oliver faced him. "I am. And I'm proud to say so."

The man's eyes widened in horror. "Men, we've been lettin' a filthy gypsy treat us. No tellin' what disease 'e's given us."

"I says we 'ang 'im!" another man shouted, spittle flying from his mouth.

One of the better dressed men pressed forward. "Now, men, let's not get carried away. We're only here to clear the camp, not murder people."

"It ain't murder. It's clearin' the vermin."

A handful of Romani men raced forward to stand by Oliver's side. Fistfights broke out as the Romani men fought to protect themselves from the mob.

"Who's got the rope?" someone yelled.

Within seconds, the men pounced, grabbing Oliver by the arms.

With a fierce kick, he forced one of the men to the ground. A blow to his head from behind dropped Oliver to his knees. He fought to remain conscious, the blackness narrowing his vision like a tunnel. They yanked him to his feet, restraining him again. He struggled, attempting to free himself, but the mob outnumbered him.

"Go to Tori. Keep her safe," Oliver yelled over his shoulder at his grandmother.

She'd never moved so quickly as she rushed back to the wagon where Tori lay sleeping. Oliver squeezed his eyes shut in a prayer of protection for his daughter. A heaviness sat like a stone in his gut at what this would do to her even if she survived. They'd only begun their relationship as father and daughter. Now hatred and prejudice would strip it away from her.

They wrenched Oliver's neckcloth away, exposing his bare skin. A noose slipped over his head, the stench of rot from the rope stinging his nostrils and the roughness scratching against his throat. Someone brought a horse over and forced him into the saddle and bound his wrists behind his back. Then, leading him to a tree, they threw the end of the rope over a sturdy branch, tying it tight.

Several other men began setting the tents on fire with their torches. People screamed and ran for their lives, others ran to the river, scooping buckets of water to put out the flames. The air became thick with smoke, creating a curtain between him and those trying desperately to save their belongings.

As he sat helpless in the saddle, he squeezed his eyes shut and brought forth the images of the women he loved. *Mami, Mother, Tori, Camilla.* His mind held on to the last as a drowning man would hold on to a lifeline. If he'd only told her he loved her. Regret, cold and sharp, cut at him. He'd been such a fool, a prideful fool, wasting precious time.

Something cold slipped into his hands, and his fingers curled around a sharp blade. Startled, he opened his eyes and twisted in the saddle to peer behind him. A man, well-dressed, with a slight hook nose gave an imperceptible nod, but didn't meet his gaze.

Too absorbed in their hate, the men surrounding him took no notice as they continued to shout slurs and threats.

Finally catching his savior's eye, Oliver mouthed the words *thank you*. Fortunately, whoever had bound him was unskilled in sailor's knots, as the one securing his hands proved loose enough to slip the tip of the knife through a small opening. He began sawing feverishly, praying he wouldn't drop the blade. If he could free his hands, he might have a fighting chance. Although small, the knife served its purpose and soon the rope began to fray and break.

Fire continued to rage in the camp around him, and horror gripped him when someone threw a torch on the steps of his grandmother's wagon. Flames licked the seasoned firewood lying at the doorstep, orange tongues reaching dangerously close to the dried kindling resting nearby.

"No!" he shouted, drawing unwanted attention back to him. He kept his hands behind his back, the rope now hanging loosely. A quick snap of his wrists would free him, but he waited for the right moment.

The horse shimmied and danced on the spot, spooked by the fire and smoke, and pawed nervously with its hooves at the muddy ground beneath. With the noose fastened securely, any sudden movement could send him flying off the saddle and snap his neck. He pressed his calves tighter, keeping himself secure as the horse whinnied in agitation. But only so much play remained in the rope above him, and if the horse were to bolt, he would breathe his last.

Blood rushed through him, his head near ready to explode with fear and panic as one of the men who'd bound him approached. Moonlight lit the whites of the man's eyes, revealing hate and malice. Oliver's time had run out. With a final prayer, he prepared himself to meet his fate. He called forth Camilla's face again, the beauty of it giving him a strange peace.

It may have been a hallucination, a wish granted to a dying man, but when he opened his eyes, he swore he saw her racing toward him as if he'd summoned her from thin air.

☙❧

Unsure what to expect, Camilla hurried behind Trentwith into the camp. Tents burned, people screamed. Smoke blurred her vision, the sting of it bringing tears to her eyes. A man sat on a horse with a noose around his neck, the end tied to a tree branch.

Dear God.

She blinked and gasped as she recognized the man about to be hanged.

"Oliver!" Not heeding Trentwith's directive to stay behind him, she shoved past and rushed forward.

The nervous movements of the horse upon which Oliver sat intensified his precarious position. She pushed against the crowd, fighting her way toward him. Hands grabbed at her, the sleeve of her pelisse ripping loose from the shoulder.

Trentwith followed on her heels. "Lady Denby, I beg of you, stay back."

Without turning, she shouted, "Can't you see? They have Oliver. We must get to him."

Someone grabbed her by the waist, pulling her off her feet, his mud-caked hand covering her mouth. The odor of his unwashed body gagged her.

Trentwith planted a facer on the man, who released his grip on her. She stumbled back, and Trentwith steadied her. "Come," he said, taking her by the hand. "Together."

As he pushed through the crowds, landing blows as needed, stony determination etched his face. Regret and love shone in his eyes as they fixed upon his son's form.

Breath trapped in her lungs when a man approached Oliver, his intentions clear as he raised a hand to slap the horse's hindquarters. She called out again, "Oliver!"

His head turned, and his eyes widened in surprise but quickly turned to fear. "Camilla! You must leave at once!" Oliver's gaze darted toward his father.

"We're not leaving, son."

The man preparing to send Oliver to his death with a strike to the horse stopped. "Son? Grab another horse, men, we've got ourselves another gypsy passing himself as one of us."

With a commanding voice, Trentwith boomed, "I am not a gypsy. I am Charles Ravenscroft, ninth Earl of Trentwith. I demand you cease this violence and release my son immediately or face the consequences."

The man cast a look to the others around him, then made an exaggerated bow. "Well, your high-and-mighty lordship, since you is demanding us to stop, I expect we should heed your warning. What do you say, men? Should we all go home and have tea and crumpets?"

His rioters-in-arms exchanged quizzical glances, then broke out in laughter.

Camilla's blood chilled.

With a swift slap to its hindquarters, the man sent the horse underneath Oliver racing forward and Camilla's heart to her throat.

Pandemonium broke out in the already chaotic scene. Events blended together in one giant blur, yet occurring as if in slow motion.

Before being completely pulled from the saddle, Oliver's hands reached up, miraculously grabbing the line of the noose above his head and attempting to lift himself from the pull of gravity. A dark-haired man scrambled forward, ducking under Oliver's legs and getting them on his shoulders to reduce the tension on the rope.

Trentwith fought his way toward Oliver, punching and kicking anyone who stood in his way, and Camilla followed in his wake. She skidded to a halt when she caught a good look at the man supporting Oliver.

"Nash! What are you doing here?"

His face red with strain, Lord Nash glared at her. "What does it look like?"

Trentwith shimmied up the tree as if he were a boy of ten rather than a man in his forties, then frantically worked on the knot tying the rope to the tree limb.

"The knife," Nash called. "Throw him the knife."

Moonlight flashed on the blade as Oliver removed a hand from the rope above him and tossed the knife to his father. A man moved forward to stop their efforts, and Camilla elbowed him in the stomach, stomped on his foot, then gave him a sharp jab to the chin with her fist.

"Remind me to never cross you," Nash said, his brow furrowed in concentration from the strain of Oliver's weight.

"Stop this at once!" a voice bellowed, and Camilla turned to discover Harry, her father, and a group of Bow Street Runners sprinting toward the camp.

Like rats racing from the waters of a sinking ship, the crowd scattered in an attempt to disperse. Some succeeded, the runners, Harry, and her father capturing those less fortunate.

With a snap, the rope holding Oliver broke in two, and he dropped to the ground, landing on top of Lord Nash. Camilla rushed forward, throwing herself to the ground beside him.

"Oh, my darling." She pulled the noose from his neck, the skin raw and red.

Harry ran over and skidded to a halt as Lord Nash brushed himself off and stood. "Nash, if you're involved in this melee, I swear by all that's holy, you'll pay." He grabbed Nash by the arms to detain him.

Nash wrenched out of Harry's grasp, pushing him back. "For once in your self-righteous life, you're wrong, Ashton. I'm here to help and stop the bloodshed."

"A likely story." Harry huffed.

"It's true," Oliver croaked, bringing everyone's attention back to what mattered.

Harry dropped to his knees beside him. "Oliver, can you move?"

With Harry's assistance, Oliver stumbled to his feet on unsteady legs. Urgency painted his face. "Tori . . . my grandmother." He choked the words out, his voice harsh, then pointed toward the wagon. Flames lapped at the sides of the wooden home, the colorful paint peeling and charring to blackened soot.

Smoke clogged Camilla's lungs and stung her eyes as she leapt from Oliver's side and ran toward the wagon, panic rising in her chest. Footsteps sounded behind her, and she turned to find her father.

"Camilla, you can't go in there!"

"Tori and Eva are in there. We must get them out."

As if sensing her determination, he gave his head a reluctant nod. "We have to protect ourselves. Give me your pelisse." He motioned with his hands. "Hurry."

She shrugged out of the torn garment at the same time he removed his own coat. After she handed it to him, he raced over, throwing a bucket of water on the garments. *What is he doing?*

"Hold it over your mouth as we go inside."

We? "Father, no!"

"If you insist on doing this foolhardy thing, I'll be damned if I'll allow you to go in alone. Now, we're wasting time."

Carefully ascending the steps ahead of her, he swatted at the flames with his wet coat, clearing a path large enough for them to pass. He kicked the door open, a feat surprising for a man his age, but she'd never been so proud—and frightened.

"Over your mouth, Camilla." He held his own coat over his mouth in demonstration, then entered the smoke-filled wagon.

Unable to see through the thick layer of smoke, she called out, "Tori! Eva! Where are you?"

The hacking cough she remembered from her visit to the old woman echoed in the small space. With her pelisse held against her mouth with one hand, she reached out with the other, feeling her way forward. Even the outline of her father had blurred.

"Over here, Camilla!" Tori's voice cried out, her own coughs ragged and faint, "Help us!"

"I'm coming, my darling." She bumped against the table where she'd sat and had tea only months ago and let out an unladylike curse.

"They're here, under the bed!" her father yelled.

On her hands and knees, Camilla crawled forward, the body of her father taking shape as he knelt in front of the bed. Two ornate doors had concealed them in the small crawl space under the raised bed. He pulled out Tori first, and Camilla held the girl against her.

"Take this," she said, lifting part of her pelisse toward Tori. "Place it against your mouth."

"I've got the grandmother," her father said. "We need to get out."

As Camilla took a step forward, Tori collapsed against her. She picked the child up and forced the pelisse against Tori's face. From the exertion of lifting and carrying the girl, and without the aid of the wet garment to aid her own breathing, Camilla struggled to pull air into her lungs. Thick clouds of smoke disoriented her. If she could only find the door.

Finally, as if answering her prayer, a light shone, illuminating the open doorway. She stumbled forward, every ounce of strength holding onto the precious child in her arms. She would save her for Oliver if it took her last breath.

When she grew closer, she realized what she'd thought was a light, was fire burning against the doorframe.

Blackness threatened to draw her under, but she fought against it. Tori's delicate hand pushed the wet pelisse against Camilla's mouth, providing blessed relief from the smoke-filled air.

"We must move quickly, Camilla," her father said, his own voice laced with panic. "Follow my voice."

The tears welling in her eyes were not from the smoke alone, but from what he did. He sang to her, a song she loved as a child, and she followed his voice as if he were the Pied Piper. Her feet like lead, she trudged forward, toward the open, burning doorway. The heat seared her face, and the fire singed her clothes. The smell of burning hair sickened her. Was it her own, her father's, Tori's, Eva's?

Wood splintered under her feet as she descended the stairs of the wagon. A step gave way, sending her stumbling forward. She braced herself, barely remaining upright before regaining her footing outside and releasing Tori from her arms. Something heavy slammed against her, throwing her to the ground and covering her. She opened her eyes to find Oliver lying on top of her.

"Forgive me. You were on fire."

250

OLIVER STARED IN WONDER AT THE WOMAN LYING BENEATH HIM. Soot darkened her face, strands of her hair stuck out in disarray, the edges singed, her clothing ruined.

"Father? Eva?" she asked, panic rising in her voice.

"Safe," he answered. "You risked your life to save my daughter. I'm not sure whether to kiss you or throttle you. If I'd lost either one of you . . ." Emotion clogged his throat, preventing the words from exiting.

"I'd prefer the former," she said, giving a quick laugh before lapsing into a coughing fit.

He rolled off of her, then helped her to her feet. "In good time, my lady, in good time. At the moment there is something I must say to you."

"Oliver, if you're going to argue about our differences yet again, it will be I who throttles you." She poked a finger in his chest.

Life with Lady Camilla would never be dull, he'd give her that much. He grinned. "No. It's not that."

"Then what?" Her glare made him love her all the more.

He paused for dramatic effect and because he knew it would vex her to be kept waiting, then stared into her eyes. He wanted to burn this moment into his memory.

"Well?" She huffed.

"I love you."

She blinked, giving him a sliver of satisfaction. Then with a quirk of her lips, she said, "I know."

CHAPTER 27—AFTERMATH

O liver and Harry assisted the injured, including those who had come to destroy and murder. Many of the mob grumbled when Oliver treated them. He may have been a little less gentle with the marauders, but he reminded himself of his oath. He was a physician first.

As things settled down in the camp and the Bow Street Runners had taken the rioters into custody, Oliver approached Lord Harcourt who moved through the burned out encampment, offering words of comfort and assistance in any way he could.

"Sir, might I have a moment?" Oliver asked, pulling him aside.

Harcourt studied him, his eyes full of compassion. "Dr. Somersby. You should rest. You're not fully recovered from this ordeal yourself."

Oliver would be proud to call this man his father-in-law. "There will be time for that. First, I wish to thank you for risking your own life and saving my grandmother."

Oliver followed Harcourt's gaze to where Camilla tended to Tori and the fierce old woman he loved. They were certainly a pair.

"No need. My motives weren't entirely selfless. A father's duty is to protect his daughter, is it not?"

Oliver understood that completely. "Yes. Sir, about that. I have a matter of importance to discuss with you."

Harcourt waited, a smile forming as if he'd already guessed what Oliver was about to say. "Of course."

"I had intended to speak with you months ago, but . . . circumstances . . . and my own pride intervened. I wish to offer for Lady Denby's hand in marriage, and I'm asking for your permission."

Harcourt snorted a laugh. "The lack of my permission has never stopped her. But you have it, plus my blessing." He turned to survey the surrounding destruction. "It takes a big man to overlook years of prejudice and mistreatment of his own people by others."

"To be fair, I haven't overlooked anything. I've simply decided to accept Camilla as a person rather than, to use her words, an institution."

"A *wise* man, then. When do you plan to ask her?"

Oliver turned, the sight of Camilla tending to Tori and Eva melting his heart. "Soon."

She lifted her head, and their eyes met.

"Very soon. Now, if you will excuse me."

He threaded his way toward her, his footsteps lighter than they should have been, considering he'd almost lost his life. A smile tugged at his lips. With her hands firmly on her shapely hips, Camilla argued with his grandmother.

Harry stood by, looking—for the first time Oliver had ever witnessed—completely helpless.

"Eva, you must allow Ashton to examine your burns. Please put the violin down."

"No. Not until I place it in Oliver's hands."

"I'm here, Mami." He bent down to where she sat on the ground, his violin case clutched against her breast with hands raw and blistering.

He sent a questioning gaze toward Camilla.

"Father said she refused to release it when he pulled her from the wagon."

"Mami fetched it from the flames, Oliver . . . I mean Papa," Tori said. "She was so brave."

"You must play it on Milosh's instrument, Oliver," his grandmother said, her voice a hoarse whisper.

Ah, my song. "Then you approve of my choice?"

"And why wouldn't I?" She huffed. "She, too, is brave. Brave enough to be Romani."

He cast a surreptitious glance toward Camilla, who seemed too preoccupied with Tori to pay heed to the conversation. Although his need to propose was urgent, he wanted it to be perfect, special, not couched in a scene of horror.

"I'm completely lost in this conversation," Harry said, as Oliver removed the violin from his grandmother's grasp.

As both men tended to his grandmother's burns, Harry asked, "Did Nash truly assist you?"

"The dark-haired man?"

Harry nodded.

"Yes," Oliver said. "He gave me the knife to cut through the ropes binding my hands and that my father used to sever it from the tree branch. Then, he supported me, keeping me from strangling." Strangely, the words *my father* didn't stick in his throat and elicit the sour taste as they had before.

He glanced up, noticing Trentwith standing at a distance and watching them intently. "Would you excuse me?"

"Of course," Harry said. "You should rest."

The concern both Harcourt and Harry had shown touched him, but resting would have to wait. He strolled toward his father, who raised his hands in defense.

"Oliver, please."

With outstretched arms, Oliver wrapped them around his father's shoulders. "Thank you, Father."

"You forgive me?"

"I'm trying. For now, I appreciate that you helped save my life."

"How could I not protect the life I created? It's about time I took my responsibilities as your father seriously, wouldn't you say?"

The sincere tone of the man's voice stirred a memory that had been buried deep under layers of resentment and hate.

A much younger version of this man had visited him and his mother at the camp, tossing Oliver over his shoulder in playful abandon. Oliver had loved him, admired him once. Perhaps the time had come to lay his hate to rest.

"Is the invitation to your wedding to Mother still open?"

In a voice choked with emotion, his father answered, "Only if you agree to stand by my side."

Oliver extended his hand. "Done."

⁂

WITH EVA AND TORI UNDER HARRY'S EXPERT CARE, CAMILLA searched out her father. People continued to cough from the smoke still circling in the sky above the camp. Her father moved among the people, offering water. His steps faltered, and Nash, who had been performing the same duty, raced to his side, grasping him by the arm and leading him to a nearby tree.

Camilla gave him a stern look. "Father, you should rest."

"I agree, Harcourt. It was foolhardy of you both to enter that wagon. Brave but foolish," Nash said.

The confusion of the evening began to clear, and Camilla remembered Eva's tale of Milosh. "Nash, may I speak with you in private?"

He placed the bucket of water on the ground and followed her some distance away from her father.

"What is it?" His tone, although not angry, was curt.

"What was your true intention this evening?" She held up her hand when he opened his mouth. "Don't lie to me. Oliver's grandmother told me what happened all those years ago. The man hanged that evening was Oliver's grandfather."

Nash's eyes widened. "I assure you, I had no idea. However, it does make my feeble attempt to atone for my past sins a bit more poetic."

"Did you have a part in Milosh's death?"

"Who?"

"Oliver's grandfather."

He focused his eyes on a spot above her head, as if refusing to meet her own. "I didn't know his name, but I was the one who took the goblet that led to his death."

"His murder." She'd be damned if she'd allow him to soften the words.

"Yes. His murder." He shifted away from her. "Roland dared me to take it and bragged about how he'd used it to rid the land of another filthy gypsy." Finally, he locked eyes with hers. "I've lived with that far too long. When I heard the rumblings about clearing the camp, I approached Roland. It sickened me to learn he had incited it, spreading lies and hate."

Dizzy from his revelation, she tried to clear her fuzzy mind and reconcile the dichotomy of the repentant man before her with the hard-edged rake she'd come to know. "Perhaps there's good in you, Nash."

He turned away. "I wouldn't go that far, and I'd appreciate it if you would keep this to yourself. If you do tell anyone, I'll deny it." He tromped off, snatching up the bucket of water along his way, to continue administering to those in need.

Footsteps sounded behind her as they squished into the soggy ground. She spun around, her nerves more than frayed.

Her hand flew to her chest. "Harry. You startled me."

"Forgive me. I merely wished to ensure Nash hadn't upset you." He cast a quick glance in Nash's direction. "Did he really assist in Oliver's rescue?"

Recalling Nash's words, she answered as truthfully as possible, "Do you doubt Oliver's word?"

Harry ran a hand through his blond hair. "No, of course not. But I don't trust Nash. He must have had some ulterior motive."

"Perhaps regret reaches even the coldest of hearts."

Harry nodded, his smile wan. "It's been a long night for everyone, you should return home."

She looked around him to where Oliver still tended the wounded. "How can I when there's still so much to be done to help?" She threw up her hands. "And what little we do seems futile. The destruction wrought on these people tonight won't be easily repaired."

With a tilt of his head, Harry rubbed his chin, his sharp mind obviously pondering a solution. "No. What if you and Maggie spearhead an effort to request funds to assist them as they rebuild?"

She shook her head. "If I've learned anything from Oliver, it's they are an extremely proud people. They would refuse charity."

"A hard lesson, I'd wager, but a valuable one. I suppose you're right."

Even in her exhausted mind, an idea formed. "Instead of monetary assistance, what if we work with them, side-by-side, to rebuild? Might you appeal to the magistrate and suggest the violators' punishment fit the crime?"

"It's a risky proposition, but worth the effort. The men who tried to hang Oliver should be punished severely, but as for the others, I would imagine, given the choice, the perpetrators would prefer labor in lieu of imprisonment. Although many in the aristocracy will balk at the idea, I could also enlist the aid of my fellow nobles. I'll call a meeting to gauge interest. I rarely use my title to my advantage, but in this case, the power I wield as duke could be beneficial to more than myself."

He gazed around him. "Hatred and prejudice often stem from misunderstandings and false assumptions. If they work together, perhaps they would learn not only about their differences but also their similarities. In effect, building a bridge between our worlds."

"It seems an insurmountable task."

"We can only try. But perhaps with you and Oliver as well as Trentwith and Oliver's mother, the bridge has already begun construction."

The hope blooming in her heart from Oliver's declaration of love allowed her to believe even the impossible. "Perhaps."

Once Oliver and Harry had tended to all the wounded, she joined them, Tori, her father, and Trentwith as they made their way to the carriages to return home.

Tori held tight to the violin case Eva had rescued. Camilla's knees buckled when her foot slipped on a patch of mud. A strong arm wrapped around her waist, supporting her.

She gazed up into Oliver's loving face.

His dimple popped, only serving to make her wobbly knees worse. "I've got you."

"Ollie . . . I mean, Papa," Tori tugged on his other hand. "Does this mean you and Lady Denby like each other again?"

In one smooth motion, he lifted his daughter in his arms. "We always liked each other, only one of us was too proud to admit it."

Camilla snorted a laugh. "How quickly you forget our first meeting."

Securely holding Tori with one arm, he slid the other back around Camilla's waist. "You will never allow me to forget that, will you?"

"No. I shall remind you every chance I get . . . especially when I want something."

He laughed, full and hearty. "Tori, I fear I've aligned myself with a blackmailer."

At the carriages, they divided up. Trentwith insisted Oliver and Tori ride with him. Camilla joined them, explaining it would be easier to retrieve Pockets from Sabina's care at Oliver's home.

"I'll return with Ashton, Camilla," her father said. He kissed her on the cheek and boarded Harry's carriage, sending a cryptic look toward Oliver.

What schemes have they concocted?

"I'm sorry we couldn't convince Eva to return with us," Trentwith said. "It would have made your mother so happy to see her."

"She's a proud woman, but I have a feeling she'll see reason given time," Oliver said.

They rode the rest of the way in silence, the swaying carriage lulling Tori to sleep as she leaned against Oliver. From her seat next to his father, Camilla locked eyes with Oliver.

"I must look a sight," she said, raising a hand to touch the singed strands of hair falling loosely about her head.

"Indeed. And a more beautiful sight I can't remember."

A muffled cough reminded them they weren't alone. "Oliver, perhaps it would be best if you accompanied Lady Denby home after we fetch Pockets. I'll stay with Victoria and your mother. You may take my carriage."

Oliver raised a dark eyebrow. "You plan to stay the night at my home?"

"Perhaps I may sleep in your room, if you would permit me?"

Now, it was Camilla who emitted a delicate cough, sending Oliver a pointed look, quite sure they both understood Trentwith's true intentions. "Oliver, I have a comfortable guest room."

The idea appeared to end Oliver's struggle, and he gave a curt nod toward his father, followed by a enigmatic smile directed at her.

Perhaps the bridges indeed were being constructed.

☙❧

An odd acceptance settled on Oliver as he stared across the carriage at his father. Or perhaps it was resignation. The man had helped save his life after all. It was the least he could offer in way of thanks.

Although exhaustion threatened to overcome him, the mere idea of spending the night with Camilla energized him, only to be soured by the thought of his father having similar expectations with his mother.

A quandary, indeed.

When they arrived at his home, he assisted Camilla from the carriage then scooped up Tori in his arms, a devilish idea taking shape in his mind.

His mother bounded to her feet as they entered the small parlor. Pockets rubbed his eyes, apparently having fallen asleep on the sofa beside her.

"Mama!" Pockets cried as he rushed to Camilla's side and hugged her skirts. "You smell like smoke." He looked up at his mother, his eyes growing wide.

"Oliver, your neck." His mother ran a slim hand over the skin left rough and red from the noose.

"It's nothing. A mere scratch," Oliver said, clasping his mother's hand in his. "I fear we all need a bath."

Tori stirred in his arms. "Mother, would you see to Tori? Perhaps allow her to sleep with you tonight? She's had a horrendous ordeal."

His father shot him an annoyed glare.

Ah, so my suspicions were correct.

"I will accompany Lady Denby and Pockets home and will return in the morning," Oliver continued.

"Perhaps Pockets needs the comfort of an adult as well," his father said, a sly smile forming on his lips. "To reassure him his mother is safe and unharmed, of course."

Blast.

"Why, Lord Trentwith, I believe that's an excellent suggestion," Camilla said.

It would appear both of them would remain gentlemen the remainder of the evening.

CHAPTER 28—TWO WORLDS MERGED

C amilla brushed a hand discreetly against Oliver's, casting a surreptitious glance in time to catch the hint of the dimple dent his cheek. Even in a crowded room, she loved those stolen moments.

Not all members of the beau monde had returned to their country estates when the Season ended. The few who had remained in London gathered in Harry's residence at the request of the duke, no doubt curious as to the reason for the summons. Lord Montgomery leaned nonchalantly against the wall at the back of the room, speaking with Timothy Marbry. Andrew and Alice Weatherby chatted with Beatrix and her father, Lord Saxton, although Beatrix seemed much more interested in whatever her brother and Lord Montgomery were discussing. Camilla's father laughed at something Lord Trentwith had said, their gazes turning toward her and Oliver.

Oliver's tall frame bent down toward her, and he whispered, "You're blushing, my darling."

"What are those two concocting? It can't be good."

His deep chuckle sent gooseflesh up her arms.

"You know something. Admit it," she said.

"Me?" He pressed a hand to his chest, his tone one of feigned innocence.

Before they could argue further, murmurs of those gathered settled to a lull as Harry cleared his throat and brought the meeting to order.

"Friends, as you know, the violence at the gypsy"—Harry flinched, sending an apologetic look toward Oliver—"Pardon me, Romani encampment left their homes in ruin. I've met with the magistrate, and with his agreement, other than those who tried to murder Dr. Somersby, the men involved will be offered a chance to make restitution through their labor in lieu of time in gaol. Not all will agree, but I'm hoping those who do will find the experience . . . enlightening."

"I fail to see how this pertains to us, Ashton," Lord Saxton said, his tone impatient.

"Father, we should hear His Grace out," Beatrix said, placing a hand on her father's arm. Although a strange young woman, Camilla had always appreciated her outspokenness.

"Thank you, Miss Marbry. I understand your confusion, Lord Saxton. But shouldn't the welfare of those less fortunate be our concern? Shouldn't we care about maintaining peace in London and its outlying areas? For our own safety if nothing else?"

Lord Saxton shifted, his gaze now focused on his feet.

"What can we do, Ashton?" Lord Montgomery asked. "Are you asking for donations?"

"If you wish to contribute for supplies, it would be appreciated. However, I'm asking for more than money. I'm asking you to set an example, to join me in working side-by-side with the Romani to help rebuild their camp."

Camilla had never seen so many shocked faces in her lifetime. A low rumble of voices echoed throughout the room, followed by an uncomfortable silence.

Trentwith stepped forward. "You may count on me, Your Grace."

Beside her, Oliver straightened, and she swore his chest puffed out.

Camilla scanned the room, a breath trapped in her lungs, wondering if anyone else would follow Trentwith's example.

Beatrix had moved over by Timothy and nudged him in the ribs. "And me, Your Grace," Timothy said.

Lord Saxton scowled, red-faced about his son's eagerness to assist the Romani.

When Lord Montgomery volunteered, Camilla caught the doe-eyed look of admiration on Beatrix's face. Perhaps this endeavor would bring more than nobles, commoners, and Romani together. She made a mental note to speak with Margaret.

The Weatherbys offered their help, but others shook their heads, arguing such action was beneath them.

When the meeting ended, only a handful of those present had volunteered. Heaviness settled around her, encasing her chest as if her stays were too tight. "I'd hoped for a better response." She gazed up into Oliver's eyes, expecting to find an even greater disappointment. "Especially for your sake. I do so want you to give the nobility a chance, to see not all of us are only concerned with our own comforts."

"It's a better result than I'd expected," Oliver said. "And the only noble I'm concerned with is you. As long as you accept me, it's all I ask."

His eyes gleamed with mischief, along with a hint of something else she couldn't name.

❦

OLIVER PLACED HIS HANDS ON HIS BACK AND STRETCHED. HE'D worked up a sweat, despite the chilly autumn day. Pleasant wood smoke now filled the encampment, so different from the scent of horror two nights before. Meat cooked on spits over the open flames, and children paused to warm their hands in passing.

Harry had brought geese from a London butcher, and Lord Harcourt had brought cheese and bread. The Weatherbys had brought some of their favorite spices from India, garnering nods of appreciation from the Romani women.

In addition to the offerings of food, the men worked alongside the Romani, repairing the wagons and bender tents. Even Lord Montgomery—whom he remembered from the night at the opera—busied himself painting the damaged wagons. Camilla, Alice Weatherby, and Margaret worked with the women helping wash and mend clothing that had suffered in the assault on the camp.

Oddly, the man who had helped save his life, Lord Nash, was nowhere to be seen, and Oliver regretted the fact, hoping to have another opportunity to thank him properly.

A constable and three Bow Street Runners watched cautiously as several of the men who had been taken into custody during the attack helped clear the camp of debris and assist with repairs.

Not all had been willing to trade a cell for a bit of labor, and those who had, grumbled and groused. They kept to themselves, careful to keep their distance from the Romani. As noble as the effort seemed, Oliver had his doubts it would lead to any lasting peace.

As he took a moment's rest, he gazed over to where his mother worked next to his grandmother, hanging freshly washed clothes on a line strung between two trees—one of which nearly had taken his life. They laughed and joked with each other, a sight that warmed Oliver's heart to near bursting.

Someone slapped him on the back, and he spun around to find his father grinning like a fool.

"It's a joy, is it not?" His father said, inclining his head toward his future bride and her mother. "Sabina couldn't stop talking about seeing her mother the whole ride here." His shirtsleeves rolled up, exposing muscular forearms, he pulled out a handkerchief and wiped his sweaty brow.

"You've been working hard chopping that wood. Perhaps you should rest awhile. You're not as young as you used to be." Oliver couldn't resist delivering a good-natured jab.

"Is that a challenge, whelp?" His lips twitched as if fighting a smile.

"I would never challenge my elder."

At that his father gave a boisterous laugh, and heads turned, including Oliver's mother's, her dark brows raised in question.

His father gave her a friendly wave. "Now, don't upset your mother. I'll consider your recommendation to rest as your professional opinion rather than an insult to my age." He strode over to Oliver's mother and grandmother, a definite spring in his step worthy of someone much younger. Oliver could only shake his head, grateful their marriage would take place in less than a month.

The sun drifted lower in the sky, signaling the end of a productive day. All had been invited to stay and partake of the meal, the mouthwatering aromas of which had tempted their nostrils during the course of the day. They gathered around, sitting on stumps and logs, the less-than contrite townspeople remaining tightly grouped together.

A young Romani woman passed out plates of food, and when she approached a man in the group of townspeople, he crossed his arms over his chest and shook his head.

"You've worked hard," she said. "You must be hungry."

"I ain't eatin' nothin' you prepared. It might be poison for all I know."

"Am I so very frightening you won't accept a plate of food?" She picked a piece of the roasted goose off the plate and placed it in her mouth, chewing dramatically. "Tastes good to me."

"I'll take it," a younger man sitting next to him said, holding out his hands. "My belly's been growling all afternoon."

Several nearby men chuckled, albeit reluctantly, from what Oliver sensed.

She handed him the plate. "My name's Marya, what's yours."

"Alfie," he said over a mouthful of food. He nodded enthusiastically. "This is good, mates. You should try some."

Several more people accepted plates that Marya and other women offered. An amiable conversation struck up between a few of them and several Romani.

Oliver's grandmother took a seat next to him, then elbowed him in the ribs. "Is he really a duke?" She pointed a bony finger at

Harry, who was in the middle of being regaled with a tall tale by a Romani man.

"He is. When I first met him, he told me not to hold it against him. I owe him more than gratitude for my position at the clinic. He's opened my eyes to my preconceived ideas of the aristocracy."

"He's not the only one who's done that." She picked at her food, not meeting his gaze, but the smile quirking her lips indicated she knew she'd made her point.

"No. Not the only one. Perhaps not even the most important one."

⁂

THE PARCHMENT IN CAMILLA'S HAND WOULD TEAR SOON IF SHE didn't stop worrying the message with her fingers. She closed her eyes, wishing Langley would spur the carriage horses faster.

Camilla,

Please come at once. It is a matter of great importance.

Maggie

The cryptic message, received late in the evening, sent a chill up her spine. Was it Edmund? Or had Margaret overdone it at the encampment the day before? God knows her own muscles ached from the work she'd performed. Camilla's mind raced through scenarios, each one worse than the one before.

Langley had barely lowered the carriage steps when she bolted out and hurried up the stairs to Harry and Margaret's home.

When Burrows greeted her, she searched his face, relieved no trace of sorrow or concern etched it.

"If you would follow me, Lady Denby."

He led her up the stairs and down the hallway from the ballroom. Soft light shone from the gap in the partially opened door, and she pushed against it to enter. "Maggie?"

Upon entering, she stopped short, finding not Margaret, but Oliver. The candlelight cast him in shadows, his broad shoulders and narrow hips sending a thrill through her. As he moved toward her, the image of a sleek animal resurfaced as it had that night at the masquerade, and he smiled, his swoon-producing dimple in full display.

"Come, sit," he said, taking her by the hand and leading her to the settee. He looked practically devious, as if he'd planned an elaborate prank.

"Where's Maggie? I rushed here in a panic."

"Margaret is fine. I asked her to send the message."

"Oh, thank goodness." She pressed a hand to her breast, drawing his eyes. His heated gaze warmed her cheeks. "What are you about?" Even she couldn't deny the teasing tone of her voice.

He laughed, sending gooseflesh up her arms. He lifted his violin from a side table. "I want to play for you. It's something I wrote myself."

"But why summon me here? Why didn't you come to my home?"

A dark eyebrow rose. "Have you forgotten so quickly? It was in this very room where we first shared our hopes and dreams."

She swallowed the lump in her throat. "Yes. I remember."

He placed the instrument under his chin, and closing his eyes, lifted the bow to play.

Unlike anything she'd ever heard, the melody hauntingly beautiful, he made the instrument sing, capturing her in its spell completely.

A foggy memory surfaced. Something Eva had said. She tried to pull it forth, but the pieces remained fragmented. When he finished, she could only stare in admiration.

"Well?" he asked, his face suddenly serious.

"There's such a sweet sadness to it, a yearning. It's left me speechless."

He laughed. "Then I shall remember to play it for you often."

"Your grandmother told me something about a song you had written, but I can't recall exactly what she said."

"Did she now?" His lips quirked, the faint indentation of his dimple barely visible as if too shy to make itself known.

"Yes, and she read my palm." Camilla held out her hand, examining it, remembering something about two love lines. "She said I would have another love, as deep as my first, but lasting much longer."

The fog around the memory cleared, and Camilla raised her gaze to meet his. "She told me you'd composed a song you would only play for the woman you wanted to marry." The unasked question hung on the air, as fragile as a soap bubble, knowing if he said no, it would crush her completely.

"Are you asking me if that was the song?" He knelt next to her and took her hands in his.

"I . . . well—"

He covered her mouth with his, tasting, teasing in a luscious kiss. "Marry me, Lady Denby. I can't promise you much. Only my heart."

Overcome with emotion, the word wouldn't come, so she nodded as tears pricked her eyes. She swallowed down the emotion rising in her throat. "Why the sadness in the melody, Oliver?"

He sighed, the sound not one of exasperation, but of relief. "When I composed it, I had little hope of finding a woman who would accept me—all of me. Exactly as I am."

"Oh, Oliver." She threw herself into his arms, no longer able to control her emotions.

"None of that." He brushed away a tear that had broken free and fallen down her cheek.

"These are happy tears."

"I'll never understand women," he said before driving all thought from her head with another searing kiss.

EPILOGUE

C amilla fidgeted as Margaret adjusted the flowers in her hair. "Are you certain I don't look ridiculous? I'm hardly a debutante, Maggie."

Margaret stepped back, and after admiring her artistry, gave an approving nod. "You look beautiful. Every bride has a right to feel special. You'll take Oliver's breath away."

"As long as he's not too breathless to repeat his vows."

They both laughed. It had been a long road to get Oliver to the altar. "So, tell me, who do you have in your sights now that you've finished matchmaking with me?"

"I have some ideas. Laurence Townsend for one. Harry and I've discussed hosting another ball or perhaps a house party. For charity, of course." The glint in Margaret's eyes indicated it was more than a simple matter of securing more funds for the clinic.

"Poor Montgomery. He doesn't stand a chance. Beatrix Marbry seemed to take a keen interest in him at the meeting Harry called."

"Oh?" The glint in Margaret's eyes sharpened. Camilla suspected Margaret experienced some guilt over breaking the man's heart when she married Harry and hoped he'd find his own love match.

Margaret's bright laughter reminded Camilla that happy endings could in fact happen. And today, Camilla would enjoy her own.

As Margaret made her way into the church to take her place, Victoria tugged on Camilla's skirt. "After today, will you be my mama?"

The word once foreign now landed on Camilla's ears like the sweet strands of Oliver's violin. She'd never tire of either one. "I would be most honored. Pockets will benefit greatly from such a wonderful big sister." She turned. "Speaking of Pockets. Where is he?"

"Over here," her father said, approaching with the blond-headed waif who had captured her heart.

Pockets grinned, revealing the space from his missing top front tooth. "Mama, I decided something."

"What is that?" She fought to maintain a serious expression.

"You can call me Philip, since everyone else in our family has a real name."

She stooped and brought him into her arms, whispering in his ear, "I may slip and call you Pockets on occasion."

"That's all right. I'll forgive you."

Moisture brimmed in her eyes, and she brushed it away. "Oh, dear. I'm crying already. Oliver will think I'm a complete ninny."

Her father chuckled, then kissed her on the cheek. "Are you ready, my dear?"

"I've never been more ready." She slid her arm through her father's and prepared to enter the body of the church.

⚜

OLIVER RAN HIS FINGER AROUND HIS COLLAR, CERTAIN HIS MOTHER had tied his neckcloth much too tight. He waited, nearly in the same spot he'd stood a few weeks before for his father and mother's wedding. For late autumn, the church seemed unseasonably warm. *Were there too many candles?*

Harry poked him in the ribs, grabbing his attention. Gathered in the pews before him, friends and family watched with expectant faces. His father, seated next to his mother, nodded encouragingly. Even his grandmother had come, grumbling about having to ride in the fancy carriage of an earl. In truth, Oliver knew she'd enjoyed every moment.

On the other side of the aisle, Margaret beamed at him, casting quick glances to her own husband. Manny squirmed in his seat next to her, apparently having the same difficulty with his own shirt collar. The Weatherbys sat behind the duchess, Andrew bending over to whisper something to his wife and making her blush.

Oliver held his breath in anticipation for the moment *she* would appear. Another poke in the ribs from Harry and a finger pointing to the entrance of the church refocused Oliver's attention. Tori led the procession, as pretty as a princess. Behind her, Camilla entered, her father on one side and Pockets on the other. Oliver's breath caught at the sight of her. Her red dress, uncommon for a bride, spoke of her courage to defy convention. Less than pure thoughts stirred in his mind, and he shook himself, remembering the sacred nature of the occasion. Everything and everyone else seemed to disappear as she walked slowly forward to take her place by his side.

If anyone had asked him about the ceremony itself, he would have been hard pressed to answer. Harry prodded him more than a few times when it came time for him to repeat his vows. He couldn't pull his eyes away from Camilla. He was completely besotted.

When the men pounded his back in congratulations outside of the church, he supposed he'd muddled through adequately. His father had loaned his finest carriage to take them back to Harry's, where a wedding breakfast was to be held in their honor.

Seated in the confines of the carriage compartment, he pulled Camilla into his arms for their first kiss as husband and wife. He breathed deeply, inhaling her wonderful lilac fragrance, and tasted the sweetness of his wife's lips.

"How long must we remain at this breakfast," he said, recognizing the husky need in his own voice.

"Aren't you hungry?" Her innocent question fueled the fire within him.

"Yes. Starving."

Her eyes widened as his meaning took hold. "I suppose I could feign a headache." She ran a delicate finger along his coat lapel. "But there is something to be said for building anticipation. Plus, it would be rude to Harry and Margaret if we left too soon."

"I have a feeling Harry would understand."

Before she could argue, the carriage came to a stop. Harry's butler, Burrows, escorted them to the dining hall where guests greeted them with raised glasses. Oliver thought back to the night almost a year ago when he entered this same home and was greeted as a lord—the night he and Camilla had their first real connection.

After filling themselves with the finest food and drink, Oliver's father rose and tapped his spoon against a crystal glass. "A toast! To my son, Oliver, and his beautiful bride, Camilla. May they live a long and happy life together."

"Hear, hear," the guests responded.

Not finished, his father remained standing. "I'm very proud of my son, not only his occupation, but the man he's become—despite me. I can't undo the past, but I can promise to strive to be a better father to you going forward."

He took his seat and handed Oliver a sealed parchment. "Although my hands are tied as far as my title and entailed property, I would like to offer this to you as a wedding gift."

Camilla slid her hand through Oliver's arm. She leaned in as he broke the seal and opened the document. After reading, his eyes rose to meet his father's.

"It's not much," his father said. "Some unentailed property and a country home in Sussex, not much more than a cottage, but comfortable. It's not far from the sea. I thought you might enjoy it, considering your time spent on a sailing vessel. My own estate is nearby, and I hoped it would persuade you to visit your mother and me frequently. I've updated my will, leaving you the bulk of my funds upon my death."

Overwhelmed seemed an inadequate word as Oliver stared at the document in his hand. "It's most generous, but my work is here in London."

His father nodded, "Of course. The house in Sussex is fully staffed and will be waiting when you're able to spend time away from the clinic."

Oliver opened his mouth to protest, but his father held up his hand. "Please, accept this meager gift. It's the least I can do for my only son."

Harry added, "Don't forget Dr. Mason is assisting at the clinic now, freeing both of us to spend more time with our families."

Oliver turned toward Camilla. "It seems my father and my employer are joining forces against me. What say you, wife?"

"Perhaps a little time away from work for a honeymoon is called for." The glint in her eyes behind her demure smile made him laugh out loud.

"It seems I'm outnumbered. I accept with gratitude, Father." He placed his hand in his father's and shook, the healing of forgiveness a sweet relief.

They bade their goodbyes to everyone and boarded his father's carriage for Camilla's townhouse. To give the newlyweds some privacy, Harry had suggested that Pockets stay with him and Margaret for a few weeks, stating Manny had missed him. Oliver's father had insisted on Tori spending time with him and Oliver's mother as he wished to become better acquainted with his granddaughter.

Once secured inside the carriage, Oliver pulled Camilla onto his lap, eager to begin married life. As he lavished her with kisses, she ran a hand against his chest, and with a gentle nudge, pushed him back.

"Have I offended you so soon?" he asked, teasing.

"No. But before you drive all intelligent thought from my head, I have a wedding gift of my own to give."

"Please, no more property or money. It's humiliating enough that I will take up residence in my wife's home here in London. A man has his pride."

"No. A price cannot be put on this gift."

"Well? What is it?"

"I am very glad we're married and I have my very own doctor."

"Camilla, you're not making any sense."

She smiled, the mere sight of it practically unmanning him. However, nothing could have prepared him for her next words.

"It seems, dear husband, that there have been . . . consequences."

৪৯৫

WANT MORE? CONTINUE THE JOURNEY ...

A viscount whose life is governed by rules. A bluestocking who circumvents them. What will break first ... his principles or her heart?

Find out in *Healing The Viscount's Heart.* Read on for a sneak peek or scan the code below to get your copy right away.

Healing the Viscount's Heart

Can't get enough of Oliver and Camilla? Scan the QR code on the next page to sign up to my newsletter and receive a bonus scene with a peek into their future as a thank you welcome gift. In addition, there will be fun contests, book news, and subscriber only extras. You may unsubscribe at any time. No hard feelings.

A Doctor for Lady Denny Bonus Scene

LASTLY, IF YOU ENJOYED READING *A DOCTOR FOR LADY DENBY*, WHY not let other readers know by leaving an honest review on Amazon. Scan the code below to take you right to the review page. Easy peasy.

Turn the page for a sneak peek of *Healing The Viscount's Heart.*

EXCERPT HEALING THE
VISCOUNT'S HEART

M ortified—the one word accurately summing up Bea's
current emotional state. It had been one thing when
Catpurrnicus attacked Lord Middlebury. But to have her one
beloved assault the other—and no offense to Catpurrnicus—even
more beloved Laurence was quite another.

Breath trapped in her lungs as she waited for Catpurrnicus to
thrust himself at her brand new fiancé. Would Laurence be as
intolerant of her pet as Middlebury? Ask her to find him another
home? Or worse, would he bolt from the house rescinding his offer
of marriage?

As if facing each other in a duel, Catpurrnicus and Laurence
stood motionless, and the challenged party reacted first.

"Hello, kitty," Laurence said, his voice calm and assured.

Bea forced herself not to follow her mother's example and fall to
the settee in a dead faint. She must remain alert to protect her
beloved!

Catpurrnicus advanced, taking slow, measured steps toward his
prey. Laurence, like the unsuspecting victim he was soon to be,
crouched down, extending his hand.

Bea pressed her hand to her chest, hoping to confirm her heart remained beating. Icy chills raced up her spine, although the sunny, late May day promised to be a warm one. She squeezed her eyes shut, unwilling to witness the horror about to unfold.

"That's a good kitty," Laurence said.

At the absence of hissing from Catpurrnicus and screaming from Laurence, she tentatively peeked through one eye. To her amazement, Catpurrnicus thread himself around and between Laurence's legs, rubbing his furry little body against the man's boots.

Picking the cat up, Laurence snuggled Catpurrnicus against his chest and returned to the settee.

Although she believed it impossible, Bea fell in love with him even more. "He . . . he likes you." Still not quite believing them, the words fell from her lips.

Laurence stroked Catpurrnicus's soft fur, and the cat purred contentedly. "One of my interests is animal behavior. I believe animals have an intrinsic instinct about people. They can sense fear, it would appear, and seem to be an excellent judge of character. Isn't that right, Catpurrnicus?"

The cat's pink tongue darted out, licking Laurence's hand.

"He didn't like Lord Fa—Lord Middlebury," Bea said.

Laurence chuckled, and Bea decided it was the most pleasant sound she'd ever heard. He leaned in closer to whisper, "Proves my theory, wouldn't you say?"

Catpurrnicus purred his agreement.

Good Galileo, she loved him. They both had forgotten her mother entirely. A rustling behind them reminded Bea of her presence. "It's a miracle," her mother said, awe evident in her voice. "A sign from the heavens above. Lord Montgomery, you have a gift."

With the crisis averted, Bea attempted to return the conversation to before Catpurrnicus's escape. "You were about to mention an article you read, my lord."

"Ah yes," he said, his voice as soothing as a warm blanket on a chilly, rainy day. "A fascinating treatise on—ah—ah—ah-CHOO."

Catpurrnicus wiggled his way out of Laurence's gentle grasp and jumped to the floor, apparently startled by the explosive sneeze.

"I beg your pa—ah-choo." A string of successive sneezes followed. Laurence's eyes began to water.

Of course, Preston took that precise, inopportune moment to bring in the tea, but thankfully Laurence's sneezing had abated.

Bea said a silent prayer of thanks to Hippocrates and tacked on a special request to keep her hands from shaking as she poured. That particular prayer went unanswered. Tea sloshed out of the cup onto the saucer beneath it. She'd keep that one for herself. Mercifully, her hands steadied, and she poured the next neatly, not spilling a drop.

However, her hand trembled as she handed the tea to Laurence and his fingers brushed against hers. Like a bolt of lightning, energy passed up her arm, making her head spin.

At the moment Laurence began sipping his tea, Catpurrnicus jumped back on the settee and rubbed his head against Laurence's side. Another bout of fitful sneezes ensued, with Laurence's tea being flung from his cup onto his waistcoat.

"Oh, dear," Bea said, rushing to grab a tea towel. As she blotted the damp spot over Laurence's chest, their eyes locked, and a vise-like grip squeezed her chest. *Oh, my!*

He wrapped his hand over hers, his lips curling in a gentle smile. "It's quite all right, Miss Marbry. No harm done. However, it seems I ha-ha-ha—ah-choo—have contracted a cold. Perhaps it would be best if I bid you farewell for today. I have no wish to expose you."

Bea's heart flipped, then plummeted to her toes, wishing he would stay a little longer. "Will you return tomorrow?" She cringed at the hopefulness in her voice.

"If I'm able. I shall send word if my symptoms worsen." He reached down and scratched Catpurrnicus behind an ear, eliciting a contented purr from the black beast. "Goodbye, young Catpurrnicu-cu-cu—choo." Wetness rimmed his eyes as he extended his hand to her. "Miss Marbry."

Gooseflesh rose up her arms as she slipped her hand into his, and he bowed over it, kissing her fingertips. He turned toward her mother. "Lady Saxton. A pleasure. I bid you farewell."

A soft meow came from the settee as Lord Montgomery strode

from the room. Bea glanced down at her furry pet. Pleased seemed too inadequate of a word to describe her reaction to his restrained behavior. She hoped fish would be on the menu that evening, for she would save a large portion for Catpurrnicus to reward him.

Then she began counting the minutes until Laurence would, hopefully, return the next day.

WANT MORE? SCAN THE CODE BELOW TO CONTINUE THE JOURNEY:

Healing the Viscount's Heart

AUTHOR NOTE

When the idea formed for this story, I hadn't planned on it taking the direction it finally did. In my mind, the class differences between Camilla and Oliver seemed sufficient.

But as I began researching the Romani, I felt compelled to add another layer of depth and conflict to the story. Their story and what they've endured in the course of history is heartbreaking.

The Romani, also known as Romanichal in Britain, migrated there in the 16th century. During the late 1500s, 105 Romani were condemned to death simply because they were Romani. Nine of them were executed.

Persecution of the Romani extended into the 20th century. Historians estimate between 250,000 and 500,000 European Romani died at the hands of the Nazi regime. The number is staggering considering that the prewar Romani population numbered between one and one and half million. Prejudice against them continues to this day.

I've taken a bit of artistic license with the encampment in the story. Although groups of Romani would settle on the outskirts of London during the winter months, they primarily traveled to the countryside during the spring, summer, and autumn for agricultural

AUTHOR NOTE

work. So it would probably be unlikely that Camilla would have found them outside of London in the summer when she visits Eva. I've tried to imply that perhaps Eva's group remained in the general area primarily because of her relationship to Oliver.

I hope you received the subplot of the Romani in the vein intended. I will admit my vision of the cooperation that occurred between Romani, the aristocracy, and the common London folk at the end of the story is optimistic at best and perhaps unrealistic at the worst. However, this is a work of fiction, and often what we hope for can sometimes be an impetus for what can be.

On a lighter note, the velocipede was really a thing. The strange contraption was the predecessor of the modern bicycle. As a mother whose son fell off his own bicycle, causing a concussion, I can relate to Camilla's skepticism of it—back then they didn't have helmets. Again, I've taken a bit of artistic license as the vehicle was primarily designed for a grown man, but I have no doubt that Lord Harcourt would have had a smaller version built for Pockets.

282

ALSO BY TRISHA MESSMER

Historical Romance

❦

❦

Contemporary Romance

ABOUT THE AUTHOR

Trisha Messmer had a million stories rattling around in her brain. (Well, maybe a million is an exaggeration but there were a lot). Always loving the written word, she enjoyed any chance she had to compose something, whether it be for a college paper or just a plain old email. One day as she was speaking with her daughter about the latest adventure going on in her mind, her daughter said, "Mom, why don't you write them down." And so it began. Several stories later, she finally allowed someone, other than her daughter, to read them.

After that brave (and very scary) step, she decided not to keep them to herself any longer, so here we are.

She hopes you enjoy her musings as much as she enjoyed writing them. If they make you smile, sigh, hope, and chuckle or even cry at times, it was worth it.

Born in St. Louis, Missouri, Trisha graduated from the University of Missouri – St. Louis with a degree in Psychology. Trisha's day job as a product instructor for a software company allowed her to travel all over the country meeting interesting people and seeing interesting places, some of which inspired ideas for her stories. A hopeless (or hopeful) romantic, Trisha currently resides in the great Northwest.

Find out more about Trisha at: www.trishamessmer.com

facebook.com/trishamessmerauthor
x.com/TrishaMessmer

Printed in Great Britain
by Amazon